TAKEN BY LIES

TRUTH OR LIES BOOK 1

ELLA MILES

FREE BOOKS

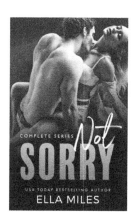

Read **Not Sorry** for **FREE**! And sign up to get my latest releases, updates, and more goodies here→EllaMiles.com/freebooks

Follow me on BookBub to get notified of my new releases and recommendations here→Follow on BookBub Here

Join Ella's Bellas FB group to grab my **FREE** book **Pretend I'm Yours**→Join Ella's Bellas Here

TRUTH OR LIES SERIES

PART I

LURED BY LIES

1

ENZO

ALCOHOL.

It can lower your inhibitions.

Transform you into somebody society accepts.

Make you relax enough to ask the hot girl at the end of the bar out on a date.

Alcohol has so much power.

The power to tempt me.

To take me away.

To make me forget.

It should be only an act of rebellion. An underage misdemeanor, done as much for attention as to feel the effects. That's all alcohol should represent. I'm only seventeen. Still a long ways from twenty-one, but alcohol has never been a healthy pastime.

As soon as I tasted the liquid, I knew it was a habit I would never give up.

Not because I'm an alcoholic. That's one thing I could never be, even when I drink in large quantities. Even when I need alcohol as much as I need to breathe.

I need it to forget.

I finish the last drop of the amber liquid in my glass. One drink isn't nearly enough for me to forget. If there were another way to erase my demons and slip me into amnesia, I would take it. But I've never found another option. This is my only option.

"Another round," I say to Zeke and Langston who are sitting in the corner booth with me. It's not a question, but a statement.

I need more, and they will both stay with me, drinking until my past is erased for another hour.

Slinking out from beneath the corner booth hidden in the shadows, I stand and cross the width of the room before climbing onto a stool at the bar. We have a waiter, but I don't have the patience to wait for her to realize we need more drinks.

I eye Blake behind the bar. He knows when he sees me to drop his other patrons and serve me immediately. His tip, along with his job, requires it. This is just another bar my family owns. It's nothing in the grand scheme of things — just a place for me to retreat to when necessary. And lately, I've found coming here on a daily basis is very necessary.

Blake spots me out of the corner of his eye. He politely ends his conversation with the flirty woman at the end of the bar and walks my way, before pouring me another glass of the finest bourbon we have. I reach for the glass he sat in front of me and wait while he continues to make drinks for my friends.

I lift the glass to my lips taking comfort in the fact that soon my nightmare will be over. My memory will be obliterated, at least until I have to meet with my father later today.

The door flies open, and a girl falls through. She stumbles once as she drops to her knees. But her cheeks don't flame with embarrassment. Instead, fear threatens her eyes

4

as she scans behind her. As if, any second, the evil she is running from will find her.

She stands quickly and brushes herself off out of habit, not because she's dirty. Her skin is a light olive color, but it's impossible to know what ethnicity she is just from the coloring. We live in Miami; everyone is tan. But her skin hints at more than just spending too much time in the sun. Hers promises a past and culture far more intriguing.

Her legs are too skinny I realize as I soak up her body and ingrain it in my memory like I do with everything. My memory is flawless, and even if it wasn't, there is no way I would forget such a spark of beauty like her.

Her clothes are too big for her. Her blue jean shorts engulf too much of her legs. Her tank top hangs like a tent instead of showing the curves beneath it. Dark black hair hangs down her neck in thick waves hiding her face.

But then she flips her head back and blows the rest of her locks from her face. Gone is the fear. Gone is the clumsy girl. Gone is the awkward girl uncomfortable in her own skin. I even forget her clothes are two sizes too big.

She's transformed from meek girl to powerful woman with one toss of her hair. Her steps are bold and robust as she struts toward the bar, only taking her three steps to reach the edge.

She smiles at the bartender, and Blake floats over to her, as under her spell as I am. I don't know what she says as she whispers to Blake, but I know he will retrieve whatever drink she ordered without verifying her age. And I'm right. Blake slides a beer to her without glancing at her ID. An ID that would either be fake or show she isn't any older than I am.

Her age doesn't matter though. The way she looks at

him with piercing greenish blue eyes and unending poise is enough to persuade him to risk his job for her.

Blake may be used to serving underage clients, but that's only because of me. I've never seen him serve anyone unassociated with me who's so clearly a minor.

The girl lifts the glass to her lips, and the foam sits on her upper lip as she drinks down the golden liquid like it is the only thing keeping her alive.

That I can understand.

I shouldn't approach her. I shouldn't think about her. I shouldn't invite more evil into her world when it's clear she running from enough herself. But I can't fight the pull. I'm not strong enough.

I leave the drinks Blake placed in front of me for Langston and Zeke. I only take my drink as I slide into the stool next to her.

Her gaze never leaves her drink as I move next to her. She doesn't realize the danger that has approached.

"What's an innocent creature like you doing in a bar like this?" I ask.

Her eyes roll gently in her head, but it's the only sign she heard me. Otherwise, I don't exist to her.

But I'm a patient man. I know she heard me, and I know she is uncomfortable with me sitting so close. She'll answer. If for no other reason than she's curious as to why I converged on her in the first place. She may not show any fear right now, but she's running from something. And the tension in her neck is enough for me to know she's terrified of me outing her and returning her to whatever she's trying to evade.

She doesn't know I would never stop her from escaping. It's a feeling I understand too well. I would never stop someone from feeling free, if only for a moment.

"I needed something to eat. There isn't anything but bars on this road for miles."

I frown. *Food? That's her excuse?*

She downs her drink, and before the last drop crosses her lips, Blake brings another bottle to replace the empty beer still in her hands.

I smirk. "It seems you need alcohol a lot more than you need food."

She shrugs. "Alcohol helps too."

"This bar doesn't serve any food. You are out of luck."

She nods. "I know." She still doesn't look at me as she speaks. It's like she's talking to a ghost. Like I don't exist to her.

"I could turn you in for underage drinking. My family is close to the cops in this town. I could have you arrested. A permanent mark on your record. But maybe that would help you. Get you somewhere safe and away from whoever you are running from."

My words finally get her attention. Her bright eyes, looking more green now than blue, finally fall on my dark orbs. Her pink lips purse, and I think she's going to yell at me or plead for me to do anything but call the cops. I expect her to beg or to dash out the door again running in fear.

"You won't turn me in, and even if you do, I don't fear the police."

My finger traces the rim of my drink instead of tracing the outline of her soft lips like I want.

"I'm not a nice man. My conscience will have no problem turning you in. I'll sleep just fine knowing I put you in jail for a night."

She licks her plump lips, and my patience teeters on the edge of a cliff. *Why the hell do I want to taste her lips?* She's just a girl. Just like all the rest of the girls I went to high school with.

I groan silently. She's not like other girls. I don't know much about her, but I know she is *nothing* like other girls.

Her bright eyes narrow into slits about to tear out my throat, and I think I finally unnerved her.

"You're not a man. You're just a boy. Just like I'm a girl, not a woman. You're not twenty-one any more than I am."

She inches closer until her face is a breath away from mine. Her lips so close I could easily take them into my mouth before she could react and stop me.

She nibbles on her bottom lip as if she knows that's exactly what I want to do.

"You may control the police, but right now, I control *you*. You won't dare call the police on me."

I exhale, my eyes squinting as I study this fascinating girl in front of me. I've never met someone who spoke so many truths and so many lies in one sentence. I lurk forward, and she stills, exhaling harsh breaths but refusing to back down.

I lick my own lip, and I watch as her bottom one trembles. Our gazes lock in a fierce battle. Neither of us will back down. I could take what I wanted without a fight from her because she refuses to show weakness. I would guess she's always this strong.

Her life is as much a struggle as mine. We would make quite a pair. But I'm afraid our lives aren't meant to do anything but intersect for a brief moment. She's here to give me a tiny sliver of entertainment. She's a distraction from my own hauntings.

Blake places a plate of burger and fries in front of the girl.

My eyes widen for less than a second, but it's long

enough for her to take it as a win. She smiles as she leans back in her chair before turning to her plate of food.

"I guess you don't know everything about this bar, *boy*," she says before shoveling a fry into her mouth.

I can't help but grin at her. The way she says boy, it doesn't feel like an insult, even though that's how she meant it. It feels freeing to seem like a boy in her eyes instead of a man who has too many responsibilities. I'm not the only one she has under her spell. This bar doesn't serve food, but it didn't stop Blake from ordering food from the nearest diner for her.

"I'm Enzo. I'm rarely proven wrong, but I'm happy to be proven wrong by..." I pause waiting for her to tell me her name.

Her eyes cut to me. "I don't give anything away for free."

"I don't either." My unblinking gaze holds hers. I gave her my name; now I expect her to give hers just as freely.

She finishes her second beer. "Buy me another drink, and maybe I'll tell you."

I finish my drink and slam it down on the bar. She jumps at the sound the glass makes as it hits the rough wood.

She startles easily.

I don't say a word, but I know Blake got my silent order loud and clear. Get me another drink and bring one for the girl.

Two minutes later, half of her burger is gone, and Blake brings another bourbon for me and another beer for her.

"Name," I command, my voice low and rumbling. I won't wait for her to follow an order. I need her to follow my demand as much as I need to drink this glass of bourbon.

She smirks. "Impatient?"

I grab her wrist as it loosely holds a fry inches from her mouth.

Her eyes widen for a millisecond before she regains her control. She's afraid of me. Or at least she doesn't like strange men gripping her wrist.

I lean forward, and my teeth snap a bite of the french fry she's still grasping.

She frowns and her body radiates anger as if me taking a bite of her fry is the greatest sin I've committed so far.

"Jocelyn."

"What?"

"You heard me."

"Jocelyn what?"

She shakes her head. "Enzo what?"

I growl, but it's so low I'm not sure it was audible.

"Jocelyn," I say again. It's a pretty name. A strong name, but for some reason, it doesn't fit the girl in front of me. I'm sure she goes by a nickname. Maybe Josie, or Jose, or Lynn. But I haven't earned her nickname. The one that only her family and friends call her. And she hasn't earned more than a first name from me.

"So Jocelyn, what are you really doing in my bar?"

Her eyebrows shoot up. "Your bar, huh?"

"Yes, *my* bar. Everything I enter becomes *mine*."

Jocelyn coughs at my words—choking slightly on the piece of burger stuck in her now dry throat.

She winces as she finally swallows the piece down, but doesn't immediately grab for her beer to relieve her throat. This girl is used to dealing with pain. It barely fazes her. And apparently speaking words to me is more important than dealing with her discomfort.

"Yours?" She drags her teeth across her bottom lip, and my dick, along with the rest of my body hardens to stone.

"You may own everything you enter, but I control everything I touch." Her hand moves to my glass sitting on the edge of the bar. Her finger lazily traces around the rim of the thick glass just as I had done before. And then her finger dips into the center, pulling up a drop of whiskey before she brings her finger to her mouth and sucks her finger dry.

I groan.

She purrs in response as if drawing me closer to her. She's playing with fire.

I grab another fry off her plate and bite off the end with my mouth, needing to regain my composure and at least the illusion of control. This twig of girl can't control me. She has no power over me. Even my father, the ruthless man he is, can't tame me.

But somehow, this girl did. If only for a moment, she claimed me as hers and made me want to do whatever I could to please her. But just as quickly the spell she cast over me broke.

She growls and snatches the remainder of her precious fry out of my hand before shoveling it into her mouth, along with the rest of the food on her plate until not even a crumb remains.

My breathing slows. *How did I not notice before?*

The spaghetti strap shirt she wears lowers, and I see the thin frame of her collarbone protruding more than what is healthy. I glance at her wrist I held only moments before. Now it seems so frail I could snap it with the twist of my hand. And I swear I can see her hip bone sticking out through the thin fabric of her shorts.

She's too skinny. Too frail. Too hungry.

I've known women like her. Some were drug addicts.

But from the lack of needle marks on her skin, I know

that is not that case. And even though she's drunk a lot of beer, I don't get the feeling that she is an alcoholic. Her body doesn't tremble at the sight of alcohol.

Others I've met were whores.

But from the innocent way she keeps biting her lip, I can't imagine her selling her body to survive.

And others...others were sold.

"Who did you escape from?" I need to know if she escaped from an enemy or from one of my own. If she escaped from my enemies, then I will have great pleasure in keeping her from them, but if she fled from one of my own...

She cocks her head to the side, studying me, trying to understand the hidden meaning behind my words.

"Answer me." I grab her wrist again firmly, showing her I won't let her go without an answer.

Her breathing speeds, and I feel her pulse skipping rapidly through her icy veins. I was right. She was sold. I just need to know who her master was. Then I can decide what to do with her.

I don't agree with men kidnapping and selling women like cattle. But right now, staring at this endearing creature, I get the appeal.

She closes her eyes, and I imagine she's picturing her master's eyes, his commanding voice, even his cock as it drives inside her.

I study her body. She's thin, but not bruised. She hasn't been broken yet. He may have not even fucked her yet. She's just hungry and hasn't been taken for long, which makes me want to break her myself.

I'm sick.

Jocelyn isn't mine. And I won't take her and be her master. I just need to know who I should return her to.

"I belong to myself. I've never been sold. And I will never be taken."

Her eyes puncture mine with sharp ice, and I realize she's speaking the truth. I've always been good at judging people. I know when someone is telling the truth or a lie.

"Then why are you starving?"

She trembles and her eyes are downcast as if that was the question that hurt her. Not the one before, assuming she was a slave.

I feel the tsunami of emotions behind her olive eyelids, before she opens them and erases any remnants of pain.

"I'm not starving. Not anymore. I'm surviving."

Jocelyn looks to where I'm still gripping her wrist, as if her eyes have any control of my hand. But somehow I can't resist what her eyes demand. I release her.

She stands. She's done with our conversation. I'm almost done too, but it doesn't stop me from getting the last word in. I stand, and our bodies collide in the thin space between our bar stools.

Her movement is fast. So fast I shouldn't even notice it. No normal person with an ordinary upbringing would notice her action. My buddies sitting in the booth deep in the corner of the bar wouldn't. And no one sitting the length of the bar would.

But I do.

It's the oldest trick in the book.

She turns to leave, acting as if nothing just happened between us.

"Jocelyn," my voice is harsh as I say her name, and as I expected, she halts. A skill I have perfected. I can control people as easily with my voice as I can with my fists.

I slowly walk to her, and I can feel the anxiety dripping off of her in thin droplets. Her body doesn't show any outward hint of worry, but I can smell the panic as it festers inside her.

I stand in front of her, and she continues to hold her head high. She won't show weakness. She won't show fear.

I shouldn't do this. I should just let her have what she took. I should be kind. It could be the difference between her eating another good meal and withering away into nothing. But I'm not kind; I'm heartless. And I don't tolerate thievery.

I hold out my hand and look down at her with displeasure. I don't have to say a word. She knows what she did.

She reaches into her back pocket and places the thick leather wallet into my hand.

I grin. "Good girl."

Her eyes meet mine, and for a second I think I see something more. Something like winning in her gaze. But she didn't win, *I did.*

"Thank you for lunch," she says. And then she's gone before I can respond or stop her from running out without paying her bill.

I smirk at my thick wallet and glance at the bar. She didn't steal from me or the bar by not paying for her food and drinks. She thought she won by stealing three beers, a burger, and fries from me. But I won't be paying her bill.

I never pay my own. That's why Zeke and Langston are here. Not that I can't afford to pay for something so inexpensive. But why should I pay? I own everything in this town. I shouldn't have to pay myself for something I take.

I walk back to the booth in the corner and take my seat.

"You let some pussy almost steal from you?" Langston says, smirking.

I glare, and the smile leaves his face. He hides behind

his drink that Lana, our waiter, must have brought him while I was entertained by the girl.

"No one steals from me."

They both nod. They know the consequences if someone stole from me.

"She your whore now? Or can I have a taste of her?" Zeke asks.

I lean back in the booth and drape my arm over the back. I don't want either of them going after Jocelyn. She's mine, even if I never get to touch her.

"I think you have too much work to do to be chasing pussy," I say.

Zeke huffs but doesn't push the subject. Lana drops off the bill that I know covers our drinks in addition to Jocelyn's tab. Langston places his credit card on the bill without looking. He knows better than to balk at paying. It's why I pay him so well. Even though my family owns the bar and I don't have to pay, it's a way for my friends to show loyalty to me by covering our drinks.

"What time are you meeting your father?"

"Three."

I glance at my watch and freeze.

Instead of the shiny silver face of my Rolex staring back at me, I see the faint tan line of where the watch used to sit.

I smirk.

I may be the devil, but Jocelyn is a thief. She left this bar knowing she had won. She never had any intention to steal my wallet. She wouldn't have gotten much from my wallet anyway. There is nothing more than a couple hundred dollar bills tucked in its depths along with credit cards I would have been canceled before she could use them and would only leave a trail for me to find her.

Instead, she stole the one thing of real value on my body. The watch is worth over ten grand.

Round one goes to the thief, but the devil only ever gets deceived once. Jocelyn has no idea who she stole from. But soon, I'll make sure she never forgets.

2

KAI

I STOLE.

I swore I would never do it again. But I didn't have a choice.

It wasn't about my survival. If it were only me, then I wouldn't have stolen. Even from someone like Enzo, who has more money than he could possibly spend in a lifetime, based on the expensive clothes he was wearing. But I didn't steal for me. I stole to save my father.

And now I owe another debt that will take me years to repay.

I hold the silver watch in my hand, running my fingers across its smooth face. The watch is warm despite it being made of metal. I make a mental note to repay Enzo when I can, but the reminder won't be necessary. I'm afraid I will remember Enzo forever.

His hair was darker than night. His chiseled jaw covered with the dark shadow of his stubble will haunt me for not feeling how the rough edges would feel when I kissed him. And his deep eyes spoke of pain and heartache that no boy our age should have ever experienced.

I glance back down the street to where the bar sits. I could still return it. Enzo doesn't deserve to feel any more pain. This watch is expensive, and although I don't know anything about Enzo, he appears not to be hurting for money. *But what if the watch was given to him by his father? Or his mother? What if it was passed down for generations? What if the love of his life gave it to him? What if it is irreplaceable?*

I study the timepiece further. It's new and barely worn, without a single scratch on it. Almost like today was the first day he wore it. *It can't mean much to him if he's never worn it, can it?*

A man walks down the sidewalk toward me. I keep my gaze down, trying not to draw attention to the fact that I notice him.

He's not here for me, I repeat to myself.

He's just a stranger walking down the sidewalk. But it doesn't stop the chill running down my spine.

I will repay Enzo someday. I will make things right. Even if I hate him.

No, hate is too strong of a word. I don't hate him. Although I've never been so tempted to kiss someone in my life. Never wanted to forget about myself more than I did when I was near him. And also never wanted to be swept off my feet by a prince charming who would take me far away from here. Someone who would protect me and ensure I never had to worry about where my next meal came from.

But Enzo isn't my prince charming, and even if he were, it's not what I want. I will find my own way out of this mess I'm in.

I may not hate Enzo, but he reminded me temptation is real. And I can't lose focus. I can't let myself fall for a boy like Enzo. I don't know anything about him except the look on his face when he taunts me.

I don't remember Enzo from school, but I know he can't be more than a year or two older than me. Seventeen or eighteen I would guess. Not that I attended much school. It's a waste of time when you need every hour to make enough money to eat.

I continue walking down the sidewalk, past the row of bars. It's mid-afternoon, so the streets near the bars have yet to grow busy, but in a few hours, they will be filled with people washing their worries away with a drink and loud music.

My feet carry me automatically, knowing these streets like the back of my hand. My fingers find the door of the pawn shop on the corner, three blocks over. I slip inside without any guilt.

I always repay my debts. Always. No matter the cost.

The door chimes loudly, announcing my presence, not that I need to be announced. Jim is standing behind the counter like he expected me. I haven't been here in a while, but I have no doubt he heard of the debt my father owes. This is the only way I know how to make enough money to pay off his debt quickly, and Jim knows it.

I don't hesitate. I walk to the counter, ignoring the smell of sweat and desperation that seems to always hang in the air here. People come here not because they are greedy, but because they have no other choice but to sell some prized possession or stolen item to survive. The same reason I'm here.

I pull the stolen watch from my pocket and lay it on the counter. Jim picks it up without a word, already knowing what I want from him.

He studies the watch carefully, running this thumb across the face's surface just as I did earlier. He looks for scratches or signs of damage. He taps the metal; I assume to test for authenticity.

I don't know how to determine if a watch is counterfeit or not. If I found this watch on the street, I would have a fifty-fifty shot at guessing its value. But after meeting Enzo, I know he would only wear the real deal. He's not fake. He has money. He's grown up in an entirely different world from me. And while it still pains me to take it from him, not knowing entirely what it cost him, I will not let the value of the watch go to waste.

"Five thousand," Jim says, meeting my gaze as he lets the watch lie flat on the counter while we haggle.

I've done a few deals with Jim before. Never for anything of this much value. I know he's a fair man, but I also know I have to be willing to lose the sale to get the full worth out of it.

I can't lose.

I don't have time to find another pawn shop to sell to. The next pawn shop owner might not be so kind. I may have to show my ID or proof of ownership. This is my only shot.

I stare at the watch, reminding me too much of the owner I only just met.

I know the exact amount I need. I also know how much I need to feed myself and my father for a month. The amount to give us some breathing room. To pay for our rent.

But this watch is only about one thing—getting one more day of freedom from my father's debts.

I won't be selfish. I won't take more than I deserve.

"Eight thousand," I counter.

Jim smiles. "That's an awfully high price for a watch, Miss Miller."

I glare back at him. "I know its worth, Mr. Wilson. I

know it is easily worth more than ten thousand, and it is in pristine condition. I know you will easily sell it for more than ten grand because you are a good salesman. You could sell a fake for that much easily. You'll sell the real deal for more."

He chuckles. "I am a good salesman, but that doesn't mean I'll pay you eight grand."

I reach out like I'm going to take the watch back. "No, you would give me ten if I pushed the subject because it's a good investment for you that you can easily make a couple grand off of and because you know if you treat me well, I will bring you more quality items to sell in the future."

I grab the watch. It feels good to have it in my hand even though I know the cost of keeping the watch for myself. But I can't stop myself from wanting the watch. From wanting *him*. I slide the watch across the counter toward me before Jim grabs my wrist stopping me.

"Seven-five, final offer."

I smile. I need seven thousand three hundred to pay off the debt. Two hundred extra. But I won't spend it on food, clothes, or shelter. It will be the first step to paying off my new debt.

"Deal."

Jim nods and then looks down at my hand still gripping the watch while he still holds my wrist. He releases me and waits for me to turn the watch over.

Instead of letting it go, I hold the watch tighter. I'm not ready to let it go. I'm not ready to let Enzo go. Not that either was ever mine in the first place. But there was something about Enzo that taunted me with a future I have always wanted. Money, protection, and adventure.

Something my current life lacks. My life is destined to become the same over and over. I have no future—nothing beyond working my ass off to repay debts. No man would ever want to take me on, not when they realize the money they would owe just to ensure we would be free.

"Miss Miller?"

I cling to the watch for a single second, reminding me of the promise in Enzo's eyes. He wanted me. Somehow I know a single night with Enzo would have been more adventure than I ever dreamed my boring life could have.

"Miss Miller?"

I turn and meet Jim's gaze.

He holds out his hand, and I raise mine over his. The watch doesn't fall out of my hand willingly. It glides reluctantly through my grasp like I'm letting my future slip away —a future I can never have.

Jim takes the watch, and my eyes burn with regret as I watch him place the watch in a small black box. Its gleam disappears beneath the lid as he closes it away from me. He then turns to the cash register.

"Cash or check?"

I swallow hard as my mind returns to my reality of what I need to do.

"Cash."

He nods, already knowing what my answer will be. He pulls out the cash and counts it into my hand.

"Stay safe, Miss Miller. I wouldn't want anything to happen to one of my best customers."

The wad of cash is large, too bulky to conceal in anything but a purse or bag I don't have. And I won't spend a dime on any of the purses lining the rack at the front of the pawn shop, even if I should to ensure I make it back home with all of the bills. I tuck a handful into each of my two pockets and then shove the remaining into my bra, not caring that Jim eyes my cleavage as I do.

"I always do."

His eyes seek mine, and I swear I see a hint of concern etched in the wrinkles that form around his eyes. "See that you do."

He knows where the watch came from. I don't know how. I didn't notice any etchings or name written across the band. But Jim knows, and he's warning me. I'm not going to get anything else out of him though—no other help or words to explain why he's worrying. I'm not afraid of anyone, including the boy I stole the watch from.

I turn without another word and leave the pawn shop, leaving only the ringing chimes of the door as I exit.

The sun blazes hotter as I step outside, causing instant blisters to form on my bare shoulders. I wish I had a car, a bike, any form of transportation to get me home faster. I would even settle on a hat to shade my head from the burning rays causing sweat to bead down from my forehead to my back. Even my ass is sweating.

The heat doesn't stop me from running. I have two miles to run to make it back to the trailer and not a minute to spare. So I run, despite my flip-flops, despite the intense heat, and knowing what awaits me when I get home.

My flip-flops slow me down, so I take them off and run, risking piercing my foot on broken glass that tends to clutter the sidewalks from drunk tourists. Risking tetanus with each step doesn't stop my feet from running.

Running should make me feel free. My feet are moving so fast, my body flying. But I only run out of fear. Only one thing makes me feel free. Only one thing brings me a moment to forget. I close my eyes as sea salt sprays my face. The ocean is the only place I truly feel free.

My body collides with that of another. The body isn't

strong enough to knock me down, just enough to make me stop.

"Mason," I gasp and fling my arms around my only friend in the world.

He holds me tightly in his scrawny arms as I bury my face in his chest, breathing in his cheap cologne so different from the rich, musky scent that oozed from Enzo. I may have called Enzo a boy, but he carries himself like a man. Mason, on the other hand, is a boy through and through. Mason is skinny, not from lack of food, but because he hit a growth spurt recently and his body has yet to catch up with his new found height. His muscles are there, but thin against his frame in long bands, not thick with years of working out. His hair hangs in long waves around his tanned face, made for the beach. But no one would ever call him anything but a boy.

I pull away and see the hauntingly worried look in Mason's face. I can't call him anything but a friend, even though I felt him sniff my hair as he held me. Even though I felt his body go rigid, his cock stirring against my flat body.

His feelings have only recently developed. A few months ago he thought of me as nothing more than a friend. More like an annoying younger sister than as a girl he craves. But things changed. I don't know how or when exactly. But they did. Mason stopped seeing me as a girl and started thinking about me as a woman. But he's wrong. I'm nothing but a naive girl and Mason is my friend. That's all.

"What are you doing here?" I ask as I pull away, out of his clutches. Mason is standing at the entrance to our trailer. He rarely comes here. When we hang out, it's at school or his home. An actual house. Not here. Not where we are both reminded of how I come from nothing, and he has everything.

"You haven't been at school in weeks. I was worried about you." He strokes my face, and I see the fret all over his.

I nod. "I've been busy working. I should have called and told you I was fine."

"You don't seem fine. You wouldn't have run into my arms that way if you were fine."

I smile making sure the edge of my mouth reaches my eyes, so it seems genuine. "I missed you, Mason. And I wasn't expecting to see you again until I go back to school."

"Don't lie to me, Kai. You're not planning on returning to school, not now that you are sixteen and not legally required to go. You've been slipping away more and more to work on that boat. To pay back debts that aren't yours to be burdened with." His fingers twist the ends of my hair between his fingers. "Stay with me, Kai. Finish school. You could live in Colton's room, now that he is away at college. My parents wouldn't mind. And then after you and I could—"

"I can't." I won't let Mason finish his thought. I don't think I can ever think of Mason as more than my friend. I don't think I can think of any man in that way. Not if I want to survive.

"You can."

I shake my head. "My father needs me."

"Your father is a grown man. He can take care of himself. Come with me."

I hear the footsteps behind me, the rough sand shifting beneath their feet and their voices echoing throughout the trailer park. This is a world Mason doesn't belong in, and I won't let him become a part of it.

"You should go. My shift starts soon."

Mason nods. "I can give you a ride."

"Dad is giving me a ride on his way into town."

Mason studies me a moment, trying to determine if I'm lying or not.

"I need to change. I'll see you at school next week. I promise." I pat his shoulder and smile. He seems to accept my words as truth. He doesn't realize his friend would ever lie to him. He doesn't understand what it's like to do anything to survive.

"I'll see you next week, Kai." He smiles back at me brightly, thinking our world will go back to normal.

He walks away with a small skip to his step. My smile drops watching him. I hate lying, but I won't let myself bring him down with me.

The voices grow closer, and I turn in their direction.

"Where's your father, *girl*?" The man who speaks can't be much older than I am. Maybe early twenties if I had to guess. His voice is harsh and demanding. He's used to getting what he wants with his threatening voice and stony stare. I see the glint of a gun at his side beneath a jacket that is too warm to be wearing here.

"My father's not here."

The man growls as he approaches and grabs my arm, pushing me hard against the side of the trailer.

I wince but quickly bring my face back to neutral. *Never show weakness.*

"I've been chasing you all day, girl. And I have no time for games. Where is your father? If you don't find him, I'll make sure *you* repay his debt."

I hold my breath to keep my body from trembling in fear. To keep him from noticing the speed of my heartbeat. I saw him earlier today. Hunting my father and me down like animals.

That's why I ducked into the bar.

That's why I stole from Enzo.

Not to keep this man from hurting me. I already know I will lose my virginity by a man like him. Repaying a debt neither my father nor I could pay.

I've accepted it.

I don't need to be a fortune teller to know my future. It's the same as any of the other girls living in the trailer park.

But I stopped it happening for one more day. I stopped my father from being beaten, tortured, and killed for one more day.

One more day.

That's all I can ever buy. That's all I can ever steal.

"I have what you came for."

The man's hand moves to my throat.

I gasp.

I can't help it. It's natural to fight for breath when he touches me like this. I can't resist my natural instinct to survive. To find air where there is none.

I recoil into my body, trying to keep my fear inside.

His eyes travel up and down my body, assessing me, deciding if my body is enough to forgive my father's debt.

He chuckles in anger. "You are far too skinny for my liking. You're not even a woman yet. You haven't filled out with curves that I can sink my teeth into."

I growl as he speaks about my body and then spit in his face.

His laughter deepens as he studies my mouth. "Although, pushing my cock into your throat so you can't speak or breathe might please me. It will not be enough to repay the debt your father owes, but it will entertain me until he returns."

He pushes me toward the trailer. I stumble into the door.

Asshole.

I feel him walking toward me, but I won't let him touch me again. I turn with a fierceness surging through my veins.

"I have the money to pay you back."

He eyes me up and down again. "I won't take a check from you, girl. I know anything you write will bounce."

"Good, because I intend to pay you in cash."

I dig into my bra and pull out the first wad of cash. His eyes grow big as he stares at the thick bundle.

"How did you get the money? Did you already whore yourself out to protect dear old daddy?"

My eyes tighten into slits. My body tenses, and I dig my heels into the hard sand to keep myself from attacking this man. "Do you want the money or not?"

He nods.

I pull the rest of the money from my pockets, careful to keep the last two hundred in my pockets away from his eyes. If he saw I had more money, he would take that too, as interest.

I shove the wad of money into his hands.

"How do I know this is everything?"

"Because unlike you I'm not a filthy liar. I keep my promises and pay back everything I owe. Now leave." I turn and march into the unlocked trailer before he says another word. I slam the door shut and stick the broom through the door handle to lock the door. It does no good when we leave the house, but there isn't anything inside worth stealing. All it does is provide some level of protection to keep men like him out.

I shake against the door, my breathing fast and heavy. Even so, I don't get enough oxygen into my lungs. Goosebumps cover my thin arms and my gut wrenches at the thought of being violated.

I close my eyes and try to forget about him grabbing my neck. About threatening to rape me or stick his cock down my throat. I try to forget it all, but I never can. It's not the first, nor the last time I'll be threatened.

A knock pounds at the door making me jump. *He got his money. What could he possibly want?*

My mind races with what to do, how to save myself. I run to the drawer in the kitchenette. I yank it open and rummage through the drawer looking for a knife. All I find is a butter knife.

The knock rattles the entire trailer this time, and I grip the dull knife in my hand aiming it toward the door. Maybe I'll be able to jab it in his eye, and he will leave realizing I'm not worth the struggle.

"Kai, it's me." My dad's voice travels through the door, weak and worried. He must have seen the man he owes a debt to. He doesn't know I paid it. That I'm still alive with my virginity still intact.

I race to the door, pull the broom handle out, and open the door still gripping the knife.

Father lets out a breath when he sees me. "Are you...?" He can't finish.

I drop the knife. "I'm fine."

It's the truth. I'm fine. I'm always fine, but never more.

Never safe.

Never happy.

Just fine.

"Good." He nods. "I can't stay. Mr. Bramble is—"

"I took care of it." I step back to let father into the trailer. He doesn't offer me a hug, although I can tell he was concerned about him. And even if he did, I wouldn't relish the embrace the way I did Mason's. Father may care about me, and I may risk my life to take care of him, but it doesn't stop the anger or pain we both feel toward each other. We just haven't been able to find our way after we lost my mother.

He studies me a moment and then nods. He doesn't thank me. He doesn't ask how I came up with the money. He doesn't tell me he's sorry for the life he's forced me in to. Nothing, but a nod.

He walks to the recliner in what most would call a living room and sinks into it, putting his feet up in the chair. He'll be asleep within minutes. The trailer has only one bedroom that is big enough for one tiny twin bed. I sleep there; he sleeps here.

We shouldn't hate each other, but we do. We shouldn't resent each other. It's neither of our faults, not really. My father does his best captaining various vessels, mostly yachts for the rich. They pay him well, but we will never get out of the debt my mother caused us.

Cancer.

She died of cancer when I was little, so young I can't even remember her. She fought a long time, over five years. But the entire time she was nothing but a vegetable. But that didn't stop my father from trying to save her. Through chemo, treatment, the nurses and doctors costing more than we could ever afford to repay.

Most men in the trailer park have addictions that have cost their families everything. Gambling, drinking, drugs.

Not my family.

My family will forever be haunted by the ghost of my mother. If only her body had given up when her spirit did, then we would just have thousands of dollars in debt to repay instead of millions.

Then my father wouldn't have to take on more loans

from nefarious people to pay the medical bills that never end.

Then I would be able to attend school instead of working all day long.

Then maybe father and I would have a relationship beyond two people merely surviving in the same trailer.

That's not life.

That's a fairytale.

I watch as my father closes his eyes. Sometimes I think he'd rather stay on the fancy yachts, away from here, where even his debts can't find him. Instead of coming home to this dump. I haven't seen him for three weeks, but it makes no difference to me. He's the only family I have and just as he works to protect me, I work to protect him.

I don't wake him as I head out the door, even though I should, to ensure he pushes the broom handle back through the door, so he's safe. I just slip out of the trailer and start my long walk to the docks. Because even though I stole over seven grand today, it's not enough.

It's never enough.

I ensured our survival for one more day. But we don't have enough for food for tomorrow. And now, I have my own debt to repay.

3

ENZO

I STEP into Surrender and my eyes automatically darken. The club's name is simple and is a little on the nose. There are no windows and very few lights. It's like stepping into darkness, forcing you to relinquish your sight, body, and soul when you enter.

My spine straightens, my lips thin, and every muscle in my body tightens as I morph into the cruel vulture I was taught to be. Gone is the boy I only occasionally let out when I think no one is looking. Everyone's eyes fall on me as soon as I step foot into the club. I'm underage, far too young to be in a place like this. But I've been coming here since I was seven. This club is what twisted my soul and made sure when I die I won't be going anywhere but hell.

My eyes don't acknowledge the stares as I walk. I know better than to give any of the drunks sitting near the entrance the time of day. They only come here to gawk at the dancing women, get drunk, and forget.

I envy them. They live a simple life, one where drinking actually makes them forget, because the worst they have to ignore is their cheating wives or inability to pay rent from their pathetic jobs.

It's the men that sit further into the club I have to worry about. They are the ones who have real money. They have power.

I walk deeper into the club, keeping my head up. I won't make eye contact with any of them, but I feel their eyes on me.

I'm the youngest man in this club and despite being younger, smaller, weaker; I'm their prince. This is all mine to collect.

Mine to rule.

Mine to control.

And because I'm the prince, every man here wants me dead.

I haven't earned the right to rule them, but I will. I don't have a choice if I want to live.

But for now, I get to continue breathing. I've made the mistake before, of staring at one of the men. It was a mistake I won't repeat. Fights don't break out in the club often; it's not allowed unless it's part of the entertainment. But each man in here feels they have to protect their pride, and when that pride is challenged, they fight. No rule is going to stop them.

I can fight. I've won plenty, lost more. Sometimes I come here seeking them out, wanting to feel the pain and adrenaline, the high that only comes when my fist connects with a jaw as blood spurts in my face. But today isn't that day.

And I've gained enough respect after my last fight that most here wouldn't dare to threaten me. At least not personally. They would send some of their minions to fight against me. Most likely sending several men to a fight that wouldn't be fair.

My lips curl up into a smirk as I think back to my last fight where I broke a glass and used the shards to draw blood against my weaponless opponent. *Not that I fight fair either.*

Deeper and deeper I descend into the abyss, into the cave of the club that will one day be mine. My heart grows darker along with the light surrounding me. There are no windows this deep into the club. The light from the lamps only illuminates how black the room is.

I don't need the light to guide me; I know how many steps it takes to get to my father's room. I know where to avoid stepping to keep my feet silent, instead of making the hardwood floor creak. I know where to walk to stay in the shadows instead of shimmering in the light.

It's not necessary to creep through the club silently, trying to be invisible. It's not possible anyway. Not with the security cameras and men everywhere. Not when every man here knows exactly who I am. But it's a habit I can't break. I'm only visible, only heard when I want to be.

The thick door is shut to my father's room, but I don't knock. I turn the knob and step inside, letting the door fall closed behind me.

My lip twitches as I see my father sitting in his favorite chair toward the back of the room. Three women, more naked than clothed, dance around and on him. Two other men sit in chairs next to them. All have two fingers of the finest scotch in the glass in their hands.

This room serves as many things for my father.

His lair.

His office.

His sanctuary.

He's fucked countless women in here and punished every man who has dared to cross him.

I don't think he'd ever leave this room if he didn't need to prowl the rest of the club and city to maintain his power.

"Gentleman and ladies, I need to speak with my father."

The women look to my father for their cue what to do. My father's gaze penetrates through me as he waves them off. They start walking toward the door in the back that leads out to another hallway. One of the women turns back winking at me as she runs her hand down her neck and across her pointed nipple—indicating she'd gladly fuck me later and wouldn't care if I paid her like my father.

I understand why. The woman is in her early twenties. Most men in this club are in their thirties or forties. Some in their fifties. She would love to go a round with a man closer to her age. I may be seventeen, but my life experience has hardened me and makes me seem older.

Maybe I'll find her later. I could use a fuck to get out some of my pent up energy. Especially after meeting Jocelyn. Gorgeous, intriguing, and a thief. Her deep sea-colored eyes will haunt me the rest of my life. Because as much as I'd like to find her and make her pay for stealing from me, I won't. My reputation is still intact. No one knows she stole. And if I found her, I would punish her.

Cruel.

Mercilessly.

Until I possessed her.

Jocelyn deserves to be punished, but I've never disciplined a woman before. Not because I'm too good, kind, or chivalrous.

One day I will. Whether by choice or necessity. And then my fall into darkness will be complete.

But I'm still young. I still have a drop of light left in my veins, and I'm not ready to relinquish it yet. Because if I touched her, I would ruin her.

Break her.

Own her.

The two gentlemen remain in their seats. I've known both men my whole life. They are two of my father's best men. Highest in rank, and trusted with his very life. But I know what this meeting is about, and they won't be privy to it.

"Alone," I growl.

I may be half their age. I may be heir to this kingdom. But I've earned my right to get to speak to the king alone. Being his son has nothing to do with it.

The threat of what I'd do if the men stayed is evident in my voice. I don't care if they are my father's men. I would kill them.

Both men start to turn to my father to ask what to do, but my unyielding glare along with the low rumble of my throat make them rethink their plans. They stand immediately, and head for the door the women exited through.

My father smirks as they leave.

"Good to know you are finally learning something from your old man," he says.

I ignore him as I take a seat in the chair his number two emptied. I help myself to the glass of scotch Baldwin left as he scurried out like a worried rat.

"You summoned me." I sip the scotch, letting the warm liquid seep through me, making my already hot skin race with the fire of the liquid. I'm always hot, ready to attack—a blaze of sweltering fire that can't be stopped.

"I did, and you came, like a good little son."

It's an insult. All of his words toward me are. He says them to get a reaction out of me, but I've long learned to pretend his insults and threats don't exist.

"Did you have a point in bringing me here? Because I

have a full schedule for today, including ensuring you make millions and the men are in line."

"Impatient fuck as always." He shakes his head. "I would have thought any son of mine would have learned to respect his elder, his leader."

My eyes darken as my lids fall, only allowing the tiniest slit of my eye to remain open. I know how to close off from this man. I know how to keep my composure. I'm seventeen. Practically an adult. No longer a boy. But around this man, who calls himself my father, I struggle to be anything but a ten-year-old boy who disobeyed. I won't be that scared little boy anymore. Not around him.

Instead, I sip on my drink like I want to be here, and I wait. I have more patience than my father ever will. I could sit here all day and all night without flinching. I know how to go deep within myself and ignore everything else. Food, drink, feelings, *everything*. I know how to shut out the world. If he wants me to be patient, I will be. And he'll lose.

He sighs. "I have a target for you."

I raise an eyebrow but don't speak. I know he has more to say.

I've killed men before, nine to be exact, so this isn't an unusual request. What is strange is that he brought me here, to the place he holds holy to give his order, instead of sending one of his men. So what's different about this one?

"How?" I know it's the right question. Does he want me to make this man suffer or kill him quickly? What kind of man am I dealing with? Am I taking out a monster or enemy? Dispatching the leader of a gang or disposing of one of our own who dared not to follow orders?

My father's body stills as he considers his next words.

"You decide."

My eyes widen, and I almost choke on my scotch. I

never get to make a decision. I may rule a group of men who will follow every order I give, but it's not the same as having free will to decide when and who we strike. I'm only following my father's orders when I give my own.

His mouth curls down at my reaction. Disappointment, I've seen it before.

I stiffen again into stone, ensuring I won't show a moment of weakness again.

"Who's the target?"

My father remains silent as he sips his drink. His pupils widen as he imagines the target in his head. Whatever this man did to deserve my father's wrath is bad. And now I decipher his meaning. I know what the real test is, why my father won't tell me how to dispose of him. Because once I know what this man did, it's up to me to prove my worth to my father, by correctly dispatching of him. By giving him the correct punishment for his crimes, and seeing that justice, at least in the eyes of my father, is done.

"What did he do?"

He turns toward me, his lips finally curling into the evil grin I'm used to seeing.

"Nothing."

Fuck.

I've killed in self-defense before. Injured many men, fighting battles to defend my family's power.

I've killed men who hurt my family or this club. Killed those who were planning to take us down. But I've never killed someone who was innocent.

It doesn't mean my father is telling me the truth either. This man could be innocent or my father's greatest foe. It makes no difference. I'll kill him all the same.

Because that's what I am—a killing machine. My father trained me my entire life to be an assassin so I could prove my worth to him. My first kill was when I was thirteen, and it has been my life ever since.

My father sees the change in my body despite the wall I put up. He knows I'll follow his every command without hesitation.

"Good." He nods at me.

My stomach drops feeling like my transformation into the devil is complete. Except the devil is still sitting three feet away from me. *How can I be the devil when he's still alive?*

"One more thing. You do this kill, *the right way,* then you will get power."

If it's possible my body stills even more. Except for my bloody heart. It thumps loudly in my chest. This is what I've been waiting for, for seventeen years—this chance.

"Kill, and you will no longer take orders from anyone. Kill, and your debt will be paid. Kill, and you'll owe me nothing. Kill, and you'll be free."

Free.

It's all I've ever wanted. Freedom.

My father is offering me what I've sought all these years.

But I doubt doing this will indeed set me free. If anything it will bring me deeper into the darkness with him. And he knows that.

It doesn't matter. This is what my whole life has been leading me toward—this final kill.

Who am I kidding? This won't be my final kill, but maybe it will be the last one I do for my father.

I growl. My father doesn't tell the truth often, at least not to his men. He doesn't have to explain himself to anyone, but he's never lied to me. So I have no reason to believe he is lying now. If I do this, then I'll be free. At least of him, but never this club. *Never this life.*

I nod, agreeing to his terms, cementing my place in hell.

He pulls out a pen from his pocket and takes the napkin on the table where his drink sat. He scribbles on it, then hands it to me.

I unfold the napkin and stare at the name before downing the rest of my scotch.

Kai Miller, you're a dead man.

4

KAI

I FEEL him before I see him.

I shouldn't know how he feels when he's around me. I've only met him once. I've barely had time to study the curves of his face. Barely had time to notice the richness of his voice. The small wave of his hair. The light scruff on his face. The way he walks, tall and strong. I shouldn't have noticed any of it, but I did. And now I could sense Enzo out of a crowd of a million. I would zero in on him immediately.

I sense him approaching easily; he sucks all the oxygen out of any room he is in, casting a dark shadow as he moves like a predator. Even though I'm standing on the front deck of a large yacht and there is air all around me, I can't breathe.

Enzo's steps are quiet, I shouldn't be able to hear his feet hitting the dock, but I do. He moves silently, a skill I'm sure he uses to his advantage to do whatever nefarious things he spends his days doing.

I try to ignore him and continue mopping the wooden floor of the yacht, but it's hard for me to pretend I don't notice him.

His feet still on the pier next to the yacht and my arms slow their movement as I stare down at his dark black boots.

Boots? Why the hell is he wearing boots?

It's summertime in Miami. Most people here wear flip-flops, boat shoes, or go barefoot. The only people who wear boots around here are those that work. Those that clean or catch fish for money to bring back to their families. People like my father or me. Not the kind that was handed daddy's money. Enzo doesn't understand anything about hard work. He's a spoiled rich kid.

I can't help but curl an eyebrow up as my eyes travel further up his body. Gone is the dark pants and buttoned-down shirt, replaced with jeans and a tight black shirt. He looks like he could disappear into the night, even though it's the middle of the afternoon.

Enzo folds his arms across his chest, and he looks at me sternly. A look I've seen plenty of times from my father when he's about to give me a whooping. The look is meant to intimidate me into doing whatever he wants, but it takes a lot more than a look to cause me to worry.

I suck in a breath and then get back to work. I've almost finished cleaning the yacht. It wasn't as disgusting as the one I did last week. That one had puke, piss, and blood all over it. I'm hoping the second one I'm supposed to clean is as easy as this one.

"Thief," Enzo says.

Shit.

But of course Enzo noticed I stole his watch. He realized immediately that I took his wallet, even though that was the plan all along. To get him to catch me stealing his wallet, so it would be easier to steal his watch. I just didn't think he would care enough about his watch to track me down.

There is no point denying what I did. I can't pretend he lost his watch or he was the victim of a desperate pick-pock-eter. We both know what I did.

I stand up straighter and stop mopping. I wipe the sweat from my brow. He's changed in the hours since I saw him, but other than tying a bandana around my hair to keep it off my face, I haven't. I look the same, except sweat beads down my skin and more dirt clings to my flesh than before.

I nod. "I stole your watch."

His eyes lighten. "You did."

Shit, he's not going to make this easy. But I'm not going to collapse and beg for forgiveness on my knees. I did what I had to, to survive.

"I'm sorry I stole your watch."

He jumps onto the yacht despite the high gap between the deck and the pier. It's a large jump most people wouldn't dare take, but he does it with ease, like he's made the leap thousands of times and never once thought of plummeting into the water if he were to miscalculate his movement.

I take a step back before I can help myself.

He grins like I just showed a weakness.

"Are you now? Because you don't look sorry to me."

"I'm sorry, I would have never stolen it if I had a choice."

He laughs. "You had a choice. You chose to steal from me. Do you have any idea what I do to thieves?"

I stare down at his clenched fists. "I'm sure I have an idea."

He cocks his head as he takes another step closer. This time, I don't step back. I let him inch closer, but I squeeze the mop handle harder. I will use it as a weapon if I have to.

"But it doesn't scare you. I don't scare you?"

"No."

He shakes his head. "Stupid girl."

I narrow my eyes into deep slits. "I'm not stupid."

He sighs. "Then why did you steal from *me*? There were countless other men in the bar you could have stolen from."

I feel the color returning to my face. This question is easy. "Because you needed the watch the least. You have more money than anyone in that bar—more money than most people in this city. You could call someone and have the watch replaced in five minutes, and you wouldn't even notice the downward tick in your bank account. You were the least likely to be hurt by my actions."

My words surprise him. It's clear in the way his body hardens, his eyebrow inches up, and his jaw twitches.

"Unless..." I start. "Unless, the watch was a family heirloom or gift. Did your father or girlfriend give you the watch? Is it irreplaceable?"

I don't know why I ask. I wouldn't rat out Jim. I can't track down the watch and get it back for him, but at least I will know how much I truly have to repay Enzo.

He laughs. Long, hard, and his voice sounds like he's gone maniacal. I don't know what's so funny, but I watch him slowly stop.

"I don't do the girlfriend thing."

Those words make me sad, because the tiniest part of me wanted him to take a chance and make me his girlfriend. But that's stupid because I don't do the boyfriend thing either. I don't have time for it, and I won't let some man take care of me.

"And my father has never given me a damn thing."

His eyes are serious as he says them and I see a pit of his pain. I see how broken he is in his dark orbs where he tries to hide his shattered pieces from the world. But he can't hide it from me, I see it as clearly as I see the sun shining in the sky.

He shakes his head again. "Why did you steal it? Planning on buying more burgers and beer with it?"

My lips curl up a little at his teasing. "It was for my father."

"Aww, I see. You're a daddy's girl. So tell me, daddy's girl, how does dear old daddy treat his daughter? Is he a drug addict? Alcoholic? Does he gamble away the money he's supposed to use to pay rent and feed you?"

"Stop."

His lips do curl up, happy he finally hit a nerve in me.

"I used the money to repay a debt my father owes, but my father isn't a bad man. He works hard and does his best to take care of me. He's not a drug addict, alcoholic, or gambler. He's just my dad."

His entire body exhales as if he disagrees with me, but knows there is no point in arguing with me.

I dig into my pocket and find the two hundred dollars extra I received from selling the watch. I hold it out to him.

He stares at the money like it's a snake about to bite him. "What's that?"

"This is me repaying you for the watch."

"If all you got was two hundred dollars for the watch, then you made a bad deal. That watch cost me twelve grand."

I shrug. I should have gotten more than the seven and a half I got. I didn't make the best deal, but I was desperate. Just like I was when I stole the watch in the first place.

"I know. I got more than that, but that's all I have left after I paid off the debt." I square my shoulders to him and hold out my hand. "I will repay you. All of it, plus interest. No matter what it takes or how long. You have my word."

He takes my hand in a dominating grip. "I don't need the money, daddy's girl."

"Don't call me that."

"Would you prefer I call you, stupid girl?"

"No, I'd prefer you call me by my name."

"Jocelyn," the way he says the name sends shivers down my spine. "But that's not really your name is it?"

I freeze. *How did he realize I'd given him a fake name?*

"You don't go by Jocelyn. You go by Josie, or Jos, or Lynn, but never Jocelyn."

I don't move. He thinks he's so smart, but he can't even figure out a sixteen-year-old girl's real name.

Enzo studies me, his thick eyelashes shading his eyes as he does. "I don't need the money Jocelyn, and as for the watch, I have dozens more at home."

I still. "Then what do you want?"

"I'm looking for someone. I was told he works down here by the docks, and seeing as you do too, you might be able to help me find him while being more inconspicuous. Help me find him tonight. And I'll forgive your debt."

It's a good deal. It will take me most of my life at my current rate to pay back the debt I owe him. "What do you want with this man?"

He shrugs nonchalantly, but nothing he does is ever casual. Every movement is planned out. His actions are orchestrated to make me as uncomfortable as possible. Make me hate him, while wanting to plant my lips on his at the same time.

"Does it matter?"

No, it doesn't. I'm heartless, but he doesn't need to know that. I don't care what happens to this man. I don't care if he beats him, extracts a debt from him, or kills him. It won't be on my conscience.

I squeeze his hand and shake. "Deal."

He smirks.

"You can tell me what you know about this man while I finish mopping. I have one more yacht to clean tonight."

"You aren't cleaning another yacht tonight until you help me."

I roll my eyes at his bossiness. "I might, if I think this man will be on it. The other yacht is on the other side of the harbor. If I think we will have better luck finding him there, then it will be more inconspicuous to be cleaning then going in guns blazing like I'm sure you plan on doing."

"You think I'll just take out my gun and starting shooting to get people to talk?"

"I don't think, *I know*." I eye the back of his shirt where I know a gun is hidden. I also do not doubt he has more weapons on him. He has a knife stashed in his boot or another gun hidden in his pant's leg.

"What world were you brought up in, Jocelyn, where you can tell if a man is carrying a gun or not?"

"The kind where I have to know if a man is carrying a gun or not for my own survival."

A calmness passes between us. An understanding of each other. He may be rich, and I may be poor, but we aren't so different, the two of us. We are more alike than we are different.

I continue mopping while Enzo scrutinizes me, studying me like I'm an alien from another planet he's just now recognizing as one of his own. When I finish, I dump the water overboard and stow the mop and bucket in the cleaning closet. Enzo follows as we both hop off the expensive yacht and onto the pier.

I can feel him smiling at how effortlessly I made the same jump he did, instead of using the ramp.

"So, who are we looking for?" I ask.

Enzo pulls out a napkin and hands it to me.

I take it hesitantly. I feel a sense of doom come over me, and I swear a dark cloud descends overhead just to cover the spot where I stand.

I unfold the napkin and read the name written on it. My name. *Kai Miller.*

Shit. Fuck. Shit.

I should have pressed harder about what Enzo wanted with the man he thinks he's hunting for. I try not to react at the name, but I feel Enzo studying my reaction. *Is he testing me? Did he know this was me all along? What does he want with me anyway, other than to give him back the watch?*

"Jocelyn? Do you know this man?"

"Yes," I breathe.

"Who is he? Where can I find him?"

I close my eyes trying to find a way out, but I don't have a way out.

I don't know for sure that what Enzo wants to do with me is bad. *Liar, yes I do.* This man oozes evil. *Is he here because my father owes his family a lot of money? What else could it be?*

Shit.

Enzo's going to kidnap me and force my father to repay the debt. Enzo likes me. He won't really hurt me. I might even be able to make a deal on my father's behalf. Promise to steal something for Enzo that he wants more than the money my father borrowed from him. He's seen how good of a thief I am.

"Jocelyn? Where is he?"

I grin. If I'm going to do this, I'm going to do it with my pride intact. "This man you are looking for. He did something to you, didn't he? Stole from you, hurt you, outsmarted you maybe?"

Enzo sighs, getting annoyed with my games. "Yes."

"So he's smarter than you?"

"I didn't say that."

"No, but you can't find him on your own, so he must be."

"Sure, but when I do find him, and I will, with or without your help, I will have outsmarted him. And if I do it without your help, you will still owe me your debt."

I nod, *men and their pride.* But I'm no different. I want my pride too.

"Where is he?" he repeats.

"He is standing right in front of you." I fold my arms across my chest and grin, my eyes daring him to doubt me.

Enzo's eyes narrow as he looks around for a man to jump out from behind me. It takes him a second to process that I'm not Jocelyn, I'm Kai Miller. Katherine is my actual name, but I haven't gone by that since I was three and declared my name was Kai. I've always been Kai.

His lips curl into a grin. "I knew you were a thief; I didn't realize you were a liar too, *Kai.*"

I smile back, tauntingly. "A liar who could have slipped through your cracks and been on the run for a lot longer than you were prepared to search for me. But I didn't run. I owe you a debt, and now that debt has been repaid."

He nods. "Your debt is forgiven. But it was a stupid trade, my beautiful, Kai." He grabs my arm. "Let's go for a ride on the waves, Kai. I have something I want to show you."

5
———

ENZO

This can't be right.

This girl can't be Kai Miller.

It has to be a mistake.

Even if she is Kai Miller, my father must have written down the wrong name.

Or there must be a different Kai Miller.

She doesn't belong in my world.

She doesn't deserve to die.

Even though she stole your watch without any way to pay you back?

Shut up, I tell the voice in my head.

There is a difference between being punished and dying. She deserves to be punished for her crime, that's all.

"Show me your ID," I say.

Jocelyn, or Kai or whatever her name is, bites her lip in the adorable, seductive way she does when she's thinking hard.

I groan inwardly, but don't let her see how such a simple movement affects me. I want to kiss her, not kill her.

"I don't have an ID."

"What? Did you leave it at home?" I ask, not sure why she would. I don't know where she lives, but surely she drove to the pier. I know she doesn't live in any of the large seaside houses that cost millions and are the only homes nearby.

"No, I don't have an ID."

I grip her wrist, not believing a word out of her mouth. "You're older than sixteen, which means you have a driver's license."

She shakes her head.

"You're not at least sixteen?" *Shit, how young is she?*

"I'm sixteen; I turn seventeen next week." She hesitates as if she's ashamed to say the rest. "But I never got my driver's license."

I narrow my eyes into slits, demanding her to tell me the truth.

"Why would I need a driver's license? I don't own a car, and even if I did, I don't know how to drive."

My heart throbs. I learned to drive when I was thirteen. No one taught me, just like no one taught me how to throw a punch or fire a gun. I learned because it was necessary to survive. But since I was sixteen, I've been driving a Lamborghini. I can't imagine never driving. It's one of the world's greatest escapes. I feel powerful and unrelenting when I drive. And suddenly, I have the urge to teach her how to drive and watch as she takes control.

"I'm Kai Miller," her words are calm and steady.

"How do I know that? How do I know you aren't lying to me so I'll forgive your debt?"

Anger flares on her face, as steam flows from her ears. She's pissed. It's cute, but not enough to make me believe her.

She huffs. "Do I look like a Jocelyn to you?"

"No."

"My name is Kai. My father calls me Katherine because he thinks Kai is too masculine sounding. But I chose the name Kai when I was little and thought Katherine was too long. It means—"

"Sea."

She nods slowly.

Kai looks like the sea. Her eyes match the greenish blue color of the ocean, and her skin thrives under the sun making her tanner instead of burning. I would guess she's grown up her whole life near the water, but instead of learning about the ocean, she's been cleaning expensive yachts...for my father, I realize. This is one of his yachts.

Fuck. She really is Kai. Whether the name on her birth certificate is Katherine or Kai, it doesn't matter. This is who my father meant when he wrote the name on the napkin. And she knows something, or my father thinks she does, which is why I have to kill her.

But I need to learn more. *So much more.* I have so many questions Kai needs to answer. I need to take her somewhere private, not here on the pier. Somewhere I can figure out what to do.

I look down at her lean body. I could grab her arm and force her to go with me. She might struggle or even scream, but it won't be enough to draw much attention to us. The sailors know who I am, and they wouldn't dare cross me or my family. Even if the police are called, it would be too late. I would already have her.

But she might answer more of my questions if I lure her, instead of taking her.

It's not in my nature to persuade someone with the carrot rather than the stick. But with Kai, I think it's the only way.

Her eyes widen as she realizes I believe her, and I want something from her.

I hold out my hand.

"I'm not going with you. Not until you tell me why you were searching for me."

I let my shoulders drop, attempting to seem relaxed. I feign a smile, and let my eyes grow soft, so I stop looking like such a demon.

"Have you ever been on a yacht before?"

She chuckles incredulously. "Are you serious? You just saw me on a yacht."

I smile more genuine now at seeing her brighten. "I meant, have you been on a yacht like this out in the ocean? Not when you were working, but when you could truly enjoy its grace and extravagance?"

"No," she exhales in sadness.

I extend my hand to her, making it easier for her to accept. "Let me take you out on one. It could be fun. Just the two of us." I wink.

Kai stares at my hand, and I know she's debating with herself. She wants to take it. She wants to have fun, have an adventure. Pretend that cleaning away nonstop isn't her life.

But she knows the danger. I don't know much about her, but this much I know. She was wary of me in the bar, and she continues to be now. She should be. I don't know what made her different than most kids our age, but I know she doesn't get to spend her days going to school, doing homework, and flirting with boys her age. Her life has hardened her to the truths of the world. She knows danger when she sees it, and I'm danger.

"Do you know how to drive a yacht?"

I smirk; I've got her. "I guess you're just going to have to trust me if you want to go out the ocean."

She ignores my hand but walks closer to me. "Let's go then."

I let my hand drop despite my urge to touch her. I need her hand, waist, or entire body in my clutches. I need to ensure she can't escape. But it's more than that. I'm desperate to feel what I know will be deliciously warm flesh against mine.

"This way then," I say as I start walking down the pier toward a yacht I know isn't being used tonight. I let her feel like she has power and is making this choice. I don't force her to follow me. But if she ran, I would chase.

I hear her hesitant steps clanking down the pier in her flip-flops. My head shakes the tiniest bit. She definitely doesn't belong in my world; she doesn't even know how to walk without being heard.

I reach the black beast of a yacht at the far end of the pier. It's not the biggest yacht in our collection, but it still looms over us, taunting us with its majesty.

Kai stops next to me, her breathing heavy as she stares up at the boat.

"It's tiny," she says, trying to lighten the mood with her joke.

A wave of her black hair has fallen on her neck, and I brush it back, feeling the iciness oozing, prickling my hot skin as I whisper in her ear, "Trust me, it's not small."

She blushes and bites her damn lip again, like she's trying to contain her excitement.

Shit, it's infectious.

Some stairs lead up to the main deck of the boat, but what fun are stairs? I jump up to the main deck and turn to tell Kai about the stairs or to help her across.

Thud.

I turn and see Kai smiling next to me. She landed on the deck, although not quite as gracefully as I did.

God, this creature intrigues me. She's made for this life on the ocean, full of thrill and risk-taking. Unfortunately, this might be the last risk she ever takes.

"This way, sweetheart." I wink at her and start walking toward the bow.

"Ugh, really? Sweetheart?" She chases after me.

I shrug. I haven't found a nickname that suits her yet.

Why am I trying to come up with a nickname for her? I shouldn't be getting attached.

I enter the wheelhouse and find the first mate.

"Out," I shout to the man I barely recognize. He's been to the club before and works for my father, but I couldn't tell you his name.

"Yes, sir." He doesn't hesitate as he exits the room. He knows the consequences.

"And ensure no crew or cleaning staff remain on the yacht. I will be taking it for a spin, *alone*."

Kai's eyebrows raise as the man scurries off.

I walk behind the wheel and start-up the yacht.

"We're really doing this?" Kai asks, her voice hitched.

"Yes," I hiss, although I don't know what *this* is. *Does she think I'm going to take her to some private island and fuck her?* She's probably a virgin for goodness sakes. And she's young. *Sixteen*. Almost seventeen. She feels far too young for my seventeen, almost eighteen years, or maybe it's the difference in life experience that makes us so far apart.

We are both too young for any of this. She may not have seen death or taken it as I have, but she's experienced pain and fear. We are teenagers who shouldn't be thinking about fucking, yet that's where both our minds are.

I don't know what I'm going to do when I get her out on the ocean, but I do know I won't be fucking her.

"Do you know how to untie us and remove the buoy?" I ask.

She gives me a wicked smile. "Of course."

"Good, do it then."

Kai tucks her hair behind her ear that has fallen from the bandana and then runs off.

I shake my head as I watch her leave, giving her another chance to get free of me.

No, giving her another chance to trust me before I ruin her.

A minute later the anchor is up, and we are pulling away from the pier. Kai's eyes are big as she watches me steer out of the marina.

With her eyes on me, I feel unsettled.

"You should go to the front and feel the breeze in your hair before we pick up speed. There is nothing like it," I say.

"What about you?" she asks, innocently.

My eyes darken. "Somebody has to steer the boat."

She sighs in disappointment.

"Don't worry; I'll have us stopped somewhere before the sun sets."

Kai smiles weakly and then does as I say. She moves to the front of the boat, where I can unfortunately still see her as I drive us out into the ocean. Her body becomes part of the wind. She throws her arms back, her eyes close, and her hair flies.

Beautiful.

I steer us out into the ocean, finding a quiet place where we won't be disturbed. And then I enable the GPS autopilot to keep us stopped at this exact location, since the ocean is too deep here to use the anchor.

"Beautiful," I whisper as I approach Kai.

"It is, isn't it?" She looks out at the ocean where the sun is beginning to set while I look at her.

"How long have you been cleaning yachts?"

She shrugs, her eyes cutting to mine and her smile faltering. "A long time."

"That's not an answer."

"Maybe you haven't earned an answer."

I grab her arm that is gripping the railing and turn her toward me. She stares at my touch. She's so cold to my fiery fingers. We both gasp before she pulls her arm away.

"I haven't earned an answer? I forgave your debt after you stole from me. I'm spending my time and money on gas to take you on a fancy joy ride. How have I not earned some answers to my questions?"

Her hand grips the railing again as she turns from me.

"What does your father do for a living?" I ask.

Nothing.

"How about your mother?"

Silence.

"How long have you been cleaning yachts?"

It doesn't matter what question I ask. She won't answer.

Does she know who my father is? Does she know who I am? Did she witness something at the club? Did she witness a murder? What?

I grab her arm and shove her back. She catches herself on the railing, her back now to it, instead of her front.

I cage her in with my arms. I've been nice, trying to butter her up to answer me, but it didn't work. Now, I need answers.

Time is ticking, and I need to decide what to do with her.

She blinks rapidly, and then her eyes grow defiant as I box her in.

"You don't scare me."

"I should."

She huffs. "You don't think I haven't been dealing with men like you my entire life. Well, I have. And you are by far the least scary. You're nothing but a *boy*. Whatever you want from me, you won't get unless I want you to."

I growl and push myself against her until her breathing stops, proving just how far I'll go to get the answers that I need.

We both stare at each other, neither of us backing down —neither of us giving in.

Her mind is whirling. I can see it going a million miles an hour trying to figure a way out of this. And she may be able to with whatever low-level men come to collect her father's debts, but she won't be able to figure a way out with me. She will answer me if she wants to live. And even if she responds, there is no guarantee of living. That was her mistake when she told me who she was, when she willingly got on this yacht with me.

"Fine, I'll answer."

I back away only an inch.

"If you win at a game of truth or lies," she continues.

I narrow my eyes, pressing my body hard against hers again. "No, you will tell me everything I want to know."

She shakes her head slowly. "I will answer any question you ask, if you win. It's clear you have questions you need to ask. That's why we are here. My father probably did something stupid, and you need information about him. But I will only answer if you win."

"No."

She smirks. "You don't have a choice, pretty boy. Otherwise, I'll refuse to talk, and you'll have to report back to your boss that you didn't get the information you need."

"And if you win?"

"Then you answer my questions."

I frown. I don't like this at all, but if I win, she will answer without me having to hurt her. And if I lose, then I guess I will torture her until she tells me.

"What are the rules?"

"We each tell two truths and lie." She thinks for a moment. "Although, since neither one of us want to reveal much about ourselves, we will play it in reverse. We each will tell two lies and one truth."

"How do you win?"

"When you correctly guess the truth."

"And if we both guess the truth?"

"Then we will both be answering a lot of questions."

I look over her shoulder and watch the sun hover over the horizon. In thirty minutes or less it will be set, and I'll be out of time. I want to determine if she deserves to die, tonight.

I look at her. Kai's street smart. She knows how to survive. She stole from me without me noticing. She's sly. But now that I know that about her, I know what to watch for. I've spent my entire life reading people; I'll know if she's telling the truth or not.

"Deal."

Her grin reaches her eyes, and then she looks down at where I'm pressed against her body. My cock has hardened against her stomach; her nipples are sharp points beneath her tank top. If I kissed her right now, I don't think she'd stop me, but then she'd never answer me.

I take a step back, and she exhales sharply.

I walk to the sliding front door of the cabin, throwing it open, disappearing inside. When I step back out, I have two glasses and a fifth of whiskey.

"Sit," I say at the table near the front of the ship.

She takes a seat hesitantly, as I pour us both half a glass of whiskey, fearing we are both going to need a lot to get through this night.

She takes the glass without a word and sips on the drink. She doesn't turn up her nose in disgust like most girls her age when they drink anything straight. She doesn't wince at the burn; she welcomes it.

I breathe in the drink before I taste it and return to the state of numbness I feel when I drink it. But somehow I don't think there is enough alcohol on this boat to make me numb when I'm around her. Every electrode in my body is firing.

"You go first," I say.

She nods.

"My first truth or lie is I've never given a blow job."

My eyes darken at her words. This is how she wants to play this. *Dirty.*

"I've never come."

Damn her, and her dirty distractions.

"I've never been kissed," she breathes.

Somehow her last one feels as dirty as the previous two. *Something so innocent, yet so delicious.*

She leans back after she finishes and puts her feet up on the table, relaxing. She said each sentence with equal weight; she's used to lying to protect herself.

"Your turn."

But I'm good at lying too...

"I've never shot a man.

"I've never raped a woman.

"I've never killed a man."

My truths and lies are darker, instead of dirty like hers. But it does the job I was hoping.

Shock.

Even if my body betrayed me on some level when I told the truth instead of the lies, she wouldn't notice, she was too busy being frazzled by my words—hating herself for getting on a boat with such a vicious man.

"Now what?"

"Now we make our choice. We only get to pick once. One chance to pick the truth."

"And if neither of us chose correctly?" I ask, even though I doubt it will happen. One of us will choose correctly and one of us won't. I have no doubt I'll be the victor.

"Then I guess we don't get any answers."

I nod, agreeing.

I think back to the three choices:

I've never given a blow job.

I've never come.

I've never been kissed.

I eye her suspiciously as I think them over and how she said each sentence. The first sentence was easy falling from her lips, meant to shock me as I had her. The second was breathy, like she was thinking about coming when she said it and how good it would feel. The third she said almost playfully, like she was daring me to kiss her.

I smile.

"Have you decided?" she asks.

"I can eliminate one easily."

"And which one is that?"

"I've never come is easily a lie. I felt how you pressed back against my body when I was touching you. You know your body well. You know how it feels to make yourself come. You know that exquisite feeling when you touch your clit and explode."

Her cheeks blush just a little, but otherwise, she doesn't show any confirmation that I chose one of the lies correctly.

"And what do you think? Do you think you know any of mine you can eliminate?"

She cocks her head to the side as if she's hiding something. "You've never shot a man. That one's easily a lie. I saw your gun. I can only assume you've used it."

I swallow hard, and she knows she guessed the lie correctly.

"Now comes the hard part though."

I nod.

We both eye each other, waiting for either to give away our secrets with a look, a breath, a word. Neither of us does.

I watch her weigh her two options in her head. Either I've never raped or never murdered. Neither makes me a saint, both make me a sinner. She knows nothing about me, but I know the hope she has will make her choose I've never killed a man, because she views that as the worse crime. She will choose the lesser of the two evils. *Wrongly*.

I think between my two options.

If I believe she was telling the truth when she says she's never been kissed, then that means she's given a man a blow job without having been kissed first. I stare up at the woman in front of me. She's not that kind of woman. She may be desperate, but she knows her own worth. She wouldn't sell herself, so she wouldn't give a blow job for money. And if a boyfriend asked, he would have had to have been chivalrous. Taken her out on date after date to gain her kiss, let alone to earn her to blow him.

"Ready?" she asks.

I nod.

She lifts her drink, and I raise mine. We both down our

drinks until the glasses are empty, our eyes never leaving each other.

"Your truth is you've never given a blow job," I say as I gently set the glass on the table, happy to declare my victory. I don't care if she guesses correctly. I will get my questions answered.

Her lips slowly curl. "Wrong."

What? She's given a blow job but never been kissed?

She leans forward on the table. "And your truth is you've never raped a woman."

My eyes glare back at her as she smirks. I don't have to open my mouth for her to know my truth. She already knows she won.

6

___

KAI

I won.

I know without Enzo confirming it. I guessed correctly, although it never felt like speculation. I've always been good at telling the difference between a lie and the truth. Enzo is harder to read than most, but even he has his tells.

He's never raped a woman.

It warms me a little to know he never did anything that horrible.

But he has.

He's shot someone. *Killed someone.*

I don't know the circumstances around either. It could have been self-defense. I have no doubt, if I could afford a gun, I would have shot someone by now and killed if my aim was good.

Somehow, I don't think Enzo has done either only in self-defense.

Enzo glares at me, frustrated I won and he lost. I expect him to argue with me about my truth and lies. I expect him to call me out and claim that surely a sixteen-year-old like me has been kissed, especially if, as I claim, I've given a man a blow job. I expect him to whip his dick out and force me to suck it, to prove I've given head before.

Instead, he's a statue, giving me nothing of what is going on inside his body.

"You're not going to question my truth?"

His head cocks to the side as if he's trying to figure out what game I'm playing. "No."

"You sure?"

He nods his head. "Yes, I know you wouldn't deceive me during the game. I know you've masturbated before. And I know you've sucked off some man's dick like a whore."

I wince at his harsh words.

His eyes meet mine, filled with want. "And I know you've never been kissed."

I bite my now sore lip, that aches to be kissed, but I'm sure is red and swollen from the number of times I've chewed it today to keep myself from kissing this boy. This very dangerous, off-limits boy who I shouldn't be on this yacht with.

Enzo stands up and walks back to the railing, where the sun is now well below the horizon. The sky has opened up, allowing the darkness to begin to overtake the heavens. Soon there will be nothing left but the stars and the moon to shine down upon us.

I consider pouring myself another drink before I approach him, but I've had enough alcohol. I need my wits about me around him. He won't express it, but I can feel the anger radiating off him as I approach. He has considerable control though to not let it show on any of his features.

I stop next to him, ensuring I don't touch him.

"Ask me."

His voice is low and rumbling. It's deepened since he was talking to me earlier. This voice is the one he uses to scare people. It should frighten me. Instead, I want to hear it again.

I know how he expects me to use my newfound power. To ask questions about the game. To ask who he's shot or killed and why he's never raped a woman before if he's done the other two.

"How did you learn to drive a yacht?"

His head turns to me, and I can see his thick, dark eyebrow raise. "I grew up around the water in this business. You were taught to take care of the yachts, while I learned everything else about them. How to drive them, maintain them, sell them. There is nothing I don't know about how a ship like this works."

I inhale and then exhale, trying to remind myself to keep breathing. *What is he doing to me?* They are just words. I shouldn't be so hot and bothered when he merely speaks. And I've let it affect my judgment. I know better than to get on a boat in the middle of fucking nowhere with a strange man. A man who has already admitted to killing someone. But his words are intoxicating, pulling me deeper until I have no brain cells left and will do whatever he wants.

"Who do you work for?"

"Black."

I stop breathing. *Black.* His name is synonymous with evil. He's a myth and a legend. I'm not even sure he's a real person, but I have no doubt Enzo works for the most dangerous man in the city.

I need to gain back some power, because even though I won, it doesn't feel like I have any control.

"Have you ever been kissed?" I ask, wiggling my eyebrows trying to break the serious mood.

"Yes, Kai. I've been kissed. I'm not wide-eyed and bushy-tailed like you." He pauses. "And before you ask, yes I've had women kneel in front of me, pleading with me for the pleasure to suck my cock."

My eyes drop to his dark jeans, and I swear I saw his cock grow against the zipper.

No, it must be my imagination. He can't be turned on.

Enzo faces me now and takes my hand in his. I watch in horror and excitement as he lifts my hand to his lips and kisses my palm tenderly. It should be innocent enough, but I feel a warm tingle cascade through my body.

"Do you have any other questions, Kai?"

I close my eyes, trying to still my racing heart. "Why did you bring me here?" My words are a whisper, but I know he hears me, despite my eyes being closed.

I feel his hand at my neck, and I gasp, opening my eyes. His body is so close to mine I can feel the electricity in his body. He's so warm; he burns me when he grazes my skin. But other than his hand at my neck, he doesn't stroke me, just thumbs my neck, melting a layer of skin from my hard shell. He's so full of restraint.

I lick my lip, because I can't stand not to feel something pressed against my lips.

"Kai," he says, his voice threatening, but I don't understand why.

"Enzo," I say his name like a curse.

His eyes tell me what he's going to do before he does it —giving me one second to stop him.

I don't stop him.

His lips crash with mine.

I always thought my first kiss would be sweet, gentle. I thought it would be the first step on the way to falling in love. I thought it might be clumsy or awkward, but the second kiss would more than make up for it.

That's not what this is.

This kiss in an explosion, setting off a desire neither of us is allowed to feel.

A second after our lips crash, his tongue sweeps into my mouth. My arms wrap around his neck like I've done it a thousand times, while his hands grip my waist, almost suffocating me with their grip.

My tongue fights with his. Both of us needing control over the kiss. He demanded my first kiss from me, and I gave it willingly. But now, we need more.

I purr into his mouth as his tongue massages mine and his body presses into me, smoldering me in the process. And I'm cursing the fabric between us, wishing we were in swimsuits or better yet, nothing at all.

We could fuck.

Here. Now.

Enzo might not be who I dreamed of being my first. But he's better than the alternative. He's better then selling my first time or having it taken from me, which is what will happen if I stay at the trailer park.

He might not cuddle with me in bed afterward or even talk to me about what happened. He wouldn't be gentle or concerned with making sure I was adequately prepared before he would take my virginity. But he would take it, and I would give it as willingly as I gave this kiss.

I shouldn't be thinking about sex. I'm too young, not even seventeen yet, but in my world, I don't have the luxury of waiting, of remaining innocent.

He bites my lip.

I feel the tingle of the blood in my mouth.

What do you want with me, Enzo?

It should piss me off, but it only turns me on more.

Dammit! What am I doing?

This is precisely what he wants, me thrown off guard.

Me, letting down my guard so he can attack. It's the reason he brought me here. To get something from me.

I might let him fuck me, but I won't let him take advantage of me.

The kiss will end soon. I can feel it. So I do the only thing I can to gain more information.

I slip my hand into his back pocket and fish out his phone. I know he didn't notice. I'm an expert at picking pockets when I want to be. I let him catch me with the wallet so I could more easily retrieve the more expensive watch.

The kiss ends.

I don't know who stops it. It just happens.

Enzo's eyes stare intently at my swollen lip. His thumb brushes across the sore. I see the blood before his thumb moves to mouth, and he sucks it off.

Neither of us speaks about what just happened. We just stare and pretend that kiss didn't change everything.

I slip his phone into my back pocket before he realizes it's missing.

"Bathroom..." I say suddenly needing a moment alone.

I don't wait for him to nod or tell me where one is. I dash away, through the sliding door where Enzo retrieved our drinks. I don't care where the bathroom is; I don't need it. I need to stop letting Enzo affect my body and use my head. I need to realize the danger I put myself in.

I open the nearest door and step inside before shutting it and locking it. I slip the phone out of my pocket and stare at it.

It's password protected.

Of course, it is.

Shit, what was I thinking?

It buzzes.

I jump, staring at it like it's just come alive.

The phone may be locked, but the message still shows up on the home screen.

The message is from Black, his boss.

Black: Is Kai dead yet?

I blink. Over and over.

I'm not reading that right.

But every time I reread it, it says the same thing.

Eventually, the screen goes dark, and when I hit the home button again the message is gone, only an alert left that he has an unread message.

Dead.

That's what Enzo is doing here. He was sent to kill me.

The door opens, but I don't have to turn to know Enzo has a gun pointed at my head.

"Do you have any more questions, thief?"

His words cut through me like glass. I may be a thief, but he's an assassin.

I turn to him with defiance in my eyes. I always knew something horrible awaited my future. He may think I'll die quick and swiftly, or I'll beg for my life.

I'll do neither because I've been prepared for this day. And I won't go down without a fight.

"Just one.

"Why?"

7

ENZO

Why?

I promised to reply to any of her questions if I lost, but this is the one question I can't answer.

"Why?" Kai asks again, her voice steady, though I can see the quiver in her lip as she speaks. A lip still swollen and stained red from the drop of blood I drew when I kissed her.

Kai won't let this go.

I hold the gun loosely in my hand, still pointed in her general direction, but not aimed directly at her. I should pull the trigger and end this. Put a stop to the questions I can't answer.

"Why?" her voice is stronger now, more determined. "You are going to kill me anyway. It won't hurt to tell me why if you are just going to shoot me. I won't be able to tell anyone."

I don't react, not even with my eyes. She's right of course, but that doesn't mean I'm going to answer her.

Her eyes grow dark and angry. "We made a bet. You played the game. You lost. Now answer me! *Why?*"

My eyes close for a second longer than they should be

closed. I expect her to take her chance and escape. She's smart, observant, and will do anything to survive, but she doesn't take her opportunity when I show the tiniest weakness. Her need to know the answer is greater than her need to live in this moment.

I want to answer her.

I want to know why myself.

But I won't lie to her, and I don't know the answer.

Her legs tremble, and she falls, the bed behind her catching her into a seated position. Her hand shakes against her chest, and if I were to feel her pulse I know it would be flying through her body, her fight or flight response kicked into gear.

"You don't know, do you?" Her words are sharp and determined.

"No, I don't know why."

"Did you even ask why when you were given this assignment?"

"Yes."

She nods slowly. "I understand. You're not high up enough in Black's crime organization to get to know why. You blindly follow orders. I knew you were a criminal. I knew you did bad things when I met you. I knew you were dangerous, but I didn't realize you were heartless and cruel. I didn't know you were a fucking coward, a nobody, a lowlife who only cared about earning cash when you took a life!"

Her breathing is hurried, but she doesn't stop. "I thought if you were to kill me, you would at least give me the courtesy of deciding I deserved to die yourself, not because some king in a castle told you to. I thought you were your own person, but now I realize who you really are. A fucking pussy with no control and no future."

"Are you finished?"

She huffs. "You're the one with a gun. You tell me."

I lower it just a little; she exhales realizing I'm not going to shoot her, not yet.

"You're right. I'm a fucking coward who won't stand up for myself. I follow orders. But you're wrong about my ability to control my future. I may not be able to control what I do on this boat, but I will after."

"How?"

"Because this is my final assignment. After this, I'm free."

She sucks in a breath, and for the first time, I see real terror in her eyes. She realizes there is nothing she can do to stop me from killing her. That my desire to be free is greater than my desire to save her.

Kai takes a second to compose herself, and then she stands. She walks to me, ignoring the gun in my hand pointed toward her leg.

Her lips pout, and her body sways as she walks toward me.

My pulse races, my jaw twitches, and my cock hardens.

I want her.

There's no denying it. It's been a while since I've felt a kiss like the one she just gave me. *No, I've never had a kiss like that one.*

It was passionate, mysterious, sweet, and full of promise. Her first kiss was everything a kiss should be. *Too bad it will also be her last kiss.*

I want Kai.

More than I want to breathe.

More than I want my freedom.

I could have both. Spend the day kissing her, fucking her, using her. Then get the freedom I'm desperate for.

As Kai moves closer, I know that is what she is offering

me too. Her body on a platter. She thinks it is the only possibility she has at keeping herself alive. If I develop any feelings for her, then I won't kill her. But that's not going to save her. Nothing will.

She reaches out hesitantly, touching my face.

My eyes stay glued to hers as I watch her tongue caress her bottom lip. And then I remember how good it felt to have her lips pressed against mine. But I've had years of training in self-control. No matter how much Kai tempts me, I won't give in.

She presses her lips to mine, softly.

"You can try to seduce me all you want; it won't save you."

"I beg to differ," she purrs back before her lips crash hard against mine.

After putting my gun back in my waistband, I close my eyes as my hands grip her body, jerking her to me. Her body is cold, soft, and so breakable in my arms—everything I've always wanted but never been able to taste. The mix of hot and cold together creating a tsunami in both of us.

The only women I've been with were whores or worked for my father. They were all skilled in how to kiss, how to fuck. It was business to them. Not Kai. She's a breath of fresh air, untamed and wild with her movements.

Her tongue pushes deeper, exploring my mouth without the finesse I'm used to. And damn, that turns me on.

"Fuck," I growl as she knees me in the balls.

I knew it was coming. Despite knowing she would try something like this, it didn't stop me from taking the brief moment of pleasure. Something I almost always deny myself, because it makes me weak.

Kai runs, but I take my time chasing after her. The ship is big, but not so large I won't be able to find her. And even if it were too large, I would still be able to find her. I'm too drawn to her not to notice her heart beating, begging me to stay away and yet still hoping I will find her and claim her.

After adjusting myself in my jeans, I feel the pain ease, and I start walking. The gun has returned to my hand as I walk.

I should be pissed and angry about what she did. I should find her and shoot her on the spot without giving her another second to breathe. But I know I won't, because she intrigues me.

I hear the engines roar.

I shake my head, knowing exactly where she is.

I walk slowly to the engine room. I try the door, but I already know it's locked.

The engines burn louder, but we won't move because the GPS autopilot is engaged and she doesn't know how to turn it off.

I kick the door in easily.

Kai stands frozen as I enter, but I don't raise my gun.

"What's your plan now?" I ask because I know she has a plan B and a plan C, etc. She won't stop until I've decided I've had enough.

She faces me stoically, with no fear. She won't die terrified.

"To cause as much pain as possible to you before I go."

I nod. "I don't think that's your real plan."

"It is."

"Liar. You haven't given up yet. You'll only change to trying to hurt me to extract revenge when you've given up trying to survive."

She frowns, hating I know her so well.

"You don't have to do this. You don't have to kill me."

I raise an eyebrow and wait. Apparently plan B is

persuading me not to kill her, although I'm guessing there's more to her plan. With Kai, there always is.

"I'm not a snitch. I won't tell anybody this ever happened."

I nod, believing if I let her go free, she would never mention this to anyone.

"I haven't witnessed anything else. I know nothing about the organization you work for. I don't know the name. I don't know who your boss is. Or what crimes anyone has committed. I've never seen anyone steal, or rape, or shoot, or murder. And even if I did, I would know well enough to keep my mouth shut to survive."

My eyes harden. I believe her. My father wants her dead, and I have no idea why. It may not even be about Kai. It might be that he is just testing me to kill someone innocent to ensure I would do anything for him.

"I will pay my debt to you. And I will pay any debts my father owes if that is what this is about. No matter how high of a price, I will find a way to pay it back. My stealing your watch and using it to pay my father's last debt should prove that to you."

I smirk. "I have no doubt you would. You're a thief. You know how cruel the world can be. But you are also a survivor. I would guess one of the reasons you've never been kissed is because the men in your life have only caused you more pain. None of them were worthy of taking something so innocent from you. You protected something so simple that most people give without thinking. You only gave when you were desperate for it. But I have no doubt you would sell your body, even your soul to survive. To protect your father. You would give everything."

She nods, her throat tight, and the vein in her neck pulsing hard. She's already relented to the fact she would eventually sell her body to survive. Like so many women from her part of town do.

I raise the gun again as anger pulses through me. I can't stand the thought of her selling herself to another man. She's mine. "You won't be selling yourself, thief."

She swallows and licks her lips.

"Don't kill me..."

I hesitate.

"...not with your gun. If you're going to kill me, then do it with your bare hands."

I smirk, both liking and hating her plan C because the only way I could truly kill her is by touching her. But her touch will end me too.

8

KAI

I TRY to look past the black metal aimed at me, to the man behind it. The gun might lead to my death, but Enzo will be the one squeezing the trigger.

I don't know why I ask him to kill me without using the gun. It will make no difference. I will be dead no matter how he does it. A gun might even make my death swifter.

I don't want to die from a bullet to the head.

If Enzo is going to kill me, I want him to do it with his bare hands. I want him to feel the life he's taking, and how desperate, determined I am to live. And a tiny part of me hopes he won't be able to kill me if he's forced to endure my heart stopping, my breathing slowing, and my essence leaving my body.

I swallow hard, trying to remain calm.

No, it won't make a difference. He will kill me either way, unless I find a way to escape. But at least this way, I will have some amount of control over when and how I die.

Enzo doesn't lower the gun.

I'm going to die.

Right here and now.

Instinctively, I close my eyes, like somehow not seeing the bullet coming will make dying easier.

I should be thinking about my mother, whom I miss. Or how my father will be lost, unable to survive without me. I should be thinking about the friends I will never get to see again. About the future I will be deprived of.

I will never fall in love...

Get married...

Or have kids...

Not that I ever thought those things were really in my future anyway.

But my brain doesn't go to any of those things. All I can think about is that damn kiss. The first one, the second one...I want *more*.

I let my lips curl up in a smile. At least if I'm going to die, I'm going to die with something happy in my head. Even if it is twisted that I'm thinking of Enzo when he's the one who's going to destroy me.

One second.

Two...

Three...

Nothing.

My eyes flutter open. Enzo's eyes darken as he looks at me. He lowers the gun, empties the ammo, and tosses the gun to the side while the bullets fall to the ground next to him.

"Why?" I ask, my bottom lip trembling.

"You ask that question a lot, thief."

"That's not an answer, killer."

"Because you asked me to. You didn't beg, you asked with dignity. And after not being able to answer the one question you want answers to the most, I owe you."

"Thank you."

"My debt has now been repaid. We owe each other nothing."

I nod. "Nothing."

Enzo steps toward me, and I reciprocate.

I should be running. I should be searching for a weapon to fight back. To kill him before he kills me.

The pull to him is too strong. I want him more than I want to live.

What's wrong with me? Am I that desperate for a small taste of what love could feel like?

Yes.

Because I know without a doubt if the circumstances were different, I could love the boy standing in front of me. He's handsome, my attraction to him overwhelms me. But it's more than his looks. He has an old soul, like me. Dangerous, yet truthful. Controlling, demanding, and merciless. He's honest, yet holds the secrets of the world. He's complicated and simple. He craves freedom, like me.

I could love a monster like him.

We both take another step closer. Neither of us knows what the other is going to do when we meet.

I hold my head high as I edge closer. My lips are parted, and my breathing is slow. Time creeps. I should be thankful. I could live a lifetime in this moment with Enzo; maybe then I could live forever.

Closer, closer, closer.

One more step...

We collide. Our bodies attach like magnets. My arms go around his waist, and his hands go to my throat.

The electricity between us is unfathomable. It dances between us like tiny fairies trying to bind us together.

We are together. Now, what the fuck do you want?

"Why?" his voice grumbles.

I cock my head, not understanding his question.

"Why do you trust me, when I've threatened to kill you?"

"You're an honest man. You may hide truths, but you don't lie. I trust you will keep your promise and kill me."

He strokes my cheek. It's not meant to be comforting; he just needs to touch me.

"I don't want to die, though. Dying would be the easy way out."

"Why?" he asks, again.

Enzo doesn't know why he's supposed to kill me, and I don't know why I keep getting close to him even though every nerve in my body is screaming for me to run away. He didn't answer me; I won't answer him.

"Kiss me," I demand.

He isn't used to being bossed around by anyone other than the man he works for. I doubt a woman has ever commanded him to do anything. But for some reason, he does as I demand without question.

Lips crash down on mine, hungrier than the last two times we kissed combined.

The kiss is reckless, for both of us. But soon all thoughts are lost, fading away as quickly as they started.

I nip on his bottom lip before he has a chance to torture mine again.

He gasps from the way I take over the kiss. And then I bite hard, drawing blood the same way he did me.

He jerks away, and I see the small pebble of blood on his bottom lip. His tongue licks over his tiny wound and the lust in his eyes deepens.

The fire grows between us. No kiss will be able to extinguish it. It will burn, long after either of us are gone. That will be my legacy—an intense fire that will reign hell down on those who hurt me.

My mouth waters, needing him again.

He gives me a predatory glare. I smirk back, tempting him to devour me again the way I want.

He does.

His lips suck on mine as his tongue invades my mouth, demanding for me to give in to his power. *Not going to happen.*

I fight right back, my tongue dipping deeper into his mouth. Our tongues continue dancing with each other for dominance. Our groans grow heavier with each lap of our tongues, and our lips are swollen from the vicious kisses.

We would make a fiery match. Both of us unrelenting and stubborn. We both have pasts that have made us ruthless and savage. We would be one of those couples with an inextinguishable passion that would turn to fighting any time we left the bedroom. The arguing would be worth it though to be kissed like this.

My hand slides under his shirt, my nails dig into his back as I push his shirt up, before tearing it off his body.

I gasp.

Enzo's hard body terrifies and intrigues me. He's not fit in the same way the football players at my high school are. His muscles aren't even or crafted in a weight room. I doubt he's ever worked out in the traditional sense, but his body is hard as steel. It's rough and sharp along the edges of his muscles that have been built with years of hard work in the streets instead of in the gym.

He's seventeen, barely a man, still a boy by most people's tabulation. Young enough to still be in high school, although I doubt he attends, he has no need for an education a typical school can provide. He's smart and sly despite little formal education. That's all the skill he needs.

I stop our kisses as my hands move over his rippled abs and up to his chest. Scars darken his once flawless skin. He doesn't have any tattoos I can see, which surprises me. Only scars. Too many for someone so young to have.

I have almost as many. Though none of mine come from being shot like his. But the knife scars I recognize. I've had the unfortunate experience of getting a knife jabbed into my arm before.

"Rape me," I say.

His velvety eyes widen as he tucks my hair behind my ear gently. How can he be so tender right now? "It wouldn't be rape," his voice threatens.

My body burns with an ache I've never felt before. He's right. It wouldn't be rape, even though that should be the only way his cock gets inside me—by force.

I want him to fuck me, to tear away my virginity, to be my first.

"It wouldn't be," I agree, my eyelids growing heavy as I trace over a scar in his shoulder that appears to be a bullet wound. My body pulsates with blistering need.

My heavy eyes meet his and the whole world stills. The ocean waves calm, the motor stops, the seagulls stop squawking. Even the wind is silent.

"Fuck me; I don't want to die a virgin."

I wait for him to tell me that fucking me won't save me. He won't fall in love with my pussy and keep me so he can fuck me again. This man has fucked plenty of women in his short life, I'm sure.

He doesn't say any of those things though.

Instead, he kisses me softer than he ever has before—a goodbye kiss.

Like hell it is! He doesn't get a goodbye kiss.

I press my body to his naked front and feel his erection thrust into my stomach. He wants me, so much. Maybe more than I want him.

I don't let him kiss me softly; I pull him back into our rough dance.

This time, it's rougher than the first.

I kiss him hard.

He slams my body against the wall.

I nibble harder on his lip.

He grabs my neck, threatening to kill me with his hands around my throat, his lips against mine, and his cock hard against my stomach. If I die, will he fuck my lifeless body?

The glare and determination in his eyes say no. He wants me very much alive.

Pain starts in my neck as he narrows his grip.

I can't breathe.

I try sucking in.

Nothing.

I gasp, which makes it worse as all my oxygen leaves my body.

My head feels dizzy, cloudy.

This is it.

His mouth pushes to me again, his grip loosens, and he breathes into my body.

He's not ready, yet. But soon, very soon...

"We could leave. Run away together. If we are both trapped, maybe leaving together would set us free," I say. It's a lie. I won't leave my father even if Enzo allows me to live. And the look in Enzo's eyes says he knows I'm lying too.

I push back, knowing my frail body can't compete against his hard one, but he lets me shove him.

I relish the space between us and hate it at the same time.

I push again, and he stumbles through the open doorway.

I storm after him.

I push him against the railing, and my hands go around his throat the same way his did mine. I tighten, knowing he can stop me at any second, and I'm not even sure I'm strong enough to strangle him, even if I wanted to.

He lets me. I kiss him and squeeze his neck at the same time, cutting off his oxygen the same way he did to me.

I don't see panic in his eyes, but I didn't reveal my terror when he did the same to me earlier. Not because I didn't think he would kill me, but because I'm stupid enough to trust I'm supposed to leave this world at his hands. I trust him to kill me in the way I deserve.

When his face starts to turn purple, I release.

And he inhales before releasing a tiny cough.

His eyes threaten mine. "Yea, we could run away and escape all of this. Or we could stay. I could protect you, make you my queen. Make you untouchable by any of my men."

More lies.

Whatever hold Black has is more than Enzo will ever hope to gain. Enzo won't give up his freedom for me.

His hand comes over my hair, removing the bandana, and letting my dark black hair fall to my shoulders.

He grabs my waist and pushes up the thin material of the spaghetti strapped shirt I'm wearing.

Yes, I moan inwardly. Take me, make me yours. I'd rather die belonging to someone than alone.

But then, we've changed positions. My body is arched over the railing as he clenches my bruised neck again.

"Why do you follow orders?" I whisper.

"Because I'm just as trapped in my life as you are in yours. I'm wealthy, I have more money than you could ever imagine, but that doesn't mean I'm free to spend it on the life I want. I do horrible things that are asked of me because I'm a monster. And even if I'm set free, the devil within will never let me go."

Tighter his hands move, just enough that the oxygen I pull through my throat to my lungs thins to a whispered breath.

"You don't seem trapped," I say—*another lie.* I may not understand it, but he's as confined as I am. If he weren't, he would have fucked me like any other boy our age would when given the chance.

He squeezes tighter, and his eyes close.

Dammit! Look at me! But my throat is closed. I can't scream at him.

He's going to kill me without even looking at me.

My hands flail, fighting against his hand taking my life. But he has more strength in his hand than I do my entire body.

I try to kick his groin, as I did before, but he has my legs pinned to the railing.

I can't move.

I can't breathe.

And I can't speak to get him to change his mind.

He's shut out the world, gone to whatever dark place allows him to kill the innocent and condemn his soul to hell.

I close my eyes as the pain overwhelms me again.

I'm alone.

I stop fighting.

I let the darkness come.

But just before it reaches me, something happens.

I can't explain it.

Maybe I'm already dead. I thought I would go to hell for the life I've lived. The stealing, the hurt I've caused my father, my disobedience. Maybe an angel saved me, and I'm going to heaven instead.

For a second, I'm floating. I must be out of my body.

And then just as quickly, I'm falling.

Down.

Down.

Down.

Until my body crashes into the cold water.

9

ENZO

THE WATER BURNS my skin as I plunge into the ocean.

My skin is always hot, like fire. The water is frigid in comparison and slices through my flaming skin like ice.

I have a love-hate relationship with the sea. I love the freedom it offers, and yet it can just as easily cause death. The ocean, for all its beauty, has to be experienced cautiously. For it can take life as easily as it gives it.

I kick hard and break the surface of the water. I suck in a deep breath, filling my lungs with oxygen.

I forget what caused me to tumble into the water. I forget everything as I breathe in the salty air. Right now, I love the ocean. I love how it makes me forget by stealing my brain cells and using my body to keep me afloat.

A gasp next to me brings me back to reality quickly.

My eyes bulge as I realize Kai is next to me, gulping for air. She's not getting enough oxygen. And then she begins floating down, under the water.

Before I think, I'm next to her. Pulling her body up, above the waves. She keeps opening her mouth, trying to catch her breath, but it's not enough.

Kai's body is colder than usual, her throat has a bruise where my hand once squeezed too hard around her precious neck, and her body is limp in my hands.

Shit.

She's going to die.

But that's what I want.

She's supposed to die.

I open her mouth and place mine over hers, giving her a breath. It's not enough.

I squeeze hard around her stomach just under her chest. Over and over I press until finally, the water expels from her lungs.

She coughs and then shivers. Her body is trying to survive in the cold water that threatens to take her life as I did.

"Shh, Kai. I've got you." I hold her against my heated body, trying to offset her temperature.

She lets me hold her. She shouldn't. She should never trust me, but she does. Or she realizes she doesn't have a choice but to accept my help for the moment, until her body regains its strength.

Her head rests against my shoulder, and her body shakes viciously trying to get warm. I continue treading water, keeping us alive.

I shouldn't be doing this.

I should let her die.

But I don't think about my responsibilities.

I don't think about what I'm going to do after I keep her alive.

But holding her in the cool water makes my heart speed up. I don't know what my heart is doing. It's never beat so swiftly before. Never pounded in my chest before her.

My body never reacts to its surroundings. I'm hot as fire, but I don't change. I let the burning build inside me, but never let it out. I don't feel pain nor happiness. I feel nothing.

Until her.

I can't make sense of what I'm feeling. *Happiness maybe? Hope? Lust?*

Something like emotion is there, stirring in my beating heart. But I can't put a word to it.

Slowly we rock in the waves, drifting further away from the yacht in the middle of the night.

Kai's eyes flicker open wide. She smiles at me.

Stupid girl.

And then the fear returns.

She begins thrashing in my arms.

"You...you tried to kill me," her voice trembles.

"I did."

"Help!" she cries out.

The ocean waves beat harder against us, giving her a silent answer. *No one will save her.*

"I killed you, but I also brought you back to life."

She pants heavily just out of reach. Her strength has returned, and her blood pumps with adrenaline.

Even in the dark of the night, I can see her emerald eyes shine with resolution.

"Why would you do that? So you can have the pleasure of watching me die again?"

Her eyes scorch mine as she waits for me to answer.

I take a deep breath. "I don't know why."

She shakes her head, and laughs gently.

Her laugh, even though it is meant to be unnerving, is beautiful and light—like her.

The waves calm as do her arms, and she begins floating

more than wading, letting the sea hold her up. She belongs here, in the water.

I can't kill such a beauty.

Not because I love her or even care for her. I just can't. Something has been holding me back from the moment I met her.

My father lied to me. There is a reason he wants her dead. She's not an innocent, naive girl. She has a secret, one I haven't discovered yet.

I can't kill her.

And that makes me weak, a coward, a fool.

Killing Kai doesn't make sense. I won't kill her, screw the consequences.

"I think you've earned the power to choose your own fate."

"Why?"

"You're asking the wrong question. I don't know why, only that I think you deserve more than to be killed at my hand." I brush against the bruises I caused on her neck.

She straightens with a stoic expression.

"How do I get to choose my fate?"

"Because I have a choice other than death. I can kill you here and now. I could drown you easily in the ocean you love dearly. It would take but a minute or two. Or, you can live, but not in Miami. You will leave and never return."

"You'll let me live?"

"Yes," I breathe.

"My father. I can't leave—"

"Yes, you can." I sigh. She continues to think of that bastard she calls a father over herself. She doesn't understand she's a million times more deserving of life than he is.

"I can't just—"

"The choice is yours, but don't worry about your father.

He has a good job, and I'll ensure his debt is taken care of." I don't know her father, but I suspect he works for my father, just as I know she does. She just doesn't realize it.

Kai doesn't speak, for a long time. The moon shines down upon us, lighting up the sky and the sea.

"Choose Kai, will you run away and live, or stay and die?"

"Live; I want to live."

"Good," I nod.

I soak her up one last time as she floats effortlessly in the water with a willpower I don't understand. I hope to remember this image of her, forever. To remember what weakness feels like and what strength looks like.

I turn and swim hard to the yacht without looking back. I'm sure she is swimming after me, but it will make no difference.

I reach the yacht first and climb up the ladder in the back. I disengage the autopilot before Kai has a chance to make it to the yacht. When I walk back to the side and look down, I see Kai has stopped swimming and is floating a couple feet from the boat.

"I'll die if you leave me in the ocean," she whispers angrily.

She looks up at me. "You weren't giving me a choice. I was going to die either way. You are just too much of a coward to kill me yourself! You'll let the ocean take me instead."

My heart does a weird fluttering in my heart again, trying to convince me to jump back in and warm her. But I can't. This is the only way. My gut-wrenches as I force myself to stay on the boat.

"You won't freeze or drown if you truly want to live."

"I'm not strong enough."

"Kai may not be your given name, but it is who you are."

"How do you know my real name isn't Kai?"

I shake my head. "I don't; you just confirmed my suspicion."

"I'll die."

I lean against the railing, getting as close as I can to her, even though we are a deck away as I stand up on the main deck, and she floats in the depths of the water.

"Kai means sea in Hawaiian. You were raised by the ocean, just like me. You know how to tame it as easily as I do. If you want to survive, you will."

Her lips part and her eyes deepen as she begins slowly drifting away from the yacht.

I could have Kai so easily. Steal her and make her mine, but as evil as I am, I won't risk my own death to take her. Only to save her.

I shake my head as I watch her float further away. She knows enough about currents to make it back to shore. I'm not the one who's saving her; she's saving herself.

"Leave Miami, if you are strong enough to survive," I say roughly into the night with a threat in my voice of what will happen if she stays.

10

KAI

MY NECK ACHES as if a thousand-ton elephant sat on it.

My throat burns with the salt of the ocean water sticking to my lips and hair.

And my core aches for a boy who left me here to die.

I'm alive, but for how long?

I shiver again in the cold water, wishing Enzo was here to keep me warm. If it were daylight, the sun would heat me, but at night there is nothing except my trembling muscles to regulate my temperature. And every second my body spends energy shivering is one less second I will have to survive. I can't afford to waste any energy on anything but swimming to shore.

The yacht speeds away, further and further until it melts into the horizon and the sound of its engines no longer vibrate through me.

Dead.

That's what I should be. He all but killed me with his hands before we plummeted overboard.

I don't remember much after I fell into the ocean. I must

have gone unconscious. And Enzo must have brought me back to life, only to wipe his hands of me.

I can't survive.

Enzo knew I would be dead before my body washed up on the shore.

I know how to float in the water, but I won't be able to with my body shivering like it is.

I'm miles away from shore, much too far to swim.

And it's too dark for other boats to find me except by pure luck. I'm more likely to get run over than found.

No, I'll drown or freeze by morning. I'm too skinny to survive in this cool of water.

If I'm lucky, a shark will find me and give me a quick death. But that's unlikely.

Fuck you, Enzo.

Fuck your evil grin.

Fuck your delicious mouth.

Fuck your masculine cologne.

Fuck your dirty, filthy mind.

Fuck your ability to make me trust you and want you, even though I knew I should never believe the devil.

I feel a cool plastic bump into me from behind.

I turn around slowly, not sure what has touched me.

A lifesaver floats amply behind me.

I eye it suspiciously for a second before throwing my body on it and clinging to it.

Life.

I choose life.

"Fuck you, Enzo!" I shout into the night, even though I know he was the one who left this lifesaver.

He wanted me to live, and he gave me all the help me could without risking his own life.

The waves pick up as does the wind, and I move a good ten feet as one wave pushes me further out to the ocean.

No.

I will not let the ocean take me, not after surviving Enzo. The sea is my friend.

I cling to the lifesaver as I kick hard, trying to move out of the current taking me further away from shore.

Kick.

Kick.

Kick.

I am strong. I can do this.

It takes everything I have, but I finally evade the pull of the current.

I pant heavily as I lay my head on the edge of the lifesaver.

Live.

Keep living.

But then what?

Can I really leave the only home I've ever known? The only connection I have to my mother? Can I leave my father, who can barely take care of himself? What explanation would I give him or my only friend Mason for leaving?

If I want to live, I will leave.

I will start over, maybe even convince my father to come with me. We need a fresh start. Perhaps someday we will find a way to return to Miami.

Right now, I just have to survive.

I need rest.

My eyes close. I'll nap for a minute; then I'll find the strength to find a current that will help guide me back to shore.

The sun starts coming up, waking me up. I slept most of the night.

Shit.

I cling to the lifesaver as I glance around. Shore is a couple of miles away.

I smile for the first time since I discovered Enzo planned to kill me. *I'm going to live.*

I consider my options. I could keep floating and hope I drift in the right direction, to shore. I could stay and wait, hoping a boat will pass by and spot me soon. Or I could swim to shore.

My first two options are the safest, but I could be out here for hours longer.

There is only one option I accept. I abandon my life-saver and start swimming.

I've been swimming my entire life, since I was a baby. It comes easily and naturally to me, but it's still difficult in my current state. I'm weak and exhausted from spending all night at sea.

Why?

The question floats around in my head encouraging me to swim harder.

Why was Enzo supposed to kill me?

Why did Enzo spare my life?

Why?

It doesn't make sense. I've done nothing wrong. I've seen nothing. I've stolen nothing from the man Enzo works for.

There is something I'm missing. Some secret I have yet to discover.

But it makes no difference now. My fate has been decided. I will leave my home, never to return.

I feel the sand beneath my fingers before I realize where I am.

Shore.

I made it.

I cough, my lungs panting for oxygen that isn't tainted with salty ocean water.

My arms and legs ache and my stomach wretches, needing food.

I smile.

I'm alive.

I lay on the shore on the edge of the water, the waves still hitting me with each push of the tide, covered in sand and saltwater.

The sun bakes me, warming my freezing core. I want to stay here lying on the beach, but I don't want Enzo or the people he works for to find me alive.

I force myself up onto my legs. Then, I walk.

If I thought the swim was lengthy, the walk is even longer.

I wish nothing more than to call my father or Mason to come to get me and drive me home. But I don't have a phone or any money. The little money I had must have been swept away with the waves.

I walk...

And walk.

And walk.

Each step is hurting more than the last.

When my trailer finally comes into view, I stumble. Falling to my knees as tears pour from my eyes down my sand covered cheeks.

I'm alive but for how much longer?

I have no money to leave with, and right now, I don't even have the strength to ride in a car, let alone walk or ride a bike out of town. I don't even have the money for a bus fare. And if I don't put food in my belly soon, I'll end up sick.

Just a little further.

I'll sleep in the trailer, hide away from all of this. I think there are some ramen noodles still in the pantry I can cook. And then tomorrow, I will find a way to leave.

I just can't find the strength to stand up.

I feel cold hands wrap around my arms, dragging me to my feet.

"Who are you?" I try to say, but the words never leave my throat.

For a second, I can see the man's face.

"Enzo?" I ask.

The man doesn't answer.

And then I feel the coldness of his hand, the wretchedness in his eyes, and the rough, unbathed smell he oozes.

This man isn't Enzo. Neither is the man to my left. They are both too cold to be Enzo.

I can't walk, but it doesn't seem to matter to them.

They drag me to a van.

I have nothing left in me to fight as they toss my broken body into the back. No strength to prevent them from tying my arms and legs with rope. And then blackness covers my eyes.

I don't understand why they are kidnapping me, and I know better than to ask, Enzo reminded me of that.

Enzo.

Is he behind this?

Or is Black, the man he works for, responsible?

It doesn't matter.

All I know now is that I'm being taken, and I no longer have any strength left in me to survive.

PART II

TAKEN BY LIES

11

KAI

Broken.

For one thousand and ninety-five days I've done everything to keep myself from breaking.

Shut off my mind off during the beatings.

Escaped the depths of the darkness in the night.

Locked down my body during the rapes.

Imagined a new life when I was tortured.

Gritted my teeth through the violations.

Tried every tactic I needed to survive.

Closing myself away.

Envisioning a better life.

Plotting my revenge.

None of the strategies worked long term.

I hate Enzo for what he did to me, but my need to extract revenge was never enough to keep me alive.

I would try blocking my reality out by pretending my stomach didn't constantly ache, and my body wasn't bruised, my bones shattered.

That would keep me alive for a few weeks.

But then came the loneliness.

Being alone was worse than the pain. Not having a friend, a family, or anyone who loved me, that was what made me give up hope more than anything.

It's been over three years since I was taken.

When those strong arms grabbed me, and the hood went over my head, I didn't know what my future held.

Nothing.

I am nothing.

I am nobody.

I am a ghost.

A commodity to be bought and traded.

I was sold for one million—that was my worth.

I look down at my naked, bruised body. There isn't a patch of skin that hasn't been colored. I doubt I'm worth as much now as I was when I was originally sold.

Who would want a pile of bones like me?

The boat rocks, and I heave. There is nothing in my stomach to come up, though. Sometimes I think it would be easier if I would just starve to death, but no matter how much I've tried, my body won't give into the sweet release. My body has adapted and learned to survive on far less food and water than what it should be capable of.

I've tried finding weapons to end my life, but there are none to be found on this yacht.

I've searched, no man carries a gun—not even a knife.

I don't understand the men who keep me.

Nothing about it makes sense. I don't even know who is in charge. *Who is my master?* They all share in the torture. They all revel in the pleasure of watching me slowly disintegrate.

No.

I won't break.

That's the only thing keeping me sane for the last one thousand and ninety-five days.

The thrill at watching the men in frustration as I continue to hold on to who I am and what I'm capable of.

Their primary goal is breaking me.

I overheard them placing bets on how long it would take and who would deliver the final blow.

Three months...

Six months...

One year...

When I made it one year, they stopped betting. I think most of them thought I would never break at that point.

I won't.

I can't.

Staying strong doesn't mean I'm safe; it means I'm foolish. Giving in to them would be easier.

They wouldn't torture me as often.

They could give me a command, and I would obey.

I would resolve that this is my life, and the last drop of hope I've been holding onto would leave.

They could keep the door unlocked. Maybe even stop at a port and get off this godforsaken boat.

But I can't break.

I'm not sure it's possible.

I don't know why.

At first, I was stubborn, defiant even.

I wouldn't give these men the pleasure.

But then, my strength left. And now, I have no idea why I won't crack.

Three years is a long time. I should feel changed, different.

When I was taken I was just a girl; now I'm a woman.

I've spent many of my formative years held captive on a boat full of dangerous, cruel men. Rapists, savages, devils.

I close my eyes as another wave hits the side of the yacht. If my body had any muscles left, I would be shivering from the cold and fever that has continuously taken over my body. I would be vomiting everything in my stomach. But all my body can do is cringe, I can't even brace myself to keep from sliding on the slick floor as the boat tosses me about.

I hate boats.

I hate the water.

I hate the men.

I hate Enzo.

Right now, I hate the water most of all as we rock viciously side to side. I don't know where we are except that it has to be deep in the middle of fucking nowhere. That's the only way the waves get this big, unless a hurricane or tsunami is chasing us. With my luck, I have no doubt a storm is afoot.

I should have hated the water from that first day when Enzo left me to drown in it. But I didn't hate it; I'm not even sure I hated Enzo then. He was just following orders from his boss, Black, when he tried to kill me. He was surviving as much as I was, and then he gave me a chance at freedom. Swim to shore and leave Miami, and then he wouldn't kill me. That was the arrangement.

It sounded like a fair deal at the time. And the night I spent out in the ocean didn't make me hate the water, I grew to appreciate it more. Its power, strength, and freedom I envied and respected.

It was when I made it to shore, and Enzo's men kidnapped me, breaking our arrangement that I could live as long as I left, that I learned what hate was.

I know more about hate than I do love.

I don't think I'm capable of love anymore.

You hear that? I can't love. You broke me! You win!

Another wave crashes, sending me against a wall.

Maybe if I told them I was broken this would stop?

No, this never stops. This never ends.

The boat rocks again, proving my point that this is now my life. Stuck on a boat with the worst of humanity.

I could end it, that tiny voice in my heart whispers again.

I can't with a weapon. I can't with food, but I could let the sea take me. With the storm pursuing us, I would be gone in seconds.

The pain would be gone.

At first, I couldn't imagine taking my life. I was too proud. Too full of hope. Filled with a determination not to let them win. That vanished the first year.

The second year, I couldn't because of my father. He is the only family I have, and even though we don't always have the best relationship, he loves me. He would find me. I couldn't give up for him.

The third year was the hardest. I had no one to live for, not even myself. I'd given up at ever having a normal, healthy life again, even if I was to escape this torturous boat ride. My father had surely given up on me, or at least, I had given up on him. The only thing keeping me alive was *Enzo.*

I can't even explain it.

It wasn't revenge; I'd long given up on getting revenge or even needing it.

I only had one question I needed Enzo to answer...*Why? Why me?*

Why when he took me out on his yacht three years ago did he choose torture over killing me? Was it the only way he could keep me alive? Because if given the choice, I wish he would have just killed me that day.

Why?

The question will haunt me forever. It might be the only thing keeping me alive.

Until now...

The yacht seesaws and lugs causing my body to slip from the wall I was leaning against and slam into the door to my bedroom.

Bedroom, ha.

This isn't a bedroom.

It's not even a gilded cage.

The room has four walls and a floor. No bed. No dressers. No bathroom. Nothing that would bring me comfort. When I first arrived, I was given a blanket and pillow, but that was soon taken away from me.

Now I have nothing, not even clothes. And in some way, having nothing is freeing.

Another quake of the boat, this time bigger than the last. I instinctively grab the door handle to keep from sliding back against the far wall. Not because it will hurt—it will—but pain means nothing to me anymore. Because despite the three years at sea, I still want to control my own fate, no matter how hard these men and the sea try to take it from me.

My pathetic grip on the door handle is barely enough to keep me against the door as the yacht is thrown again in the waves and wind of the sea.

Fuck.

We are going to die.

We've never experienced a storm quite like this. *This is the end.*

Dammit.

This is not how I want to go. When I die, it will be when and how I decide.

"You hear me! I decide when I die!" I shout out.

Yelling like that used to get me a beating from one of the men. They tried to get me to give up my voice along with my body and soul.

I never ceased. Eventually, they stopped responding, learning being alone was harder for me than dealing with their brutal violence. But today, even if they wanted to hear me, they couldn't. The wind's cry is too sharp to hear anything except its wicked howl.

Another creak and bang of the boat sound as the yacht violently slaps against the water.

My door flies open, the door handle ramming into my stomach knocking all the air out of me.

I gasp for breath as I fall to the floor in agony.

Even the sea wants me to break.

"Never!" I cry when I finally catch my breath.

I get to control how this ends.

Another sway and my body slides into the opening of the door. I inch out into the darkness of the hallway. I'm used to darkness, my hole of a room has no light, no electricity, and no windows to the outside. My eyes have adjusted to the pitch black of night, but the hallway almost always has light. The storm must have taken out our power.

I smirk, taking comfort in the fact that the men who held me captive for years won't survive past tonight either.

They don't deserve a quick death. Tonight I hope the storm traps them in this vessel as they slowly suffocate or starve. However, it's unlikely that they will suffer a slow death. The odds are far greater that they will be knocked out by a massive chunk of the ship or the water will drown them quickly, but I can hope.

I move one hand in front of the other as I begin to walk.

I feel my shattered bones crunch into more and more despair with each movement. My bruises burn into my body with each brush against the floor begging me to stop.

I won't stop. Not until I take my last breath.

The yacht lurches forward sending me the length of the hallway to the stairwell.

Shit, stairs.

I have to make it up a flight of stairs.

I haven't climbed in months. *Can I really ascend stairs?*

I bite my lip, more determined than ever to choose how I'll die.

I stare down at my broken toe I earned after I shared my food with one of the other women the men kept on board. I haven't seen or heard another woman on board in weeks. If I did, I would have to free them as well, so they too could choose their own fate and how they will die.

I grab the railing and pull myself up. I wince as I again put pressure on my broken foot that hurts like a moth-erfucker.

Broken bones are the worst. Nothing but time will heal them. And I have nothing to set the bones correctly. The fingers in my left hand won't bend fully because they healed crooked. The broken ribs are worst of all, because the shat-tered splinters slice into my lungs making every breath painful.

Stop wallowing in self-pity and do something to end this.

One step, then another, then another.

It's painstakingly slow, especially since I have to stop each time the yacht veers to the side, and I use all of my energy just holding the ground I made up the stairs.

The door is the last obstacle before I'm on the main

deck. But one simple turn of the knob and the door bursts open in my face. It hits me hard, but I smile.

Almost there.

I'm thrown onto the main deck as the boat jerks forward again and then stops suddenly, like we're traveling in a car that has just thrown on its brakes to narrowly avoid hitting a child playing in the street.

But we don't have any way to control how the yacht moves, not in this storm. Mother nature decides when the boat moves forward or stops. Or even if it stays afloat at all.

The rain pelts down on me as I lay on the main deck. I tilt my head upward feeling the cold droplets cascade over my face in one heavy stream.

Kai means sea in Hawaiian. You were raised by the ocean, just like me. You know how to tame it as easily as I do. If you want to survive, you will. Enzo's words come back to me. I knew before he told me what the name I called myself when I was three means. I was born Katherine but never felt like it fit. Kai is more fitting.

I shake my head.

Kai means sea. I was born by the sea. I will die at sea, I say in my head, already knowing my fate and how wrong Enzo's words were. How wrong the name I chose for myself was.

Unlike three years ago when Enzo tossed me overboard and I eventually saved myself, this time I won't be coming back up. I won't have a buoy to hold onto through the night. I won't have the strength to swim for shore. We are in the middle of the fucking ocean—no one can save me.

And that brings me peace.

I let the rock of the boat push me to the railing on one side of the boat. *Thank you, gravity.*

The railing is the hard part. I won't let the waves push me over; I want to do this myself.

With the rain pouring down, it's hard to feel like I'm not already letting the ocean take me. I grip the slippery railing cautiously, one wrong step and I'll be gone.

Slowly I climb up on the railing with my feet on the bottom rung, my hands gripping the top.

I suck in a breath, but it's mostly water entering my throat at this point. It burns down my lungs, making me cough and gasp for a clean breath.

I don't have much time if I'm going to be the one to decide.

Carefully, I hike one leg over the top of the railing and then the other until there is nothing between me and the ocean but letting go.

A wave splashes hard onto my body, knocking me back against the railing. I don't know how the surge didn't take me then. I shouldn't be strong enough to hold on and fight the wind, rain, and waves.

I close my eyes, trying to feel one moment of freedom. One moment that's mine. One where I can forgive the sea for the pain it's caused me and let it take me in mercy. In one swift pull, I'll be gone.

I have no one to say goodbye to. Nothing left to think or worry about.

I don't think of heaven or hell.

I've been living in hell, and I can't imagine such as place as heaven after what I went through.

No, I long for darkness to take me and never give me back. I ache for a long sleep where I never wake up.

Peace.

I feel it for a moment. The sea seems to calm as if accepting me and preparing me to take the plunge.

"Take me," I say. I let go.

I fall for only a half a second, before a hand grabs my wrist. My feet didn't even leave the bottom rung.

"What the hell?"

I turn back and see Jarod holding my wrist. When I first arrived, I thought he might have the most empathy. He was the one I tried to break and persuade to show me compassion, but it only made him try harder to break me—more determined than all the rest. And if I had to say who the leader is, it's him.

He's the captain of the boat, the leader of the crew. *But only here.* Enzo is the leader back home.

No, Enzo isn't a leader either. He follows orders from Black. Black is the one I should hate the most.

"Let me go," I cry, knowing one slip of his hand and I'll be free.

But Jarod is strong. One sharp pull and I'm back on the other side of the railing, but not to safety. I've learned there is no such thing. But I'm no longer on the edge of death like I was before.

"You crazy bitch," he curses.

Another wave crashes and knocks us against something sharp. My head pounds, and now along with the water flowing down my face, I feel the ooze of blood.

My eyes grow heavy, and the world turns foggy.

"Shit," Jarod curses.

He tosses me over his shoulder as he carries me inside. To my surprise, he doesn't take me to my room. It's the only room I've been in for months. No, instead he brings me to another room—to one with a bed.

A bed?

Why would I need a bed?

Are they going to rape me in a bed instead of on the floor?

I should fight, but I have nothing left.

I've given up.

I have no hope.

I have no fear.

I am nothing.

I don't shiver.

I don't react.

I'm not even sure I'm breathing.

Jarod tosses me on the bed, and I don't move, not even to cover my naked body or gain warmth.

My eyes are open, but I don't see the men standing over me. I see nothing except darkness. *Am I dead or dying?*

They say you see a white light before you die, that your entire life flashes before your eyes. That isn't my experience. I see nothing but gloom and death.

"Is she dead?" a voice asks.

"No," Jarod answers.

I'm not dead. I almost feel like crying at that, but I don't. I'm still alive, and as much as I wish I were nothing, I still have hopes and dreams. My dreams are no longer shiny and pleasant. I hope to be dead.

"She's broken," Jarod says.

What? Broken? I'm not broken. Am I?

"Broken." The word travels through the men like a ghost of a whisper. Each mutters it, not sure that it is true until he gets a chance to speak the word himself.

Broken.

I'm not broken. I feel no different from before. My wounds might be worse, and I might die if I don't recover, but I'm not broken.

Never.

But one by one they test the word themselves.

Broken.

Broken.

Broken.

Each time they say the word, I begin to believe it myself more and more.

I'm broken.

They finally broke me.

This is what it feels like.

"Does that mean...?" one of the men asks tentatively.

"Yes, we can go home now. Our job is done," Jarod answers.

What?

Their job was to keep me until they broke me. *That makes no sense.*

What are they going to do with me now? Are they finally going to kill me?

No.

They won't. Otherwise, Jarod wouldn't risk his life to keep me from killing myself.

Men start filing out of the room, and for once the heavy rock of the boat begins to return to a gentle sway as mother nature agrees that she has broken me, and there is no reason left to keep tormenting us with her wrath.

I feel a blanket go over my skin.

I want to fight it. I don't like it touching me. I've yearned to be touched, to be comforted, to feel a soft, warm blanket for years. But now that I feel it, I hate it. I want it gone.

But I don't have the strength to say anything or even remove the blanket from my body. I'm a frozen corpse.

Jarod looks down at me grimly. "You're broken," he says almost like he's trying to convince me I am.

I'm not, comes the tiniest of voice. *I'm not broken.*

I know Jarod sees the defiance in my eyes. It's the only thing I can give him to show how wrong he is. Any other time it would be enough for him to fight me and try again to break me. He knows he didn't truly break me, so why is he saying it.

So they can go home.

The men had one job: to break me. For years they failed in their task. None of them thought the task would last this long. The storm shook up more than just me. They all thought they were going to die. They want to go home. I just don't know what they are going to do with me.

Jarod leans down and whispers in my ear, "You're broken, now you're free."

12

KAI

Home.

I never thought I'd be returning home.

I thought I would die at sea.

But here I am, lying on a park bench in baggy shorts and a T-shirt.

I look homeless.

That's because I am.

Miami isn't my home anymore.

It hasn't been my home for over three years.

I'm not sure it was ever really my home, even when I was living in Miami. The trailer I inhabited with my father barely ensured I had a bed to sleep in and a roof to protect me from the rain. Most of the clothes I owned had holes in them. And my belly was never fully fed. Although, I would go back to that time in a heartbeat.

Back then I wasn't really starving. Back then I'd never experienced pain or understood loneliness. Back then I wasn't completely alone. Sure I only had my father and Mason, my best and only friend. I felt lonely, but I wasn't really. I didn't understand the word until recently.

Loneliness isn't about being alone. It's about realizing you have no one. No one who loves you. No one who misses you. No one who even cares to talk to you.

It's what leads you to be so desperate as to talk to the spider in the corner of your room like they are your best friend. Then you talk to your shadow. Then you start talking to yourself like the little voice inside you is another person and not yourself.

It's when you realize no one will ever talk back; no one will bury or mourn you if you die. That's when you understand what true loneliness feels like.

I slowly sit up, as the sun burns my now pale skin. I haven't seen the sun in years. I used to wear a tan year round, but after spending three years locked in a dark cave, the hint of sunlight scares me. I will blister immediately if I don't find shelter.

I don't remember coming back. My last memory is falling asleep on the lumpy bed on the yacht. It should have felt like a luxury; instead, it felt too soft to fall asleep on. But the pull of exhaustion made me sleep, despite the lack of comfort I felt lying in the five hundred count sheets.

I don't remember getting dressed.

I don't remember leaving the yacht.

I don't remember the swaying stopping.

As I sit up, I realize the swaying truly hasn't stopped. *Maybe I'm still on a boat after all? This is all some dream.* I used to dream about Miami a lot that first year. I tried to remember what the sun felt like even when I was cursing it for causing me to sweat so much. This is a dream.

I stand up, and the ground shakes.

Shit.

I grab the back of the bench to steady myself.

The ground seems real enough. Grass tickles the bottoms of my feet.

I stare down at my bare toes. I may have gotten dressed, but I'm not wearing any shoes—*not that I want shoes*. I can't remember why people would ever want to wear such things.

I take a step, and the texture of the grass is intense. It tickles and itches the bottom of my foot.

So their feet don't have to feel this, that's why people wear shoes.

One more step, and I let go of the park bench. The ground still shifts back and forth, and I'm sure I look drunk as I walk, but I don't care.

It's early in the morning, and other than a few early morning joggers and homeless people, there isn't anyone around to judge me.

I keep walking, slowly at first, and then my steps become more regular as I get used to the wobbling. I know the way without thinking. My past has been buried for years, but now it blasts back into my consciousness as if I was here yesterday.

I don't take in my surroundings as I walk; the sounds and noises would overwhelm me if I did. Instead, I let the sounds of the cars honking and whizzing by drift into the background. I don't focus on the grass, or sand, or sidewalk changing under my feet, making it more difficult to walk with each change in the terrain. I keep my eyes down, so I don't have to register the bright sun or the vibrant colors all around.

All I want to do is make it to the trailer and lock myself up in my room for days.

Finally, the trailer appears in front of me in the same place it's been parked for almost twenty years. It never occurred to me, as I walked over here, that father could have moved or sold it.

The ratchety old door creaks open, and I realize the door still doesn't latch properly. My father never fixed it.

And then, as if my thought of him called him to existence, my dad stands at the top of the three steps that lead up to the door. Enzo kept one of his promises to ensure my father stayed alive.

We both eye each other, standing tall and stiff. Neither of us breathes. We just look. I don't have to speak to tell him what I've been through the last three plus years. He can see every mark and hand that was ever laid on me. If he thought I ran away from home, that doubt has now been pushed away.

I've changed completely; he looks the same.

If there were ever a time where we would react differently than our usual, unaffectionate selves, now would be that time. But that isn't who we are. We don't do hugs. We don't do warmth. We may love each other, but we don't stoop to such weakness. It's not who we are. I doubt my father even hugged me when my mother died.

I can't remember ever hugging this man.

I don't know how long we stand just looking at each other. It could be seconds or hours. My ability to comprehend time was taken from me, along with my body and sense of worth.

Finally, my father moves. He takes the three steps down the stairs and stops in front of me.

"You shouldn't have come back," his voice cracks.

I agree, I shouldn't have.

I don't speak though. I don't nod. I just let his words fill me.

Is there a tear in the corner of his eye?

No, that can't be. My father doesn't show emotion, ever. He doesn't cry.

But yet, I think that's precisely what he's doing.

And then he's gone, walking away from me. Our reunion is over.

"Kai? Is that you?"

Mason.

I turn and look at the boy I grew up with. Even he hasn't changed much. His body is a little thicker, his hair a little longer, his voice deeper. There are a few thin lines around his eyes I don't remember before, but otherwise, he looks exactly the same. He's the same boy I've been friends with since I was five.

I should speak, reassure him, because he looks like he's seen a ghost. And after he realizes it's really me, he will see the bruises, the scars, the broken bones. He will see how frail I am and then he will lose it.

He'll rush me to the police or the hospital. I'll have to answer questions I never want to explain.

I'm not ready to speak. I've talked plenty of times, mainly to myself, but talking right now feels like opening myself up to let someone in again. And as much as that person should be Mason, I can't.

He hasn't changed, but I have.

And a part of me hates him. For not finding me. For not preventing me from being taken. For not saving me.

Mason and my father were the only people who would have missed me. My father could barely feed himself. I don't blame him, but Mason has money, resources, connections. He loved me. He wanted more from me. He could have found me.

"Jesus, it is you." Mason runs toward me with open arms threatening to engulf me.

His fingertips barely touch me, and I wince, taking a step back. The light touch feels like fire against my ice cold skin.

"Christ," Mason curses as he runs his hand through his long blonde surfer locks.

My eyes turn downcast. I can't watch him realize what happened to me. I can't take his empathy, his concern, his anger. *He has no right to feel any of those things!*

"What happened?" he asks.

No answer.

"Kai? You can talk to me. I won't hurt you." His hand brushes against me, and I jump out of my skin.

I can't. You can't touch me, I shout inside.

My eyes meet his, telling him to stop with a sharp glare as a dog would warn a stranger thinking of coming onto its property.

"Okay, no touching. Can I drive you to a hospital or police station?"

I freeze. *No.*

"Kai? A doctor should see you. You could have broken bones. I will pay for everything."

I do have broken bones, you idiot.

Slowly, I shake my head no.

He sighs.

"Okay, I won't push you. Let's go inside though. Maybe after a bath and food, you might reconsider going. I could even have a doctor come to you if you prefer."

Mason puts his hand out, offering it to me like a crutch to walk with.

He thinks I'm weak, *maybe I am?* But I don't want his or anyone else's help.

I ignore his hand and walk to the stairs and then enter the dilapidated trailer.

I take a deep breath, and everything returns—the smell of bacon and coffee, my father's usual breakfast. The stench of cigarette smoke, alcohol, and bad decisions hangs in the air.

I don't hear Mason behind me, but I'm sure he's followed me into the trailer. He's never come inside, not once in all the years I've known him. I was always embarrassed of my home. I didn't want him near it; now it doesn't matter.

Mason may think we have a future together if he doesn't already have a girlfriend. I glance behind me, spotting his left hand. No ring. He's not married, but he could be dating.

It doesn't matter.

I don't have a future. And anything I do from here on out won't involve him.

Mason slowly moves by me to the single bathroom at the back and then returns a moment later.

"I started the water for a shower. I wish there was a tub to soak in, but a shower will have to do for now," he says.

Shower.

How long has it been?

I reek, I'm sure, but I can't tell anymore. This is how I smell, like rotting flesh and death.

"Do you want help?" his voice shakes a little as he asks.

I shake my head. I'm not even sure I want a shower, but I want to be alone. I spent years yearning for someone to talk to, and now that I have someone, I want nothing more than to hide away by myself.

"I'll make you something to eat."

I don't answer. I should eat, but my stomach no longer cries for food. It's used to surviving on nothing. It doesn't matter if I eat or not.

I walk past Mason and head into the tiny bathroom. I

pull the door closed and strip the dirty clothes off my body. The shorts were so baggy. I'm not even sure how they were staying on my body.

The steam begins to fill the small room, and it draws me to the water.

Water—*my enemy, my friend, my everything.*

It reminds me of the ocean and angers me that I never got the end I wanted. I'm alive when I shouldn't be.

I step into the small corner shower. I don't bother to pull the curtain closed as the water drips down on me in thin streams. There was a time when I thought the water pressure wasn't enough, certainly not enough to wash the shampoo out of my hair. But now, it's too much. It feels like it is dumping on my head, the same as it was the night of the storm on the yacht.

The warm droplets are too hot for my icy skin, and I immediately want to retreat. But that means facing Mason again—something I'm not ready for. So I force myself to stand under the heavy stream.

I don't use shampoo or soap. I don't try to remove the caked on dirt, sweat, or filth. I just let the water do the work.

Time passes, again, I don't know how long. But eventually, I turn the faucet off. I let the water drip from my hair down my skinny frame. I've always been thin, but now I can see every bone in my body. I should have curves; instead, I have protruding bones.

There is a towel lying by the sink, and I use it to dry off before stepping out of the bathroom and then walk to my bedroom.

Sleep; I need sleep.

I fall onto the bed in a heap still wet, but it doesn't matter. The bed feels too soft. I'm not going to be able to sleep on it, I realize instantly.

"I made you soup." Mason steps into the small room. "Oh my god! I'm sorry, I should have knocked first."

He stops and shields his eyes.

I look around the room, confused by what he is shocked and sorry about.

It takes me too long to realize I'm naked. The towel that was wrapped around me has fallen open. My nakedness doesn't bother me, but it does Mason.

So I reluctantly wrap the towel around myself.

Mason peaks from behind his fingers and then straightens to bring me the bowl of soup he prepared and a cup of tea.

"I wasn't sure if you could handle more than soup, but if you can keep this down, I can get you whatever you want to eat."

I look at him with big wide eyes. *Food.* He would get me anything, anything I craved. *Doesn't he realize I don't crave anything anymore?*

Mason sits on the edge of the bed next to me and holds out a spoonful of the soup to my lips. I look down at the cup of tea he sat on the small end table. I take that instead, lift it to my lips, and drink slowly.

He sighs in exacerbation and sets the bowl next to me.

"I will do anything to help you, Kai. I don't know what you've been through. I don't know who took you or what evil you've experienced. But I..." He takes a deep breath. "I love you, Kai. I have since we were five. I've just never had the courage to tell you. Not having you all these years, thinking you ran away and never called was hard. Realizing the truth is harder. I love you. I will never stop loving you."

His words should comfort me. Make me stop feeling so alone. They don't. I don't feel anything anymore. All I feel is numbness.

So I don't speak. There are no words to say back. And if I speak, he might ask questions I don't want to answer. I don't want to talk about what happened. I don't want to see a doctor or a therapist.

His eyes travel over my body again. They slowly meet my eyes.

Broken.

He thinks I'm broken.

He sees my frail, ruined body. He thinks my spirit has been crushed; my heart ripped out of my chest. My soul trampled on.

I'm not broken, I say inwardly. *I can't be broken.* I swore they would never break me.

He doesn't hear or see that though. All he sees is a broken doll he thinks he can fix.

I don't need fixing. I need answers.

This is who I am now. I need acceptance.

I finish my tea and then eat some of the broth soup before I pull the covers up and close my eyes, pretending to sleep.

Mason eventually leaves me alone in the room and shuts the door.

Finally, alone.

I stand out of the bed, letting the towel drop, and curl up on the carpet floor. Even that feels too soft.

I want cold.

I want ice.

I don't want comfortable and warm.

But the floor is better than the bed. And my body is too tired to find a better, harder bed.

So I sleep.

The next morning, everything happens again.

Mason is still here. He must have slept on the recliner.

He feeds me. He encourages me to talk. He talks. He tries to get me to shower. To eat. To go to a doctor.

The only thing I do that makes him happy is eat.

Otherwise, he looks at me with pity in his eyes. He winces when my bones creak. He swears when he sees new bruises. He tries to take care of me, but it's not what I want.

Mason is a good man; I should have dated him before. He would have made a good boyfriend. Maybe if we were together when I was taken he would have tried harder to find me?

Now, I'll never know.

Now, we can never be.

Time passes, and our routine stays the same.

I sleep.

I eat.

He asks questions and pushes.

I don't know how much time passes, except eventually I don't feel like sleeping so much. My bruises and pains are still there, and I haven't gained much if any weight, so I doubt much time has passed. But some did.

Enzo.

His name floats back into my head again.

Why?

That becomes my new focus. Not on avoiding Mason, but on thinking about Enzo.

Not the good. Not the adrenaline at stealing Enzo's watch when we first met.

Not when he took me on my first yacht ride, the last one I will ever enjoy.

Not when we played our two lies and one truth game, and I won.

Not when he gave me my first kiss.

The only thing I think about when it comes to Enzo is why?

Why me?

Why didn't he kill me, when he was ordered to?

Why did he have me kidnapped and sold, instead?

Why did Jarod let me go when I was his favorite plaything?

I need answers, to so many questions.

But it is all really one question. *Why?*

I don't know how to find Enzo. I don't even know his last name or if he still lives in Miami. I don't know if he's even alive anymore. He worked in a ruthless business. He could be dead.

No.

I feel it.

He's alive.

He's why I'm still alive.

He's why I'm here.

I need answers.

Not necessarily revenge, although I'll take that too.

I can't think past what I'll do when I figure out my answers.

I listen carefully and hear Mason sleeping in the other room. The faint sound of the old television blares and skips. I'm surprised the television still works.

I need to get out of here to get my answers.

But where?

First clothes, then where.

I go to the rod in the corner of the room that holds my old clothes. I stare at them. I don't want to put them on, but I need to if I don't want to get arrested or sent to a psych ward.

And I need them to cover my body. My scars and bruises need to be covered.

I pull on a pair of jeans and a long-sleeved sweater. It's summer, but it's the only thing that will hide my body.

I run a brush through my midnight black hair and leave it down, even though it descends far down my back almost to my butt. It needs to be cut; the ends are uneven and frayed. It would look better up, but I need my hair down to cover my neck and cheeks. Now people will only notice the bruises on my face if I look up.

I take a step, and the jeans fall off my hips.

Shit.

I rummage through my drawers until I find a belt.

The clothes itch and burn against my skin, but I don't take them off.

Shoes.

I need shoes.

I try on tennis shoes, closed-toe shoes, flip-flops, even heels; but I can't. It's too much for my feet. They all feel like a vice grip.

People go barefoot in Miami all the time; this is a beach town after all. Hopefully, no one will notice my feet.

I open my door and listen carefully. Mason is still asleep.

I tiptoe through the small trailer, ensuring my feet don't make a sound.

I should feel bad for leaving Mason without talking and without a note. A reasonable person would, but I don't have feelings anymore. *Those were taken.*

I get to the door, knowing this is the most dangerous part. I could wake him up, and then how would I leave without him following?

I touch the handle and pry it open inch by inch.

The creak softens, and I stare intently at Mason. He's

out. Exhausted from trying to take care of me and break through my walls—walls no one will ever knock down.

When I'm outside, I breathe again.

I'm free, at least of Mason.

Now, where?

I rack my brain, thinking hard for the first time in forever. My mind is foggy, and it hurts to use, but the thought finally comes to me. Where the most dangerous people in town go...

Surrender.

The name of the darkest underground club in town floats in my hazy brain.

It's for the wealthy, the secretive, the criminals.

It's shady, but it's where all the elites and those that cater to them go.

My clothes won't get me into the club. Even if I were dressed up, I wouldn't get in. It's invitation only.

But somehow, I know that's where Enzo is. If he's there, he'll let me in. And if he's not, then I'll find a way in. I'll find someone who knows him.

Because Enzo is the only way I'll get my answers. The club is where all the darkest creatures that crawl the earth lurk. If Enzo is still alive, he'll be there.

I shouldn't go. I should stay far away from the man who sold me, but I can't. I need answers more than I need to live. I'll be breaking our deal by coming back to Miami, by not staying away, but Enzo broke our deal first when he had me taken.

13

KAI

THE DOOR to Surrender looms across the street from where I stand. I can't make my legs move toward the door, but I can't walk away either.

There is no sign above the frame—no advertisement as to what sins men partake in behind the door.

There is nothing to indicate that anything happens here or that this is even a club.

It's simply an unmarked door. I shouldn't know it exists, but when I was fifteen, I was desperate for money. To eat. To survive. And to pay off my father's debts. Debts he accrued when my mother fought a long battle against cancer.

I found a boy at school who sold drugs and offered to help him to make some quick cash. So I sold weed; I couldn't bring myself to sell anything harder. But this is where he wanted to meet me, outside this club. This is where most of his clients were, and that's how I knew this place existed.

It's exclusive and private.

No one knows about the club or gets in without an invite.

There is no way I'll get in.

But I have to get in.

I try not to seem too interested as I stare at the door. I'm sure a hundred security cameras are looking at me right now, cameras that extend well beyond the door of the club. A place like this needs to know who is approaching. They need to know if the person is dangerous or one of their members before they even decide if they are letting them in or not.

I scan the top of the brick building but don't see any cameras. No guard stands outside the door, but I have no doubt there is one inside. I may make it through the door, but that may be as far as they will let me go. They could kill me for just knowing about the club when I shouldn't. And even if I make it to Enzo, even if I get my answers, he will kill me.

This is a suicide mission.

But at least I'll have my answers.

I stop stalling, and I walk slowly toward the door, like Enzo might jump out and aim a gun at me at any moment.

Nothing happens.

I hesitate at the door. I have to be the old Kai. The one who could walk and talk her way into anything. I didn't have curves, or a body men would die for, but I knew how to exude strength and confidence.

I close my eyes. *I am her.*

I open my eyes as I open the door and push myself inside the den of the most evil men in the world—men who kill, torture, and sell women.

I expect arms to grip me. A man to tackle me. Some movement to try to throw me out. So when I feel nothing but the warm air of the club against my cold skin, I exhale sharply. I'm emitting steam and ice in a place built of fire.

I force myself to keep my head high and meet the customers' eyes as I walk into the large room holding men seated at tables with drinks and half-naked women dancing around them.

I don't belong here, but maybe they will think I'm one of the dancers who hasn't changed into her stripping attire yet.

If they looked at me at all, they would know that isn't the truth. They would realize I'm just a broken bag of bones and flesh.

Surrender is precisely what anyone would expect a club to look like. You would never know these men are more dangerous than the average. Other than the furniture being more luxurious and talent of the dancers being better than most, I've stepped into numerous clubs like this along the Miami coastline.

This isn't where I'll find Enzo. This isn't the deepest, darkest place of the club. This is for appearances, so if anyone like me stumbles inside, they won't realize what they found.

I don't think Enzo is these men's leader, but even if he were, he's proud enough not to bother mingling with the men at the bottom. At least he was three years ago.

The covered clothes I'm wearing feels like a mistake. The sweater and jeans are suffocating me and make it impossible to pretend to be a dancer or a waiter, which are the only role a woman has in a club like this.

But I keep walking, and no one stops me. No one asks me a question. No one even raises an eyebrow.

It's eerie how the men continue on. I feel like a ghost. *Maybe I am? Maybe I did die at sea, and I've come back to haunt Enzo's ass?*

I make it out of the main room and find myself in a hidden hallway darker than the main rooms. The blackness should scare me; the amount of light here only makes the wickedness harsher. It does nothing to brighten my way.

But I prefer the dark, the night. The black trapped me for years, but it taught me how to see even without the moonlight.

I walk easily, somehow feeling more at ease as I walk down hallway after hallway.

I should be stopped. I know I'm on camera, but no one stops me.

It's like Enzo wants me to find him.

I see more light pour through at the end of a hallway, and I hear music again for the first time since I left the main room at the entrance.

This, this is where I'll get my answers.

I stand in the shadow of the door, wishing I could see what is going on in the room without being seen myself.

I wish I could steal my answers from Enzo as easily as I stole his watch the first time I met him.

Instead of recoiling, I step forward out of the shadows and into the doorway.

Enzo.

He's seated in a large, red chair at one corner of the room. It looks like it was made for royalty, not his traitorous ass.

His eyes meet mine the instant my body appears in the doorway, as if he knew I was walking down the hallway toward him. No one else notices me. Just him.

Rage, like I've never felt before, explodes like shock-waves through my body. This is the man responsible for my years of torment, pain, and suffering. This man chose to sell me to Jarod and his men. This man ensured I hated the sea forever. This man took my life and twisted it into something

I'll never be able to claim as my own. He took my freedom and exchanged it for retching pain.

This man.

This fucking gorgeous, evil man.

Last time I saw Enzo, he was a boy. Tall, his muscles strong, but young. He looked older than his age of seventeen, but now he's all man. He's grown into bulk muscle, hardened into a monster of beautiful veins and cords twisting through his body. A shadow of his dark hair covers his rigid chin, sharp lines form his cheeks, and slits for eyes that resemble a snake. His hair is a little longer than before, twisting into black threads weaving his victims under his spell, making it appear he's innocent when he's the epitome of evil.

My air is gone as he stares at me. I've imagined this moment for years, replaying this moment in my head and all the ways it could play out. With me slapping him, yelling at him, giving him some of his own medicine when I tortured him. I imagined so many variations of what I would do when I first saw Enzo again.

I never expected to freeze like a pussy. I'm strong and fearless. There is nothing left to fear when everything has been taken from you. But standing in front of the man responsible for my breaking is too much for my brain to process.

Enzo stands, brushing off a well-manicured hand that was tracing over the lapel of his suit jacket. A suit that melds over his sculptured muscles like a second layer of skin. I thought he looked good in his clothes before, but now he radiates confidence as he moves like nothing and no one will stop him from getting what he wants.

My eyes widen, their attention drifting from Enzo to the women lounging and dancing around him. Five women, all in various states of dress. Skin tight clothing revealing their breasts and asses, to lingerie, to completely naked. Then I see the men. Two of them wear suits like Enzo's although they don't fit as well. And three wear jeans and hoodies. None of the men acknowledge the women, treating them like they are inanimate furniture and decorations instead of real people. It should disgust me, but these women are treated like queens compared to the women on the yacht I've spent too much of my life on.

Everyone's focus is on Enzo as he stands, still gawking at me like he doesn't believe I'm really here. I doubt he even recognizes me. It's been years, and I was nothing to him but a paycheck he collected when I was sold to ensure I kept our deal and stayed away. He's probably just amazed that one of his slaves made it through his security to his door without being thrown out.

Enzo walks toward me, and the room falls silent as their eyes shift to me. I should be terrified of being in a room full of so many predatory men. Men who probably knew about my fate or have helped Enzo do similar things to other women. I don't feel anything about the other men, only Enzo.

"Out," Enzo says without tearing his gaze from me. He's not speaking to me though, he's speaking to everyone else in the room. His throat growls as he says the word in his deep, authoritative voice. His voice was always strong and powerful. It sounds much the same as I remember, but somehow deeper than before.

The women scatter, but their eyes give me a curious glance before leaving. I watch them from the corner of my eye. They are all beautiful and unbroken, unscarred, untouched.

The men in the hoodies and T-shirts leave next through doors in the back of the room.

The two men in suits linger. One opens his mouth as if he wants to question Enzo's authority, but he resists the urge. They leave slowly after the rest.

Enzo worked for one of the most powerful men in all of Miami, maybe the world—definitely one of the most dangerous. It seems in the time I've been gone, he's gained more power in the organization. He told me once if he killed me, he'd be free.

He didn't kill me. So I guess he never got free.

What did selling me get him? *Power*, women who dance for him, men who shoot without asking questions.

Now that we are alone, my heart speeds. The last time he touched me, he almost killed me with his bare hands on one of his yachts. Then he saved me from drowning when he threw us overboard. I'm not ready for him to touch me again.

But I can't back up and show my fear.

I take a deep, painful breath as my ribs expand and the broken bones dig deeper inside. I push my chest out, standing as tall as I can in my loose jeans and pale colored sweater.

"You should have killed me," I say, my first words in days.

Enzo stops a foot in front of me. He doesn't react to my words, but his eyes read recognition. He knows exactly who I am. The girl he should have killed, turned woman. Because now that I survived, I will get my answers. And I will ensure his life is hell.

I don't know why Jarod set me free. Maybe Enzo gave him instructions when he sold me to him that I could only go free if I was broken enough to never want to return to

Miami. Jarod grew bored of me and set me free, thinking I was broken. But I wasn't. I'm not. That was his mistake.

"That can be arranged," his voice is harsh.

I grit my teeth as my legs begin to tremble beneath me. I don't even have the strength to keep standing. *Why would I think showing up here and demanding answers was a good idea?* He'll sell me again or dispose of me with a click of a gun. I'm nothing to him.

No, I'm something. He was supposed to kill me, not sell me. Whether he thought selling me was a better fate than death I have no idea.

And I'll ensure he kills me before another man touches me. I'm not afraid of death. And I'm not afraid of Enzo.

"Then what are you waiting for—kill me," I say. He won't. I can see he has as many questions behind his eyes as I do. He wants to know what happened to me. *How I escaped my master? Why I'm here?*

He tilts his chin as if that will give him a better angle to view my thin-as-a-toothpick body. That's all he can see though: how skinny I am. The broken bones, the bruises, and the scars are mostly hidden. Unless he examines my toes or fingers, he won't see any broken bones. My nose has been shattered several times, but my left eye has a deep bruise that would be impossible to hide even from makeup.

"I could kill you," he nods as if considering it. "Or we could play a game."

My heart stills. I know exactly what game he is talking about—truth or lies. The same game I taught him last time. The game I won. Winning the game didn't matter though. I ended up an empty shell of the woman I once was.

"I think I'd rather be dead."

His eyes narrow and his jaw tenses. "Why?"

"Because in death I might finally be free."

He walks toward me again, and I still, silently begging him not to touch me. My body screams on the inside to stay away, but I'm afraid if I speak, he will stroke me intentionally. My skin crawls at that thought.

He doesn't touch me as he circles me like a hawk determining how to snatch its prey. After circling he stops in front of me.

"Death won't free you." He steps back, giving me space to breathe.

"Yes, it will. I'm broken, can't you see? I am nothing. When you sold me to those men, you ensured my death. I should have died three years ago when you had your men take me before selling me, even after our arrangement. You didn't give me the chance to leave Miami. You lied. You did this to me..." my voice cracks in a high pitched squeal, and I know tears are threatening. *Do not cry.* Not in front of this man.

I think back to when I was first kidnapped. I was exhausted after swimming to shore all night, and then the hands came around me. At first, I thought it couldn't have been Enzo. I thought it was one of my father's debt collectors.

After Enzo spared my life, I thought he had compassion. There was no way he would have done this. And then I overheard the men talking about Enzo, about his boss Black. When I was brought to a room full of wealthy men, plodded out on stage like cattle, and sold to the highest bidder, it was Enzo's name who was given as the seller. He may not have been there, but it was by his order that I was sold.

Enzo must have realized I would have never stayed away from Miami and my father. But he couldn't kill me, so he sold me.

I swallow the tears back down. "You ensured I was broken, by selling me to the worst men. It's my turn to give an ultimatum: kill me or answer my questions, because I will not live another day in this hell without understanding why you didn't kill me that day. Why you were tasked with killing me in the first place."

I spit my words out, but he doesn't flinch. Each word is like a punch to his gut. But he's invincible; he can't be fractured. He has a natural armor I would die to possess.

"You're right. I sold you, not to the highest bidder, but to the cruelest man to ensure you a life of pain. One who didn't even want you, but loved knowing he would ruin you for any other man. Now that you are broken he has no use for you, so he dumped you on the nearest shore."

I should sob at his words. Or feel validated for confirming my suspicions. Enzo is responsible for my pain, and I have a chance to hurt him for hurting me.

"You are wrong about one thing," he says.

"I doubt it."

He smirks. "The men failed. I've seen shattered women. I've tortured enough men to understand when that last bit of desire to live leaves, when the whites vanish from their eyes, and they relinquish their souls to me. I know what it takes to drive a person to the edge of existence and ensure they never want to hold on. Your body may be in agonizing pain, your mind clouded with fear, but you, Kai Miller, are not broken."

I gasp.

I'm not broken.

I've known it the whole time, yet I needed confirmation from someone else to believe it. My father didn't say it. Mason couldn't even imagine it. But Enzo said it without me even asking or pleading with my eyes. It's what I needed to hear to survive.

"I know I'm not broken, despite what everyone keeps telling me."

He nods slowly with a tiny twinkle in his eye.

"Now that we've settled that, you don't truly want me to kill you. It's time to play a game."

"No, no more games. Even if I win, you'll find some twisted way to deceive me."

"And you never deceived me?" he asks.

"No, not during the game."

He nods. "I never lied to you during the game either. You won the game. I answered all the questions I could."

"All but the one that truly mattered." *Why? Why did he come to kill me?* The one question he never answered and I need to be answered more than anything.

"I was a boy with little power then. Now, I'm a king." He gestures to the grand room that looks more like a lair than a room.

"You will answer any question I ask if I win the new round?"

"Yes, if you win, I will answer any question."

This is why I came. To get answers to my questions. To understand why, of all the millions of women in the world, the devil found me. I can't trust Enzo, but this might be my only chance to get answers.

Why was Enzo assigned to kill me?

Why didn't he kill me?

Why did he take me?

Why did he have his men sell me?

Why was I tortured to the edge of breaking?

Why?

"You'll tell me why?" I ask, not including all the questions, knowing his answer would encompass all the questions.

"Yes, I'll tell you why."

Enzo may be evil, but he'll tell me the truth if I win. He wants answers too. He's itching to ask me endless questions. To tie me down, beat me, and force me to answer. I don't know why he doesn't go with that method. It wouldn't work; I know how to endure the worst torture imaginable. Maybe Enzo senses that. I have nothing to hide. Losing and having to answer his questions isn't really a loss.

"And if I lose, I'll answer your questions," I say.

"No."

I wait with bated breath for him to speak his next words. His wolfish eyes and growl of his throat already giving way to what he wants. *Me.*

"No, if you lose, I win you," he says.

14

ENZO

I thought Kai was a ghost.

I thought I was dreaming, imagining her standing in the doorway to my lair.

But then she spoke, and I knew Kai was real.

She's been gone so long. I made sure she would never appear in Miami, in Surrender, in my life. Yet, here she is...

Skinny.

Beaten.

On the edge of death.

Kai shouldn't be alive. I don't even understand how she's standing.

I remember how tiny she was before, but this is on a different level. The years that have passed since the last time I saw her have turned me into a hard machine of muscle. No one would ever mistake me for a boy. Kai should have filled out the curves of her body; instead, she's thinned into almost nothing. A strong breeze could blow her over. I could snap her frail neck between my thumb and fingertips.

Her clothes hang baggy; her bones poke out beneath long sleeves and pants that I'm sure hide the unconceivable

—bruises, scars, pain. Her midnight dark hair has grown in length but is uneven and frazzled. The swelling around her eye is what has me entranced the most. Black and blue coloring around her now pale skin, lightened from lack of sunlight and nourishment.

For years, I've done my best to forget what happened. Forget her beautiful pouty lips, her gorgeous wavy black hair, her silky skin. I tried to erase her snark and tenacity from my head. I pretended that night was all a dream. That I never put my hands on her and threatened to kill her. That I didn't force her out of Miami and into a world of pain.

As much as I tried to forget, it was impossible. Not because she was the only girl I've ever wanted and couldn't have. A girl who intrigued me and sparked a stirring inside me I didn't know could exist. But because getting rid of Kai gained me power.

I'm no longer a prisoner to my father, but a ruthless, free man.

I decide my destiny now. And I have men who will fight to the death to ensure I get my way. And I've never forgotten what it cost me to gain that authority—Kai.

She was the sacrifice for my freedom. She was never supposed to return. I was never supposed to deal with the consequences of my sin. But here she is.

Kai was stupid to come back. She was free. She could have gone anywhere, and saved herself. Rebuilt her life. It would have taken time, but she had that choice. She chose to come back here, to me.

It's clear from the look in her defiant eyes she wants to destroy me, but she wants more than that. She wants answers.

I sigh.

I understand her need for truth, to make sense of what

happened to her, but it's a stupid reason to give up her life. When the answer is simple—I sacrificed her to save myself.

But I'm not going to enlighten her. Not unless she wins.

"Sit," I say, indicating to the chair Langston, my right-hand man, was occupying before.

Kai's eyes cast down to the chair, but she doesn't move. If she doesn't sit down soon, she will collapse from exhaustion.

"Sit," I practically shout, my voice bellowing throughout the room. I'm not used to my orders not being followed immediately and completely.

Kai doesn't shutter at the loudness of my voice, but my command finally registers. I expect her to fight and argue with me at every step. Instead, she steps toward the chair. He legs wobble and shake, barely keeping her upright with each step. But she doesn't seem to notice her flawed body shutting down.

She stumbles, and I reach out my arm to catch her, but she pivots at the last second, catching herself instead of tumbling into my grasp.

I sigh and move my hand to the back of my neck, rubbing hard, trying to get the frustration out on my tense muscles.

I shouldn't want to help or even touch her, but I can't help the pull this woman has over me.

I need a drink. Kai needs food. I don't know when the last time she ate was.

Fuck.

How could I let this happen? I'm a cruel, sadistic bastard, but I never meant for this betrayal to take over her life. I hate how hollowed-cheeked she is. I hate how much pain she's in. But most of all, I hate that any man ever touched her.

She's *mine*.

Then why'd you let her go?

Because I didn't have a choice.

I leave Kai in the room as I walk to the kitchen to get some food. I should be worried about what Kai will do in the minutes I'm gone. What secrets she will find in my private room. I'm more concerned that her weak heartbeat will stop or her lungs will give out and she'll be dead before I return.

I don't know what food is nourishing for a person who has been to hell and emerged on the other side. So I just throw the first things I find onto a plate: strawberries, old pizza, crackers, and olives.

I jog back to the room, my feet silent as I move.

When I enter my lair again, Kai is still sitting in the chair, her fingers brushing against the hem of her shirt.

She startles when I enter.

I should apologize. I should make her feel better, but I don't. I want her to eat, but I also want her on edge. I want to win our game of truth or lies. I want to take her and secure her as mine.

I don't know why I suggested the game, when I could just as easily take her by force. She's too weak to fight. I could toss her over my shoulder and take her to my home. Lock her away forever.

But it doesn't seem fair. I like giving her a fighting chance, even if the result is the same in the end.

I set the plate of food on the end table next to Kai and then pour us each a glass of water. I'd offer her alcohol, but I'm afraid it would burn what little lining is left in her stomach after years of eating itself in order to survive.

"Eat."

She stares at the food, like it's a pile of worms and bugs I'm asking her to eat.

"Kai, eat," my voice warns.

Her eyes flutter up to me as her breathing slows. "I didn't come here to eat; I came to get answers. Are we playing the game or not?"

I sigh. She's the most frustrating woman. "When we play, and I win, you will eat. You will do everything I say, because I own you."

She releases a breath. "You forget that I won last time. And now I'm more determined than ever to win again."

"You may have won before, but by the end of tonight, you will be mine."

"I will belong to no one, but myself," she snarks.

I grin. "There is the fighting girl I remember."

She huffs. "She's gone. Kai Miller drowned in the ocean."

"So you're Katherine now, then?" I ask, remembering the name she said her parents called her before she declared her name was Kai.

"No, I'm nobody. I don't even exist."

We breathe in unison, both needing air, but I'm not sure the room has enough for both of us. And what's left of the air is pushing us together. We both try to resist, but somehow I'm leaning toward her, reaching my hand up to brush a strand of hair that has fallen into her face.

Kai brushes it away glaring at me before I can touch her. She hates me, of course, she doesn't want me to touch her.

"The rules?" she asks.

"Same as before. We each get one guess to identify the truth from the lies correctly."

She nods. "I win; I get my answers."

"I win; I get you." I expect her to ask questions. *How long would I take her if she were to lose? What would she be expected to do if I take her?*

She doesn't ask. Being taken no longer scares or concerns her. She's lost her life before, because of me. This is no different to her.

And I need to win for so many reasons. There is the attraction, the pull that begs me to take her, make her mine, fuck her and show her pleasure she's never experienced before, while ruining her more than she already is. But I need to take her for more than just my own sexual desires. The power and life I've gained require her to stay hidden. I can only do that one of two ways. The same two choices I had before: kill her or take her.

"You can start."

I sit back in my chair, sipping on my water like it's scotch. I should have poured myself a drink, but I want to be acutely aware of her. Ready to tell when she's lying or telling the truth before she even speaks. Last time we played, I was naive. I thought I had experience, and that she didn't. Time has changed us both. Me into brawn, her into vengeance. We both have the skills needed to win the game, but hopefully, her brain is too clouded to think clearly.

Kai clears her throat as her head drops to her hands. She's covering her face as she thinks about the lies and truths she will reveal, hoping that by hiding her face, I'll be less attuned to her.

My lips curl—*as if not feeling her was possible.* I feel her more than I see her. Her icy breath pierces my burning heart with each exhale. And my blood pumps slower through my veins matching her slow, irregular beat. Even thousands of miles apart, I would occasionally feel a chill down my back or a sharpness in my side and think of her.

We are connected, and right now I feel her pain, along with her determination.

Slowly, Kai reveals her face to me again; she reaches for the water takes a sip and then stares straight at me.

"I hate my father.

"I hate the ocean.

"I hate you."

I smile loving the theme she chose this time. The last time we played she chose lust, temptation. She tricked me by making me believe she was more innocent than she was. This time, she's chosen her strongest emotion—hate. It's easiest for her to fuel into every sentence equally, making me believe every word out of her mouth.

She wants to play with the strongest emotions to win. Then I will too.

"I love my family.

"I love the ocean.

"I love money."

"I didn't think you were capable of love," she snarls.

I shrug. "Everyone is capable of loving something."

Her face darkens. She doesn't think she's capable of loving, not anymore.

I stare down on the deep purple colored bruise on the inside of her wrist, exposed as the sleeve pushes up her arm. Then to her bare feet where several of her toes bend the wrong way.

I doubt anyone who has been through what she's been through is capable of loving anything anymore.

"Which is my truth?" Kai asks, impatiently.

"So eager to lose."

"I want my answers."

"Which do you hate the most, Kai?" I pick up my glass and swirl the water around as I contemplate my choices.

"The easiest and most obvious choice would be that you hate me. I tried to kill you. I left you in the ocean. I told you if you survived, to leave Miami. And then I caused torment worse than death."

I pause, waiting for her to argue or yell at me for any of those points. She doesn't.

"But the most obvious choice doesn't mean it's your truth. Although, I have a hard time thinking you could hate anyone as much as you hate me." But maybe she uses a different word in her head for what she thinks of me. After all, hate and love are two sides of the same emotion. And if she hates me, then it means she has the capacity to love me. She could never love me; therefore she could never hate me.

"Your father would also be easy to hate. He was supposed to protect you. Or at the very least rescue you. He didn't." But she's too much of a daddy's girl to truly hate him. Not for his incompetencies, even though she should.

"The ocean is worthy of your hate too. I left you in it to drown. Who knows what hardships you experienced on the sea?"

Her eyes dilate a millimeter.

"Have you made your choice?" she asks.

"Yes, have you?"

"I still don't think you are capable of love. But between loving your family, the ocean, or money the choice is easy."

I smirk. *Bingo, I have her.*

And I know her truth.

"You go first," she says.

"You don't hate your father. And as much pain as I've caused you, you don't hate me. You hate the sea." It's plain as day. She hates the sea. Sea equals Kai. She hates herself. She hates what she's become. She hates being broken and weak. She could never hate her father, and she sees me as nothing but a soldier following orders. Who ultimately kept her alive, even though she was tortured because of it. She hates the sea.

"And you love the ocean," Kai says.

Neither of us blinks. Or breathes. Or moves. Neither reveals who the winner is. The thread of connection between us looms revealing our winner. One of us chose correctly, and the other wrongly.

"The ocean represents freedom for me," I say.

Her eyes widen, realizing her mistake. "But you don't long to be free anymore; you are free," she whispers.

I nod.

"And you don't love money," she says.

I nod.

"You love your family."

I nod. "I love my family. Those men, Langston and Zeke, are my family. Maybe not my blood, but they are my family in every other sense of the word."

She nods. She doesn't call it cheating. We both chose our words carefully. Family means whatever it truly means to me, not the technical definition of the word. Family means Zeke and Langston.

"The ocean represents everything I lost," she says.

I nod.

"I could never hate my father for not being strong enough to rescue me."

I nod.

"I don't even hate you..." her voice cracks. "Hatred requires me to feel anything toward you, and I don't believe you are human enough for me to hate. You're a beast who broke every promise and then sold me to a bigger monster."

Her bottom lip trembles. "I hate the ocean because it

took everything from me, and instead of letting me die and be free, it sent me back here to you."

I should be kinder. I should feel empathy and let her go. I won't, but I should.

"I lost," she whispers while she holds her head high. Her lips purse and her icy cheeks pale.

"And now, you're mine."

15

KAI

I LOST.

I won't get my answers.

This was a one time deal; no way will Enzo give me this chance again to get the answers I seek. And now, because I was blinded by the need to understand why I endured punishment and pain for years, I'm his.

I traded one unknown master for this man.

I should be scared, terrified.

He could take me and sell me again. He could beat me, rape me, kill me. He could do whatever unthinkable things he wants with me, and I couldn't stop him. Enzo could have taken those things anyway, whether I won the game or not. But he didn't have to resort to that. I offered myself up willingly, all so I could win a bet. And now I've lost everything.

No, I didn't have anything left to lose. That's why I could offer up everything.

Enzo devours me with his hungry glare. My stomach aches, but not from the lack of food, but because of the lust that stirs inside me every time I'm around Enzo. It shouldn't be there. I should hate him with every fiber of my being.

Instead, my body longs to feel something, anything, even an ache for a monster.

Maybe it's because he spared my life that I don't feel the hatred I should feel towards him? Maybe deep down, despite how devastatingly difficult life was on that yacht, some part of me preferred to live rather than die. I just need to find that piece of myself again.

"Come," Enzo says.

I consider fighting him, but as he stands and inches toward me, I know if I don't follow his directions, he will grab me and force me to obey his orders. Something I'm used to. But not something I will allow anymore.

I stand up.

Enzo raises an eyebrow in surprise and then starts walking toward the back of the room. I follow slowly, wincing as my broken toes swell with each step. He pushes on the back wall, and a hidden door opens.

He steps through the door.

Then I do. And then we are back in the darkness.

Enzo knows his way as we weave down unlit hallways, much the same as when I made my way to his room. He doesn't stumble or bring up a light on his phone to see the way. It appears he can see in the shadows as easily as I can.

He turns his head back toward me once, but not to see if I'm still following, we both can sense each other more than we'd like. There is an attraction, a pull. Like magnets that pull as much as they push. His fire and my ice begging to be brought together, while knowing the second we touch we will explode. Cold and heat aren't meant to mix, just exist close to each other.

And then the light is burning my retinas as we step into the light. He was warning me with his gaze, I realize, now that the sun is burning down on me.

Enzo studies my every movement as I recoil into my sweater. I hate the fucking sun. Ridiculous thought, after spending so many years begging to feel its warmth. Now it's too hot, too bright, too much.

"Get in," Enzo says.

That's when I notice the car. The very fancy, blacked out car. It's a two-seater, shiny, and very fast looking.

And suddenly I don't want to get in the car. I can't remember the last time I rode in a car. A car looks claustrophobic. It looks dangerous. It looks—

"Kai, get in the car."

Fuck.

I will not let Enzo see my fear. It's just a car. I've ridden in them countless times before. I can handle it—even a tiny, suffocating car like this one.

I walk to the passenger side, open the door, and slide in. My foot instantly relieved to no longer be standing on it.

I close my eyes and try to take a few deep breaths.

"Afraid of the car or my driving?" Enzo asks.

My eyes pop open as I snarl at him.

He chuckles. "It's not my driving you should be worried about."

I still. I know exactly what I should be worried about. This isn't my first rodeo. He isn't my first capture. But Enzo isn't like the other men who took me. We have a connection that saved me last time; I'm not sure that link will save me a second time.

I'm jerked backward, slamming against my seat as Enzo speeds off.

"Seatbelt, Kai. We wouldn't want anything else to happen to damage your pretty face."

"Really? You're making jokes now?"

He shrugs as he zips around another corner.

I grab the seatbelt and clasp it across my body despite hating how trapped I feel.

"I wouldn't call them jokes. I enjoy watching you squirm. And the faster you learn you are no longer in control, the easier your life will be."

I will never confess I've given him control, just like I never admitted I was broken. My life may have never been my own, but it doesn't mean I don't have some control.

"So stubborn," he says, turning sharply.

"Motherfucking bastard. Fucking slow down. I'm weak, I feel trapped in this car, and I'm about to hurl all over the upholstery."

He smiles and then slows. It seems that is all he wanted: for me to show weakness.

I close my eyes again as my stomach churns from the turns and being in such a small space. I can barely breathe. Bile rises in my throat; I'm going to vomit.

"Open your eyes, Kai."

I don't want to open them. *Why does he want me to open them anyway?* So he can see the terror on my face he's causing. He's sick.

His voice softens, "Open your eyes."

I open them.

"Look at the road ahead. It will help."

I watch the road and notice our speed has slowed tremendously. Cars are now passing us, speeding down the highway. I watch the road in front of us and the pressure building in my stomach subsides a little.

"Good, just like that. Now breath in through your nose and purse your lips as you breathe out."

I do what he says, my breathing calm. He's so nice, so kind.

"And if you need to puke, tell me. If you thought those

men tortured you before, you haven't felt wrath until I punish you for destroying my car."

I frown—*from cruel to nice in the flip of a switch.*

He notices my reaction. "I was joking."

"It wasn't funny."

He sighs and then turns back to driving, ignoring me for the most part. I do occasionally see his eyes cut to mine when my breathing grows erratic again, whether for the safety of his car or for me.

I expect us to drive to some underground society. Or to a condo high above the city. I assume Enzo might live in a mansion high up on a cliff. Or worst yet, a yacht. What I don't expect is the house we stop in front of before Enzo cuts the engine in the driveway.

"This is your home?" I ask, as I stare at the modest house on the beach.

"Yes. Were you expecting something grandeur?"

I look at the modern, sleek looking house that can't be more than two to three thousand square feet. I'm sure the home is expensive, it sits on a large private piece of beach property, gated and secluded, but it still seems modest compared to what I figured he could own based on his fancy suit and expensive car. But somehow this fits Enzo— no magnificence is needed to show his power and attraction.

"No, this was exactly what I was expecting."

"Welcome to your new home, Kai."

Home.

This will never be my home. I don't have a home.

Enzo steps out of the car and doesn't wait for me to follow. He jogs to the door and opens it, smiling as he steps inside.

I look around as I sit in the car. He never gave me an

order. I could continue sitting in the car for the rest of the day, and he couldn't get angry at me for disobeying. I don't know why he trusts that I will stay. I lost the bet, but that doesn't mean I'll make it easy for him. I never promised not to run away.

I get out of the car, my eyes scanning, trying to find my best method of escape. A habit I've developed after years of being captive. But one step on my injured foot and I realize why Enzo isn't worried about me running and escaping. I can barely walk, let alone run. I would have no chance against him.

So, reluctantly, I follow through the door where Enzo went.

"Mr. Black, welcome home. It's been a while since we've seen you," a man in a suit who appears to be a couple decades older than us says to Enzo.

Black.

I frown as I try to make sense of what the man said. Enzo said that Black was who he worked for. But he never told me his last name.

Enzo turns to me and reads the confusion on my face. But he doesn't answer my question.

"This is Mr. Westcott. He works for me and takes care of this house while I'm away. If you need anything and I'm not here, he can assist you," Enzo says.

"It's very nice to meet you, Kai," Mr. Westcott says.

"How do you know my name?" I feel out of the loop, like everyone else knows the answer to a secret, but I'm not even aware of what the secret is.

Mr. Westcott smiles. "Mr. Black texted me that he would have a guest by the name of Katherine Kai Miller, but that you preferred the name Kai."

I glance between the two men. The story checks out.

"I'll leave you two to tour the house. Mr. Black, please let me know which rooms you would like prepared. The fridge is fully stocked, but if you need anything else, I'll be in my office." Mr. Westcott says before walking away.

"Mr. Black?" I ask, staring at Enzo with my hands folded across my chest.

He narrows his eyes. "You need to eat, Kai."

"I want my question answered, *Mr. Black.*"

"Eat first; then you can ask questions."

I frown. I don't like this tit for tat game, or him expecting me to win a round of truth or lies to get a question answered.

Enzo turns down a hallway and like before, he doesn't ask me to follow him. He walks, and I'm expected to follow like a trained dog. Reluctantly, I do.

He stops in the kitchen and has his head buried in the fridge, pulling out all manner of food. He frowns after pulling a platter full of fruit and raw vegetables out. "I don't have any meat, which might help you heal faster, but eat this for now, and then I'll get you something more substantial to eat."

I stare at the mound of food as I stand next to the island. "I can't eat all of that."

He laughs. "Eat some of it while I talk."

"Okay."

He smiles and slides the food on the island in front of where I stand leaning against the counter.

I pick up a grape and gnaw at it. "Talk."

"There isn't much to say really. My last name is Black. I'm Enzo Black."

"How?" I mumble, my mouth still working on the first bite of grape.

"My father's name is Black. He owned the empire. The bars, the yachts, the men."

"Owned?" I ask, realizing he used the word in the past tense.

He nods. "Yes."

"And now? Who rules the empire now?"

"Me." I can see it in his eyes. How he got the power he now wields. *Me*. I don't understand how disposing of me gained him control over his father's empire, but I know I had a lot to do with it. And he won't tell me anything further than what he just told me.

I swallow, the sour taste of the grape lingering on my tongue. I stare down at the platter, trying to pick a fruit that has the least flavor, but I can barely remember the taste of any of the fruits. I haven't had anything this fresh in years. Instead, I opt for a snow pea stalk. I take a bite off the end.

And then anger fumes inside me. "He was the king, and you were the prince. You had more power back then than you let on. You could have decided I didn't have to die or be sold. You could have convinced your father."

He shakes his head. "No, I would have ended up dead. I traded your life to save mine. I did all I could to save you. I'm sorry you aren't grateful for that."

"Grateful! You expect me to be grateful! Do you have any idea what I've been through?"

He looks at me sheepishly, his face fallen and hurt. It wounds him, what has happened to me. Yet another thing that doesn't make sense about this man. He can't care for me. Not if he sold me to cruel men. That's not caring; it's the opposite of caring. It's savage.

He's silent though, not giving me any more insight into his thoughts or reasoning.

"But you're the king now?"

"Yes."

"So you have the power to decide my fate? You could let me go."

"Yes."

"But you won't?"

"No, you controlled your own fate when you offered up your life to me. Now you're mine."

"To what? To beat? To rape?"

He shrugs. "If I like."

My eyes flitter, looking deep into his. He might decide one day to rape me, but that isn't the purpose of him taking me. At least I don't think it is.

"Or will you sell me when you get bored of me?"

His eyes dilate, and his nostrils flare at my words.

"You. Are. *Mine.* I won't sell or share you with anyone."

That warms my insides. I'd rather be with the monster I know than one I don't.

"Besides, I wouldn't get my money's worth now that you've already been touched and broken."

I shudder. He's right, but I hate his words. *Why isn't that enough for me to hate him? Why do I still feel like there is more to the story I'm missing—like why me?*

I stop eating and turn toward the large window behind me that overlooks the ocean, trying to process what's happening. Enzo is callous yet considerate. Merciful yet punishing. I have no idea why he took me or what he intends to do with me.

"It scares you, doesn't it?"

"What?" I ask.

"Being so close to the ocean."

I nod. There is no point denying it. I'm in one of the most gorgeous, secluded places on a private beach, and I won't go near the ocean for however long I'm here.

"What happened to you, Kai? What made you so afraid? Of the water above everything?"

I freeze.

"You were afraid of the car. Wounded by the sunlight. But both of those you were willing to face. With time you will stop fearing them. But the ocean you look at like it's the enemy. You look at it with a hatred you don't even give me."

"Jarod, the man you sold me to, you had no contact with him after you sold me? He never told you what happened?"

Enzo looks at me wide-eyed. "No, I had no contact with the man who owned you."

I nod. Then he won't be getting the truth from me. He doesn't deserve to know what happened to me. He doesn't get to understand my fears. There is nothing that can fix me anyway. And I have a sinking suspicion that the only reason Enzo would try to heal me would be so he could ruin me again himself.

"Kai..." His hand reaches out and touches my wrist. I don't know why or what purpose, but everything else falls away but his touch.

It burns.

The heat overwhelms my body, and it feels like fire is flaming my skin. I stare down at the spot wide-eyed, expecting red blobs of fire to be flying from his fingertips to my wrist.

It's too much.

His touch.

My body.

It's too damn much.

I step backward, trying to get out of his grasp. *Don't touch me. Let me go*, I plead in my brain, but I can't form the words.

Everything goes dizzy.

Cloudy.

Then black.

I feel myself falling.

Like before.

I'm falling.

Down.

Down.

Down.

Maybe this time, if the ocean catches me, it will keep me, drown me until I'm gone.

16

ENZO

WATCHING Kai collapse to the ground shouldn't affect me. It shouldn't bother me in the slightest. *But then why do I have this gut-wrenching, heaving, gnawing feeling in my stomach as I watch her ailing body fall and then bounce against my hardwood floor?*

I should have moved faster; then maybe I would have caught her and prevented the forceful impact of her body. But I was too focused on the bruise on her wrist. The blues and purples drew me into her pale skin, but I couldn't tell if it was fractured, sprained, or just a bruise. The desire to hunt down Jarod, the man who dared to hurt her flooded through me, while simultaneously wanting to tie her down and fuck her, giving her more wounds and scars from the ropes I would use to tie her up.

Fuck, there is something wrong with me.

"Kai?" I bend down to offer my help for her to stand, even though I know she won't take it. She all but hates me. She thinks I'm going to torture her and rape her like the last man who owned her. She should think that way. I'm not safe. Although it's not my style to force a woman against her will, women line up to be fucked by me. I pay the most beautiful women in the world to work in my club, and they have no problem extending their services to me when their shifts are over.

Kai's different; she wears the battle she's endured on every piece of her flesh. And all the scars do is make me wonder what she sounds like when she screams with tears running down her cheeks. Because I'm a sick, fucking monster.

I don't know how she ended up on the floor. I reached out wanting to touch her bruise and wanting to see if the cold still pulses through her veins. And then she was on the floor.

I don't know how...

Did exhaustion finally catch up with her?

Lack of food?

Or was it panic I saw in her eyes at the thought of me caressing her?

"Kai," I say louder, keeping my hands by my side instead of touching her, in case my almost brush against her was what caused the panic attack.

She doesn't stir.

Shit.

"Kai," I scream.

Westcott runs into the room, "Enzo? What happened? I heard a scream." His face is full of shock as he stares down at Kai's lifeless body.

"She just collapsed," I answer.

"I'll call 911," Westcott says.

"No," I hiss.

Westcott frowns, and I know he will disobey me if I don't do something soon. He's worked for my family for a long time. He's one of my most loyal employees, but he doesn't put up with my shit. He doesn't have to worry about me firing him; I won't. And even if I did, I pay him well enough that he could retire now even though he's only fifty.

Westcott pulls out his phone, threatening me. He's the only person in the world allowed to bully me and not get reprimanded or killed for his trouble. In some ways, he was the father I always wanted but never had.

What do I do?

"Kai, wake up!" I scream as I roll her over onto her back.

Ice. Her body shoots off frosty sparks through my warm body. She's as bone-chilling as I remember, possibly colder. I shudder for a second as her cool combines with my fire causing the hair on my arm to stand as goosebumps form.

I survey her, looking for any sign of the injury that would have caused her to collapse and not wake up. But other than the bruise that was already covering her eye, I don't see any visible head injury.

And then I watch her chest rising and falling. She must have knocked herself unconscious when she fell. I know I shouldn't move her, but I can't keep her lying on the bare floor. She needs a bed; she needs sleep and food. She needs medical support and therapists to heal, but I'm not sure I'm willing to let anyone else see or touch her even to help her. *She's mine.*

Gently, I cradle her head and scoop up her legs. Having her in my arms does something primal to my body. It arouses an urge I haven't felt since the last time I kissed her. I feel alive even though her skin prickles mine—a steady, calmness pulses from her thin veins to my thicker cords. I feel more settled and more urgent at the same time. An awakening builds inside as my stomach clenches at what I let happen to this beautiful woman in my arms; she still seems like a girl to me in so many ways.

"What are you doing to me, Kai?" I whisper into her ear. Her breathing is still slow and constant in my arms.

"Sir?" Westcott asks with concern in his eyes.

"She's breathing. I think she just collapsed from exhaustion. Is the master bedroom ready?"

He nods.

"I'll call an ambulance."

"No," my voice cuts through the room. I won't have anyone take her away from me. *Not now.*

I rush past him to the bedroom I usually occupy when I'm staying here. This is my favorite house out of all the ones I own. If I can't be on the sea, then I'll take this beach house as a close second. But I just got back last night and slept at the club before coming here. None of my stuff is here or unpacked.

Kai can have the master; I'll take one of the spares, I decide as I climb the stairs to the second floor. She doesn't stir the entire time I hold her.

I kick open the door to the spacious master bedroom. An oversized white canopy bed sits against the far wall with white linen sheets giving off a beach vibe as it gets the perfect view of the ocean out the floor to ceiling windows—one of the windows pushes out as a concealed door leading out to the private balcony. There isn't much else in this bedroom. I like to keep everything simple and elegant. Only a door impedes the bare walls and leads to the deluxe bathroom suite where the walk-in closet is.

This room will serve as the perfect gilded cage for Kai. I haven't figured out what I'm going to do with her yet. Killing her would be the easiest, but as I've already determined from our last encounter, I can't kill this girl. Locking her away is the next best thing to ensure I keep my power. This room isn't exactly a prison, but to her, it will feel like one.

I carefully lay her down on top of the covers on the bed. A quiet moan escapes her lips, but otherwise, she doesn't stir.

I walk quickly to my closet that is always filled with the basics for when I stay here and pull out one of my shirts for her to sleep in before I return to her side.

She's still breathing, still knocked out when I return.

So I begin the slow, torturous work of removing her sweater and jeans. Her feet are already bare, filthy from spending days walking barefoot, swollen, and covered in deep lesions. The only parts of her body I can see are her hands, feet, and face—and if they are any indication of what lies beneath her clothes, I'm not sure I can bear it.

I pull her sweater up her smooth stomach attentively as I'm not sure what I will reveal.

I'm not a squeamish man, but when I see the cuts, bruises, and scars marking her skin, I want to hurl. I force myself to stay put and continue removing the sweater from her frozen, defeated body. I finally get the sweater over her head, and I lose my mind.

What the fuck did Jarod do to you?

What did I do?

I thought death was the worst thing that could have happened to Kai, my pretty girl, but I was wrong. This—this is the worst thing anyone could ever experience.

Every inch of her skin is covered in her anguish and pain.

Scars.

Bruises.

Cuts.

All of her is broken.

Misaligned.

Torn.

Injured.

Jarod didn't spare one inch of her precious body. Every part is marked.

He fucking claimed her. He made her *his*. He ruined every part of her body, and there is no telling what he messed up inside her, both internally and in her mind. I don't know how anyone recovers from this.

I understand now why Kai thinks she was broken. She is broken, but somehow, an essential part of her spirit remains. Despite what her body has gone through, the fight persisted. She wouldn't have come to find me if she didn't want to battle—to take back her life.

I have no doubt when her body is strong enough; she will once again fight for her freedom. She might even win.

I can't let that happen. We are both two parts to a whole. We both can't survive in this world. If she escapes, I'll cease to exist. The only way we can both live is if the world thinks she's dead—at least my world does.

I try to purge the fuming rage that has built up inside me and is now exploding out of me with passion from my body. I want to call on all of my men to hunt the bastard down who did this and make him wish he only had to experience the pain Kai did after what I plan on doing to him.

But if I send my men to find them, it would be admitting Kai is alive.

So I push the feeling down, something I'm an expert in.

I take the T-shirt in my hand and pull it down covering her stomach and the tops of her thighs. Only then do I undo the jeans and gently pull them off her body. I want so badly to lift the T-shirt up and catch a glimpse of her gorgeous cunt I've dreamed about for so long. But I'm not a sick fuck who dreams of corpses, which is basically what she is in this state. And if I see that her pussy is as broken as

174

the rest of her body, I'll throw all my rational thoughts out the window, and I'll do something that will get me killed in the end.

So I quell my dark desires, locking them deep inside the cage where I keep everything else.

I tuck Kai under the covers as her breath continues to rise and fall.

What am I going to do with you?

I reach into my back pocket, and I call Westcott.

"Sir?"

"Call a private doctor to the house for Kai. The best, one who specializes in her condition."

"Absolutely, sir. I'll have a doctor here right away."

I end the call. Kai won't want a doctor to see her. She won't want the help, but she doesn't always get a choice in her life. She'll die if not.

I don't know what to do, but stand over her and ensure she continues breathing until the doctor arrives.

"Enzo?" her voice croaks.

"Yes, I'm here," I moan back in agony at seeing her in pain.

Her eyes don't open, and I'm not even sure she's conscious.

"I'm so cold," she whispers.

I nod. I love her arctic skin against mine. I love how it centers me and makes me crave her.

"Hold me, Enzo. Make me warm."

Fuck.

I stare at her a minute, not sure she wants me to touch her. But then she shivers despite being under the pile of blankets.

I kick off my shoes, remove my suit jacket, and loosen my tie before climbing into bed next to her. I don't dare take off any more clothes. My self-control is already hanging on a thread as it is. I can't feel her skin to skin.

But as I wrap my hot skin against her cool ice, I feel every part of her connect with me.

Body.

Heart.

Soul.

What are you doing to me, pretty girl? And why do you have this hold over me?

I pull her tighter to my body, our skin regulating each other's temperature and bodies as we doze while we wait for the doctor to arrive. My cock hardens, pressing against her ass.

Not going to happen, I try to convince my cock, but to no avail.

And I know that as I hold her, I can never touch her again. I'm the devil, but I'm done being a monster to her. I will stay far away. She will be safe as long as she never leaves these four walls. And I will continue to be the monster with power over the world, and control everything, except her.

17

KAI

THE CHILL RETURNS to my body. My eyes fly open.

Where am I?

What happened?

I'm in the most magnificent room I've ever seen in either real life or a magazine.

The bed I'm lying on is enormous. Much bigger than a traditional king. It's a white canopy bed with white linen sheets softer than a pile of feathers. Floor to ceiling windows line the wall, giving me a view of a balcony most people would pay a fortune to sit on, because it has the most unobscured, private view of turquoise blue water I've ever seen. You can't even see any sailboats on the horizon, that's how reclusive it feels. Like you are on your own tranquil piece of paradise.

But I want to sprint over to the curtains and pull them shut, blocking out the fucking sun and the divine view that makes my stomach want to hurl.

I chuckle to myself when I notice the see-through curtains. There is nothing in this room that will block out the sun's rays.

I stare down at the stark white sheets and comforter covering my body. They may be made of the softest fabrics known to earth, but they irritate my skin—making me feel like I need to scratch my reddened flesh like I have the chicken pox.

I can't decide if I'd rather bury myself under the covers to block out the sun or throw the scratchy covers from my body.

I try to remember where I am and how I got here.

Enzo.

I remember the club. I remember losing the game. I remember collapsing.

Shit.

I collapsed. Passed out. That's the one thing I never wanted to let happen. Because when I'm unconscious, I can't control what happens to me. I can't fight. I can't prevent the torture.

My body stills. But I don't feel the usual pain that comes after being abused. I don't think I was touched...

But I remember being warm.

How is that possible? I never feel warm. Even with the light shining in and the mountain of covers on top of me, I'm not warm.

Now, I'm cold. It must have been a dream of feeling snug.

I actually feel colder than usual.

That's when I take in more of my body and feel the stick of the needle in my hand, pouring the biting liquid into my body.

My eyes widen, and my body trembles. I want it out. *Now.*

I look around the room, searching for someone to explain what the fuck happened and why I have an IV. I don't need an IV. I don't need a doctor. I don't need anyone.

"It's good to see you awake, Miss Miller," a man sitting in an armchair on the other side of the bed says.

I shake at the unexpected sound.

"I didn't mean to startle you; I'm Dr. Gould."

Fuck.

I recoil further up on the bed, inching to the farthest corner away from this stranger, covering myself with the evil covers.

The doctor's smile drops when he sees my reaction.

"Mr. Black brought me here to help you, Miss Miller. I won't hurt you. You can trust me."

Liar.

I can't trust anyone.

The doctor purses his lips when he sees my reaction.

"You've been passed out for three days. I inserted an IV to give you proper nutrition. And I only did the bare minimum of examination to ensure you didn't need any further treatment while you were unconscious. I didn't think you would appreciate anything more while you were out."

He's right; no one should touch me while I'm passed out.

"Where am I?" I ask, even though I already know the answer. I want confirmation.

He eyes me carefully, trying to study my reaction. "Mr. Black's beach residence."

He doesn't say more, but I know I'm in Enzo's room. I can smell and feel him everywhere. His musky cologne and ocean salt scent covers the room.

Why the fuck does Enzo live in a box of light?

He should be living in a dark cave in a hillside—*not this.*

I need the dark, not the light.

The doctor rounds the bed to the side I'm hiding under. I want to move to the other side, but he moves faster than I can crawl away.

His sad eyes stare down at me as he stands tall overhead.

"Miss Miller, can you tell me what you remember?"

I frown and huff steam from my nose.

He nods.

"Can you nod and tell me you remember, though? I'm worried you might have brain damage."

I nod. *I remember.*

"That's good. I know you've been through a lot these last few years. I need to give you a more thorough exam. I believe you have several broken bones and some have started healing while not aligned. After I examine you, we can talk about getting some x-rays and prioritize your injuries. I promise you will recover from this. I've helped countless women heal from similar situations. You will get through this."

I raise my eyebrows as a chill runs through me. Enzo didn't just get any doctor to look after me; he hired one who knows exactly how to treat women like me.

I can see in the doctor's eyes he wants to touch me, comfort me in some way. He tells me with his body first, then his words.

"Let's start with something simple. I'm just going to check your pulse. Is that okay?"

I don't answer. I can't. I'm frozen.

He hesitantly reaches his hand out, and his fingers press against the inside of my wrist.

I jump.

I can't fucking stand the touch. No matter how

comforting he intended it. It feels like he's trying to stab my body. To ruin and torture me.

My body springs up like a scared cat, my body on alert, my claws out, and a hiss from my mouth.

"Miss Miller, I'm sorry. Come back to—"

I can't hear the doctor's words. I can't be here a second longer.

I spring from the bed, feeling the tug of the IV trying to keep me in.

Fuck that.

The pain of the needle barely registers as it pulls from my hand. But I feel free as I leave the bed. The covers no longer trapping me, and my body safe from being touched.

I don't know where I'm going. Enzo started the tour of the house yesterday, but he never finished it. Instead, I collapsed like a pussy. Enzo will think he can take whatever he wants from me—that I won't fight back. I won't be surprised if he comes to my room tonight and takes whatever he wants from me.

I can't think about that. I'll figure out how to protect myself soon enough.

I run to the stairs.

Fucking stairs.

I'm so tired, but the adrenaline from needing to get away from the doctor is stronger than the weakness and dizziness I feel.

Down the stairs I go, half running, half falling.

When I stumble down the main floor, I keep moving my legs, still not sure where I'm headed or why. My fight or flight has kicked in, and I can't stop until someone slows me down.

I keep going, sweat soaking my body, chills shooting up and down my spine, panic weighing down my legs.

Keep running, flee, escape.

Those thoughts play on repeat through my head.

I can't stop.

I can't get a reprieve from the exhaustion I'm feeling. Nothing will stop me.

"Stop," a deep, authoritative voice echoes in the walls.

What? Stop? I can't.

"Stop."

I feel my legs slowing, although I don't understand why.

"Stop, Kai."

My legs come to a halt as if I hit a brick wall.

I didn't, but I came close.

Enzo is standing less than a foot in front of me.

I pant heavily, knowing I can't catch my breath. I've pushed my body too hard. I'm about to faint again.

"Breathe," comes the same steady voice. I hang on to that voice, letting it fill my lungs as if it were oxygen.

The fog covering my eyes lifts, and I see Enzo, really see him for the first time.

He's so close to me, yet I don't get the urge to run away from him. He's not attempting to reach out or touch me in any way. His eyes are locked with mine, and it's almost like he can see inside my head. Our stupid connection, I don't understand. One we've had for far too long and needs to be severed, immediately.

Enzo nods, encouraging me to continue to slow my body down until I'm calm again, or at least my version of composed.

Once he sees that I've returned to my less erratic state, his eyes darken, his lips twitch, and the vein in his head pops out.

"Why aren't you dressed?" Enzo hisses at me.

My fists clench at his harshness, but I don't step back. Neither does he.

I stare down at my body for the first time. I was wearing an oversized shirt when I left the bedroom. Now I'm wearing nothing. I don't remember removing the shirt, but I must have on my way down the stairs, needing the itchy clothing off me as much as I needed the sheets to stop constricting my body.

I huff. "Does it matter? I've seen the way you look at me. It doesn't matter that my body is broken. That other men have touched me. You're just as sick as them."

He growls and then steps closer to me.

I don't retreat, even though I feel the blood frosting my body as it pumps faster. *Don't let him intimidate or threaten you.*

"You will wear clothes anytime you leave your bedroom," he fires into my ear.

I grow rigid. "Don't you mean, *your* bedroom?"

He shrugs. "It doesn't matter what it *was*, only what it *is*. You can pretend it's your sanctuary, your cage, my bedroom, or whatever fantasy you create in your head to make sense of what is happening to you. But while you are here, it is *your* bedroom."

He takes three giant steps back, and I can breathe again. Then he does something I don't understand. He removes the T-shirt he's wearing.

My eyes hone in on the rippling muscles over his stomach, so defined and tight, then jump up to his hard pecs. He would be a perfect specimen if it weren't for the healed scars that cover his body—like mine. His make him look stronger though, more rugged—nothing like mine.

He tosses the shirt to the floor a foot in front of me.

I cock my head.

"Put the shirt on, Kai."

My eyes narrow, not understanding why he cares if I'm dressed. He's seen my naked body before. He must have, how else would I have gotten out of my clothes? I doubt the good doctor would have undressed me. *That means Enzo has touched me.*

Fear rakes through my body at that thought. He just touched me; he didn't violate me.

I finally take the room in. It appears to be a large office, but it is not just occupied by Enzo. Two other men stand behind him. All three men are wearing jeans and dark shirts, and I can see sweat on all of their brows. They've been working.

I recognize the two men standing by Enzo; they were the same men at Surrender with him. One of the men tries hard to avoid eye contact with me or gazing at me at all, as if he thinks looking at me will burn his retinas. The other man only looks at my eyes, ensuring his eyes never drop lower to my naked body.

A tiny smile crosses my lips. Enzo is mad because he doesn't like these men staring at my naked body—whether because he wants me to himself or because he's embarrassed by the state of my body and them knowing he wasn't the one to break me in. I don't care. I kind of like that he wants me to himself instead of sharing me with others. Unlike my last master, I won't be shared around like a whore.

Enzo's body hardens as he notices my carelessness about my body. I've had disgusting men stare at my body and violate me. I don't care that I'm making him uncomfortable now.

But my eyes return to the two men. They seem to be Enzo's right-hand men. They might have the answers I seek.

They might be able to tell me why Enzo's father ordered him to kill me.

The only way I'm going to get a chance to ask is by putting clothes on so they can all stop acting like they are innocent men who have never seen a naked woman before.

I step forward and pick up the shirt, and quickly pull it over my head. It's warm like Enzo, smells like salt and sweat, and covers most of my body. I don't hate it against my skin, but I don't love it either.

"Who are you?" I ask the two men.

"I'm Langston."

"And I'm Zeke."

Enzo motions with his head, and both men disappear without a command.

Damn him. I forgot he can practically read my thoughts.

A knock on the door startles me.

Enzo's nostrils flare as he looks behind me. I turn as Dr. Gould enters.

"Miss Miller, you really should return to bed. I won't examine you now if you need time, but I would recommend an exam sooner than later if you want to ensure you heal a hundred percent back to your previous state."

Enzo rushes past me, and hurries the doctor out of the office—leaving me behind. I fold my arms across my chest as the cold nip returns. I'm used to being cool, I thrive in it, but the shakes are different. It reminds me of how weak I am.

I try to distract myself by inspecting the office. But there isn't much to look at. A large desk with multiple chairs all made of modern materials. White walls and gray floors. And of course a stellar view of the ocean from behind the desk.

I suspect every room in this house was built around the spectacular views. Views I long to erase from my head.

And then I hear their voices.

"I did what I thought was best to care for the girl. She needs immediate medical attention. It can't wait!"

"I hired you because you were the best. That you wouldn't hurt her, but it's clear you couldn't even do that right."

Muffled voices continue.

"You're fired."

My mouth falls open as Enzo returns to the office.

"You fired him?" I stutter out.

He nods.

"Why?"

"Because he wasn't very effective in his job. He's supposed to do no harm, but he hurt you."

I swallow hard. "Will you hire another doctor?"

He doesn't answer, and it's clear he hasn't decided.

"You need to put a bandaid on your hand," Enzo says, holding one out to me.

I glance down at my hand where the IV was and see blood slowly oozing out. I take the bandaid from Enzo, careful not to brush our fingertips together, and then I apply the bandaid.

"Thank you."

He smirks. "Don't thank me, Kai—for anything."

"What do you want with me?" I ask, my voice shaky, afraid of his answer. Because I can see the heat in his eyes. I already know the answer.

He shakes his head. "I want you to go upstairs to your room, keep your clothes on, and eat the food I provide you. And the next time I hire the best doctor in the world to examine you, you take the help."

He moves out of the doorway for me to leave.

"Why are you keeping your distance? Avoiding touching me?"

His body darkens as he steps closer. "Because I will *never* touch you. Never. Why would I want to claim what has already been tainted? Why would I want you?"

I feel the tears behind my eyes. I should be happy to hear he won't touch me, even if his words are harsh and cruel. He can't hurt me if he doesn't touch me. But then that means I'm nothing to him.

"Why keep me? Why keep me alive?"

"You didn't win the game. You didn't earn your answers. You are mine for as long as I want to keep you. Now go to your room and don't come down until I can no longer see every fucking bone in your body."

"So I'm a prisoner to my room?"

"Until you learn to obey the rules, yes."

I feel the sickness take hold of my body. I don't want to give in, but I don't have a choice. If I stay defiant, I will blackout.

"Go, before I'm forced to carry your body to bed again, myself."

I storm past him and then reach the stairs.

Shit.

Now I wish Enzo would really carry me upstairs, because I will have nothing left in my tank by the time I reach the top. But I'm too stubborn to return and ask for his or anyone else's help.

So I climb. It's ruthless, unforgiving, and I feel new bruises forming as I knock myself against the stairs as I move upward. But I make it.

I walk down the hallway to the bedroom he calls mine, and I stare at the bed. I won't get in that cloud of heaven.

Instead, I stumble to the farthest corner of the room from the windows, I remove the shirt, and lie down on the smooth hardwood floor. At least his home is floored with hardwood instead of carpet. I curl up on the ground, tucking my knees to my chest, and close my eyes.

Sleep will easily overcome me. But Enzo will haunt my dreams. He was the boy who saved me, only to sell me. He was my first kiss. My first taste of what falling in love could feel like. He was freedom to me. And now he's my master, who's so disgusted by me he doesn't even want me.

I thought I knew loneliness, but loneliness is only now coming for me. Because even Enzo can't hate me. I am nothing. I am no one. I should be dead, but no one will kill me. Instead, I'm trapped in this cage of gleaming light until I find a way for it all to end.

18

ENZO

I watched as Kai climbed the stairs with bated breath.

It took her twenty minutes to reach the top, something that should have taken her thirty-seconds to do. It took everything in my body to restrain myself, to keep my feet planted at the bottom of the stairs hidden in the shadows, instead of tossing her over my shoulder and carrying her to bed. But I can't touch her, for both our sakes. *Never again.*

If I touch her, I would fuck her, rape her, hurt her. That's a line I won't cross, no matter how my twisted brain wants me to. I won't harm her.

That's a lie. I'm hurting her by keeping her captive—by not telling her the truth.

She reaches the top, and I wait for as long as I can stomach before heading up the stairs. For one, I need a new shirt, my clothes haven't arrived yet, and the only ones I have are hanging in the closet off the room she now occupies. And two, I need to know she isn't passed out again.

I run up the stairs and creep at the doorway to the room. Kai didn't bother shutting the door, so it's easy for me to loom in the dark. She's not in the bed.

Fuck.

I walk inside, expecting to see the worst. Instead, I hear her snores.

I shake my head as I see her curled up in my shirt on the floor. I don't know what she's been through to prefer the hard floor to a comfortable bed. To prefer walking naked than be clothed. To prefer to be left alone than touched.

I want to grab a blanket from the bed and cover her. I want to support her head with a pillow. But both would wake her up, and she needs sleep above everything else.

She slept for three days straight after she first passed out. I spent most of the night holding her in her sleep, keeping her warm, as she requested when she was unconscious. I close my eyes remembering how good it felt to not be burning hot all the time. To let the rage inside me cool. To feel comforted even though she wasn't awake to hold me back.

Never again.

I leave her and head to the closet. I grab another black T-shirt and pull it over my head. And then I walk back over to Kai. She's still asleep on the floor. I need to call another doctor to monitor her. To provide an IV if she starts sleeping for days again, one who will be more cautious when she tries to persuade Kai to do anything.

I need to touch her. To feel her. She's like a drug pulling me to her. Too bad I can't have her. Too bad she's going to be trapped here for the rest of her days. Because she could be the one person who could save me.

My fingers graze her hollow cheeks, and I suck in a breath at the power that pulses through me at the connection.

Fuck, I could live off this feeling.

I can't keep doing this. If I keep touching her when she's

unconscious, I won't be able to resist caressing her when she's awake. And the faster I can get her to trust that I won't touch her, or hurt her beyond keeping her here, the faster she will heal and settle into her new life. Then I can leave her in Westcott's trust. Then I can be free of her, forever.

I take the stairs two at a time as I try to put my thoughts of Kai behind me. Not an easy task.

Langston leans against the doorframe leading to the living room. His arms are crossed across his chest, his muscles bulging and revealing tattoos wrapped in black ink around his bicep. His lips wear a knowing look.

"What?" I grumble.

"Nothing." Langston smiles.

I roll my eyes. I don't have time for whatever games he wants to play.

"Who's the girl?" he asks.

I glare at him. "You don't get to ask about my life."

I storm past him and head to the kitchen to get a bottle of water to calm me down. I feel like I'm about to boil over and no one is safe when I let my temper loose. I can't control what happens. I'm worse than a hurricane running through town. I destroy everything in my path; I don't leave anyone behind.

"Actually, I think we've earned the right to know everything about your personal life, boss," Zeke says entering the kitchen.

Great, they are ganging up on me.

I down a bottle of water, crush the plastic, and toss it on the ground, my anger palatable in the air.

"Are you running a hospital or something now? Taking in the sick? Or is she something more?" Langston asks.

Both men stand on either side of the island in the center of the kitchen. I stand between them. *Trapped.*

Kai is more. She's everything. Everything I ever wanted. Everything I ever dreamed about: her strength, her influence over me, her resilience.

She's also everything I hate. She revealed my own weaknesses. She's the only one who could take away the power I've gained. And I won't go back to being the powerless boy I was when I met her.

My eyes cut back and forth between the two men. They are my best men. And my best friends. Not always a good mix. Since they are my friends, they think they can pull shit like this. Try to force me to talk to them.

I've known them since we were kids. Zeke was always the brute force in our little group. He could kick anyone's ass with his size alone. Langston was never as gifted with muscle as Zeke, although he's worked hard and gained plenty of muscle, he was more of the brains. He preferred security and doing surveillance. And I was the leader of the group. The decision maker even before I had any power in my father's organization.

I blow hot steam from my nose as I glare between the two men.

Langston laughs, throwing his head back like it's the funniest thing in the world.

"What's happening?" Zeke asks confused.

"Black here, has it bad," Langston force out between laughs.

"Has what bad?" Zeke asks.

I groan. "Langston thinks I have the hots for the broken girl currently occupying my bedroom. I don't. And even if I did, it doesn't matter. I don't fuck another man's goods."

Langston cocks his head. "There is so much more to this story. And I'm dying to know. But right now, we have a decision to make. Reko has been breaking the rules. He's been smuggling drugs without your consent. He needs to be dealt with."

I nod, my blood cooling as I think about work and let the taunting about Kai go.

"Who is his lead man?" I ask.

"Warwick," Langston answers.

"Good, I know the man. He's a regular at Surrender. He will be easy to snatch."

"And what are we going to do when we snatch him?" Zeke asks, I can hear the itch in his voice to do some damage.

"Torture him until he either gives up his boss or he's dead. Either way, it will send a message."

"How long?" Langston asks.

I smile. "Two weeks." I need out of this fucking house. Westcott will be able to handle Kai for two weeks, especially in her weakened state. And I need to get to the ocean. We always do our business on the sea. It's easier to clean up and dispose of the bodies. We throw a lavish yacht party while doing business. It gives us a good alibi, and we can continue to learn about what goes on in the city and on the sea, my jurisdictions.

I don't love the party part, but it's the easiest way to get information out of people. Surrender is good, but the yachts are better. At Surrender, people aren't really trapped. On the yachts, they have no place to go until I say. Not unless they want to take a dip in the water.

But there is another purpose to wanting to be gone. I decide against my better judgment to pay Jarod a visit. Repay him for how he took care of Kai.

Langston and Zeke both smile. They love the water as much as I do.

"Maybe after a day or two of being apart from the girl,

we'll be able to get more information out of mister romantic here," Langston teases.

I growl, threatening him.

But Langston runs off, like he knows exactly what he's doing to me. He knows me too well. I've never brought a woman here. This is our place. It's as much Zeke's and Langston's as it is mine. We have all crashed here at various times. But we have one rule, it's just us. No girls. I broke that rule, and they know it was for a very real purpose.

I've broken too many rules for Kai so far. By my rules, she should have died a long time ago. I won't break any more rules for Kai. From now on, I do everything by the book.

———

"What did this Jarod guy do?" Langston asks suspiciously.

He destroyed what was mine—Kai. He brutalized her, burned her flesh, stabbed her, broke her bones, raped her. He did so many unthinkable things no man should ever do to a woman. But I don't want Langston or Zeke to know the real purpose for tracking Jarod down for the past two weeks.

"He destroyed some property of mine to the north," I say keeping my words vague so I'm not technically lying to my best friend. I hate lying if I can avoid it.

My words seem to be enough for Langston. Neither he nor Zeke need much to follow my orders. They trust me with their lives. They will do anything I ask with zero questions.

"So what's the plan?" Zeke asks as we crouch down on near the railing of my own yacht staring across the black sea to Jarod's yacht.

"We sneak onto the boat silently, then take out every man until we find Jarod," I answer.

"And when we have Jarod?" Zeke asks.

"I send a message that no one touches what is mine," I say.

Zeke and Langston's exchange knowing glances. They are more than capable of getting their hands dirty without me being involved. My father would have let his men carry out his orders, but I prefer to be more hands on. It sends a better message. And this is personal.

Langston stares across to the boat. A light flickers off. It's time. This is as unguarded as the yacht will ever get. There are only three of us and who knows how many men on Jarod's yacht, but we will win. I could have sent Langston or Zeke by themselves on this mission, and they would have slaughtered everyone on board with ease. The three of us doing this job together is overkill.

"Let's go," I say as I silently jump into the water with the tiniest of splashes.

They both follow as quietly into the ocean. And then we begin swimming, careful with our movements to hide in the waves and avoid making a wake, but quick and efficient.

I reach the ladder leading up the back of the boat first. I ascend, my blood boiling with need for revenge. I should have brought Kai with me. Let her take out the man who hurt her so viciously, but that might lead her to believe I am a good person. I'm not. I'm not doing this for her. I'm doing this for me, so I can sleep better at night. I should have never let Jarod touch her in the first place.

I hit the deck of the yacht, and pull my silenced gun out from my waistband. I don't find a guard right away. Amateurs.

I don't wait for Langston or Zeke to come up the ladder.

I start moving like a ninja in the night. My body blends with the shadows and creaks of the boat as it rocks gently in the sea.

My first target doesn't appear until I walk inside. A man asleep at the helm. I shake my head as I shoot him in the head. He almost deserves to die solely for being so poor at his job, not just for having a part in hurting Kai.

I hear a couple quick fires in the distance. Zeke and Langston have boarded the ship and taken out their first men.

I smile.

I always come alive in moments like this. When I'm hunting deserving men. Giving them their justice. I don't always kill evil men. Sometimes the men I kill are just mixed up in the wrong business, but the cruelest are my favorite to end.

I creep deeper into the yacht and open the first bedroom door. A man asleep in the bed. I sigh as I pull the trigger. This is almost too easy. I really should have come alone.

Another door, this man is up, having heard the sounds of the men dropping and our guns firing softly. He draws his gun, but he's too slow as I shoot him in the chest. He falls with a thud.

I open door after door and find no one. I open one door that sends chills down my spine. The room is empty—not even a bed. I should leave, not step inside, but I do. It pulls me in.

It's then I see the scratches on the door, walls, floor. I see the marks where a body hit the wall. Blood stains the floor. I trace my fingers over the scratches on the door.

Fingernails.

Rage fills me. This is the room Kai stayed in. The room

Jarod kept her in. Tortured her in. No wonder she hates my bed. She's been used to the floor.

I storm out. A hurricane force beats inside me, yearning to do damage to the man who hurt Kai. How the fuck could I let this happen? How could I have been the reason for this cruelty?

Because I was a stupid, fucking coward.

"Zeke has him tied in the room on the end," Langston says when I enter the hallway.

"Good, stand guard on deck," I say.

I throw the door open and see Jarod tied to a chair. His eyes burn in confusion when he sees me. Sweat covers his forehead and fear rakes his body.

Good, he should fear me.

"Black," his voice trembles as if he's seeing the devil himself.

"Good, you know who I am. I didn't think you would."

I give a look to Zeke, and he departs us immediately.

"Black, I'm sorry. I didn't—"

I punch him hard in the jaw. I don't want to hear his apologies. His body careens as he falls sideways to the floor.

He spits out blood. "I didn't do anything wrong. I was just following orders. I don't deserve to die for doing what was commanded."

He's right. He doesn't deserve to die for following orders. "Too bad I don't believe in being fair. You touched the girl, that alone means you deserve to die."

His pupils dilate in terror.

I grin.

I love this part.

I spot the tape Zeke used to tie Jarod to the chair. I tear off a piece and cover his mouth with it. I don't want to hear him speak anymore. His muffled screams will be enough to excite me.

"You deserve to feel everything you did to Kai. Too bad I don't have years to spend torturing you. A few hours will have to do."

I kick him hard in the stomach. He gasps and wretches. Possibly even vomiting in his mouth.

"I'm sure you kicked Kai when she was down. I've seen the bruises and broken ribs."

I kick three more times for good measure as his body slams against the wall, breaking him free of the chair, but his hands are still trapped behind his back. He stumbles to his feet.

Good, I'll enjoy the fight more now that he's standing.

I slam my fist into his jaw over and over in quick succession. His face coloring and swelling before my eyes as blood swells from the cuts.

"Did you punch her like this? Bruising her body repeatedly? Did you enjoy it like I am?"

He twists away, but he has nowhere to escape.

"What about stabbing?"

His eyebrows raise as I pull a knife from my pocket and extend it. He tries to retreat back, but I grab his arm and thrust the sharp blade into his shoulder and twist.

He cries out, but it's muffled.

"How many times did you stab her? Three, four, five times?" I ask, pulling the knife out before jabbing it back into his other shoulder, extracting more vengeance.

Tears start down his eyes. Stirring more energy in me to continue as I know how many tears he pulled from Kai. Zero. She would never cry in front of this monster. She kept them all buried inside. One day she will explode, and I will curse myself when those tears fall.

"You burned her too?"

I find a lighter on his nightstand and hold the flame to his neck. He screams as the flame sears his skin—music to my ears.

For hours I continue the torture well into the night until I've lost track of time. I let the devil live inside me all in the name of getting revenge for the pain Kai lived, but I don't do it for her. I do it for me. Because the evil inside me needs a life to defeat.

Jarod lays broken on the floor. A mess of blood, tears, and piss.

I lean down close to his ear, knowing he is seconds away from begging for a conclusion. For me to kill him.

"I think we've covered everything you did to her, except one. Rape."

He sobs and closes his eyes in fear.

"Don't worry; I'm not a sick fuck like you. I won't rape you."

I pull the gun from my waistband. "But I am done with you."

I fire—killing him. And closing the biggest mistake of my life. I let this man hurt Kai, and now I've rectified the situation. It won't matter to Kai. She'll still think I'm a monster for what I did, and rightfully so. But at least now I took back what was mine.

19

KAI

Enzo's gone.

He has been. For almost three weeks.

He vanished. It's like he wasn't even here. I imagined him.

No.

He was real. He is very, very real. Otherwise, I wouldn't be trapped in this fucking, gorgeous beach house. I shouldn't complain. I'm being treated better than I have ever been treated in my entire life. And that includes before I was kidnapped.

My father had nothing. And my mother died when I was little, leaving behind a legacy of hospital bills for us to spend our entire life paying off.

And for the first time in a long time, I don't know what my future holds. When I was living with my father in his trailer, I knew what my life would entail. I would live in the trailer with him, and clean yachts for a living. Until one day the debt collectors would come and demand more from me. And then I would sell my body to pay the bills. I knew my destiny, and it didn't look bright. It wouldn't include school or a career or a husband and kids. My life outlook was bleak, so I never dreamed.

And then I was kidnapped, and my future changed. I no longer worked to put food on the table. I was lucky to get a scrap of bread on that yacht. I knew what my future was. Death.

But now that I'm trapped in a house on the beach, I have no idea what my future holds. I can guess...rape, beatings, death. Maybe a little bit of everything I thought my future held before. But if my future here does include those things, it will be behind the glow of the modern walls of this beach house. It's too pretty for anyone to think anything heinous happens here.

And Enzo... I have no clue what to think about that man. He's dark, dangerous, and powerful. I should be scared of him. He's worse than any master who could ever own me. Killed more men than an army. But he hasn't hurt me. He specifically said he would never touch me. *Never*.

But then why am I trapped here?

Why keep me?

Isn't that the question? One I'm afraid I will never get an answer to.

A light tapping rattles on the door. It's Dr. Miranda. She's been overseeing my progress these last few weeks. And when I say overseeing, I mean overseeing. She's never touched me, not even to place an IV. She did convince me to use one for the first week to increase my strength and nutrition without overwhelming my stomach. But instead of inserting it herself, she taught me how.

"Come in," I say, knowing she will stand outside my door all day and never enter until I give her permission.

The door creaks open as Dr. Miranda pokes her head inside.

She smiles at me sweetly when she sees me sitting in my usual corner of the room on the floor. She doesn't berate me or tell me my bones would heal easier in the bed. She also never asks how I'm doing—realizing that even if I'm doing better, I'm still in a dangerous place and that isn't an encouraging question to ask.

Instead, she sits cross-legged on the floor in front of me.

"How many hours did you sleep last night?"

"Three or four."

She nods, showing no reaction to my answer. She never does.

"Still getting nightmares?"

"Yes, I woke up three times from them and after the last one, I just decided to stay awake." I went from sleeping twenty-four hours a day from exhaustion to only sleeping three. My body doesn't know how to react. So I go from one polar extreme to the next.

"Have you been able to keep food down?"

"Yes."

She never asks how much I've been eating. I eat enough, but not as much as she'd like, I'm sure.

"How is walking?"

"Still difficult, but the swelling in my foot has gone down."

"Would you like to show me?"

I bring my foot out from beneath me and show her. She nods at the progress.

"How is your pain overall?"

"Manageable."

Miranda looks to my bottle of painkillers that have been sitting on the nightstand. I haven't taken a single one. Not because I enjoy the pain, but because I'm afraid they will knock my frail body out. It's one of the reasons I don't sleep well either.

"Would you like me to prescribe you something to help you sleep?"

"No."

She purses her lips, obviously wanting to tell me something, but not sure she should say it. She doesn't like pushing me. I don't know if it's because Enzo threatened her, or if she just realizes if she pushes she might lose any progress we have made.

"What?" I ask.

"I was thinking about your sleep. Sleep is the most important part of your healing process. Of course, I would like you to eat more. I would like you to take more medication and get some x-rays done. But if I had to choose one thing to focus on for you, it would be sleep."

I sigh. "I can't control when my nightmares come or how much sleep I get. And I won't take anything. It doesn't make me feel safe."

She nods. "I'm not asking you to take anything."

"Then what are you asking?"

"I'm asking if there is anything that would make sleeping safer for you?"

I look at her wide-eyed. I'm pretty sure there is something, although I would never ask for him. I'm not even sure if it was a dream or reality. But the first few nights I was here and slept for hours uninterrupted, Enzo slept with me. He held my body all night, keeping me warm without overpowering me. I've never slept so peacefully, but maybe it was just because I was so exhausted and it had nothing to do with him.

"Maybe a stronger lock on the door would help you? Blackout curtains? Sleep during the daylight and staying awake at night, if that is more what you are used to. Take a relaxing bath before you sleep. All I ask is that you try to get more sleep. It's the most important thing for your body to heal."

"I will try."

"Good, thank you."

Miranda studies me a second longer. "For what it's worth, Kai, you are healing. Your cheeks are filling back out into light shades of pink, your eyes aren't empty holes anymore, and you have fat and muscle returning to your body. I know the healing process can be frustratingly slow, but be patient with yourself. You will get better. And you will heal in ways you didn't even realize you needed healing —just be patient."

I nod.

She stands. "If you need anything at all, give me a call. Mr. Westcott has my number. Otherwise, I'll come back in a couple of days."

Miranda doesn't wait for a goodbye or acknowledgment from me at all. She leaves without expectation of a hug or a handshake or a verbal goodbye. I like her as much as I can like a person, which isn't much, but I'm thankful to have someone watching over me and ensuring that I'm healing. Albeit slowly and on my own terms.

I lean my head back against the wall. I know what comes next, and I'm not sure I can handle it. I wish everyone were as gentle and understanding as the doctor.

A loud tapping rattles the door.

I don't have to welcome him in, he just enters.

"Good morning, Miss Miller," Westcott says with a large tray of food.

"It's Kai," I say for the millionth time.

He ignores me and sets the tray on the nightstand.

"I brought you pancakes, eggs, bacon, sausage, and toast. There is also a side of fruit. A smoothie, yogurt, and orange juice. And then I brought you both coffee and tea since I wasn't sure which you preferred and you still haven't told me." He looks resentful.

I haven't told him because I don't even know which one I prefer. Not anymore.

"Would you like to eat out on the balcony today? It's a beautiful day. It would be a shame to waste the sunshine. Vitamin D is essential for healing you know."

I frown. If it were so important, then the doctor would have recommended it.

He sighs when I don't answer and lifts the tray to set it down on the spot on the floor next to me, knowing this is the only way he'll get any food in me, if it's within my reach.

I take a piece of the bacon off the plate and start nibbling on it. Its probably not the best for my stomach, but it tastes good.

"Is there anything else I can get or arrange for you today?" he asks.

"My freedom."

He ignores me as he always does.

"Actually..." I sit up straighter. "You can do something for me."

His eyes grow big and an automatic smile forms.

"Can you arrange for blackout curtains to be installed in the room? And several locks on the door that can only be locked from the inside."

He frowns.

"Westcott? Can that be arranged?"

"Yes, of course. Mr. Black wanted you to have anything you requested."

"Except my freedom. I'm to stay locked in this room?"

"The door is never locked. You are not a prisoner in this room as much as you think you are. You are welcome downstairs or on the balcony or to visit the beach if you so wish."

I smirk. I can go anywhere on the grounds where they can keep an eye on me.

"When is Enzo coming home?"

Westcott doesn't answer me. But I think it's because he doesn't know, not that he was told not to tell me.

"Anything else, ma'am?"

I shake my head.

Westcott leaves me to try to muster down some of the food and drink. I decide to test the coffee and tea today. I should know which one I prefer. I taste both, and my stomach feels like hurling, the bitter taste they both leave in my mouth is too much for my bland tastebuds.

Gross, how do people drink either? I know some people want an IV of coffee hooked up to them, but I don't understand why.

I sigh. I don't like coffee or tea. I'm not sure I can like anything anymore.

I nibble more on the bacon. I guess I like the bacon.

I continue my best to eat, and within an hour there are men in the room installing curtains and more locks on the door. I try not to hide and shrink away when they enter the room, but I can't help it.

They won't hurt me, I repeat to myself. *They won't hurt me.*

As soon as the men leave, I run to the door and close all the locks. Each one is different and uses a different mechanism to close along a different part of the door. Some high, some low, some in the middle. It would take a lot to get through the door.

Then I move to the curtains and close them tight. The room descends into blackness.

I smile.

Finally.

I might be able to sleep.

I go back to my corner of the room where it's now dark enough to try to sleep even though it's the middle of the day. And that's what I do. I sleep.

————

My body is shivering uncontrollably in the tiny room the men left me in. It's so fucking cold. I'm used to the cold. My body always runs cold, and our trailer doesn't have heat. Not that we need it much in Miami, but we can't afford jackets or blankets either.

I'm somewhere much colder than Miami.

I was unconscious when they brought me into the room.

The room heaves.

What the hell?

We keep rocking, and it takes me a minute to realize I'm on a boat. The water—my favorite thing in the world, and also my enemy.

I hear men's voices outside of my room, and I remember.

I was kidnapped.

I was sold.

And now a man owns me.

I don't have to be told why a man would buy a woman. I know the purpose they have for me.

The door opens, with a loud thud as it slams against the wall. A toothy man steps inside. He doesn't look particularly strong. He doesn't have defined muscles, but he's a heavy-set man, that could throw his weight around and hurt me.

"It's time to break in the new whore."

No.

My shivering changes to uncontrollable trembles. My body is not prepared to be raped. I can't. I don't want to become a shell of a woman who can't function after this, if I ever get free.

The man comes into the room, and I inch backward, looking for a weapon, for anything I can use to hurt him. I find nothing.

He smirks, like he knows what I'm doing.

I can't hurt him, but I can run.

That's what I do as he moves forward. I'm faster than him, so I run around his body. I dart out of the room, not sure what my next step is. I just won't let them take me easily. I won't let them hurt or violate me.

I make it to the hallway, and I see another man with arms crossed smiling at me. "I win the bet. I told you she would try to run."

"Fine, fine," *the man from the room says as he closes in from behind me.*

My heart races, and my body continues to shake violently like that is going to help. I'm more scared than I realized.

No, don't let them have my fear. *I will fight, and they might still claim my body, but that's it. I will keep everything else. I will not be a broken, scared girl when I leave here.*

I force my body to still, which only makes the toothy man smile brighter.

"You're a fighter. Good, it's been a while since we had a fighter. It will be more fun when you finally break. I give you a month."

"Nah, I give her three. She's more determined than you think," *the man behind me says.*

Each man walks closer, and I don't know what to do. Which man is weaker? Which do I attack and hope I can break free of?

I don't get to make a decision. Both of them grab an arm at the same time.

I fight—viciously. My legs start kicking, my arms flail, my nails dig into their skin, and I try to bite their skin with my teeth.

I can do this all day.

Until the fist makes contact with my jaw.

Black dots surround my vision as a pain in my head overwhelms me. I've never felt anything like this before. And I know I can't keep fighting. Not when the fight is so unfair.

They can do whatever they want to me. I'm weak. I have no strength.

They start pulling me to a different room—one filled with men. The shakes return, and my eyes widen. I thought only one man would take my virginity. I thought only one man would rip me apart, violate, and ruin me. But there are six men in the room.

I don't know what they plan, but I'm outnumbered. I turned seventeen yesterday. Still too young for anything like this to happen. But being too young won't stop it.

I don't know what I expect. But I don't expect this. I feel a kick in my side, then a slap to the face, followed by being thrown into a wall.

When they said 'break' they literally meant break.

And my body starts the slow process of turning into a shattered pile of bones.

Another hit.

Another kick.

A yank of my wrist.

I try not to cry out, to keep my voice and pain to myself, but I can't.

I scream.

———

My eyes fly open. *It's a dream. It was just a dream.*

I pant heavily as cold sweat covers my body.

My body burns as it did that night. I don't know if that night was the roughest they were on me, but it was the hardest night for me. It was the beginning. The not knowing what to expect. The unfamiliarity of the agony with each hit, putting fresh wounds onto my body for the first time. That was what destroyed me.

I scream at the pain. Even though I'm awake, I can still feel it, still hear their grunts, still see their smug smiles brighten at the enjoyment they got from hurting me.

"Kai." A loud pounding comes at the door.

I still.

"Kai, open the door."

Enzo.

He's back.

And I don't know how to feel.

He came back. That should make me shrink in terror, but I like that he came back. It means I'm not alone anymore.

I should go open the door and let him in, but I'm pissed. At him for keeping me captive. For leaving me alone. For letting me endure my nightmares when he could easily stop them by sleeping here with me.

So I don't open the door.

Enzo doesn't get to see my pain, my tears. He doesn't get to see what leaving me did to me. Because as much as I want to be free, this is the only place I have a chance of healing.

I pull my knees tight to my chest as I rock myself in the corner, trying to calm myself. I can't. My icy veins are pulsing so hard I'm afraid my heart is going to give out from the speed.

I close my eyes even though the room is already dark from the blackout curtains. The darkness often saves me, but it can't save me from this.

I hear the door handle rattle as Enzo tries to get inside.

I don't know why he wants into my room so badly. *Is he pissed I had men install locks on the door? Did his business dealing go badly and now he wants to blow off steam on me?*

He can't get inside. There are six locks on the door, none which have keyholes on the other side. They are all various chains and bolts keeping anyone and everyone out.

I'm safe in here.

My eyes focus in on the locks. *I'm safe, but then why do I feel anything but secure?*

Sweat continues to ooze from my pores like my body is trying to expel the nightmares through my skin. My mind tries to shut off, but it can't block out the men. And I can't get rid of the shakes that ricochet through my body.

The door handle stops rattling. I exhale. Enzo realized he couldn't get in.

I'm alone.

And I don't know how to feel.

I'm alone to face the demons in the dark. Alone to heal myself. *What if I can't heal myself? What if I just stop eating and drinking until my body finally gives out?*

Dr. Miranda wouldn't allow me to do that. Neither would Westcott or even Enzo. Enzo would hire someone to break through the locks and force feed me before he let me wither away into nothing. I still have my suspicions that the only reason I'm here is so he can heal me and then get more money when he sells me.

But for now, I get one more day alone.

I hear a loud crack.

I jump.

The door.

Another pound against the door, followed by another crack.

Shit.

I grip my knees tighter as my teeth begin to chatter.

Pound.

Pound.

Pound.

Then crack.

The door splits along the edge. Enzo pushes the door open wide enough for him to step through.

He's dressed in a black suit; his tie has loosened around his neck like he just came home from a normal day at the office. But that's where the normalcy stops. His dark hair is ruffled and longer than the last time I saw him; he could use a haircut. The shadow of hair on his sharp jawline has thickened. Sweat trickles down his forehead.

Blood.

Tiny droplets of blood rest on the collar of his shirt, tie, and cufflinks.

What have you been doing Enzo? And do you plan on doing the same thing to me?

I had so many questions of why he wanted to break down the door before. Most ended in something horrible happening when he made it through the door. But now seeing his face, those worries vanish.

Enzo is shattered.

His eyes are dark with fear, his brow wrinkled with worry, and his lips tight with anxiety.

He's concerned about me—about what he would find when he opened the door.

My lips open to comfort him, to tell him no one was

torturing me, it was just a nightmare, but I can't, because I'm not fine.

His eyes travel over every inch of my body, inspecting, trying to figure out where I'm hurt and where I've healed.

We both continue to stare at each other, like whoever stops first loses.

Neither of us knows what to say.

I don't offer up any information about what I'm going through, and he doesn't tell me whose blood stains his clothes.

But despite the connection of our gazes, I long for more. To understand this man, who for one second shows he cares only to show later how monstrous he can be.

His body wants me. I can see his cock lengthen and harden in his pants at the sight of me this way. Sweaty, scared, and broken.

That's how he likes his women.

Yet, he denies himself the one thing he seems to want—*me*.

Finally, he swallows, and our connection is lost. He glances around the room at the curtains and then to the locks that were preventing his entry.

"I see you did some redecorating while I was gone."

I snarl.

He ignores my response and cocks his head to the side.

"You are supposed to be dressed."

"No, I'm supposed to be dressed when I leave this room," I snap back.

He smiles a little at my firey response.

"There was no need to barricade yourself in this room."

"Why not? I was told not to leave this room until I had fully healed. Might as well ensure no one gets in. Although, I see my plan backfired."

He winces at my words, and I explode.

"You're a fucking asshole! You've kept me locked in this fucking room, this house, for weeks!" I stand feeling my anger from him leaving me, and the nightmare overtakes any other thoughts.

He doesn't blink as I yell. He just lets me berate him.

"You don't tell me fucking anything! You just give me mixed signal after mixed signal. You were supposed to kill me but didn't. You should have sold me or raped me by now, but you haven't. You want me to heal, yet you spend your time yelling or ignoring me. You're a fucking coward! Nothing has changed since you were a boy."

"Are. You. Done?" I feel his temper rising with each word, but he doesn't let it free. This man is practiced in self-control.

"No, I'm not fucking done!"

I realize I've taken several steps toward him as my anger took control of me. I'm dangerously close. Close enough he could touch me. Last time he did, I passed out for days. I won't let that happen again. I know how much his touch burns.

But I won't retreat either.

The shiny piece of metal captures my attention. He has a gun.

None of my previous captors had a gun. At least they never wore their guns around me, as if they sensed I would steal it if the opportunity presented itself.

Here's my chance.

I'm risking everything by doing this.

I'm out of practice with pickpocketing.

My movements are slower than usual.

He could touch me in the process.

Or realize what I'm reaching for and shoot me before I

have the chance to shoot him, if he no longer thinks I'm worth keeping alive.

But I have to try.

"You're a cruel, evil monster. Don't think I didn't notice the blood of your victim on your clothes."

"Who said the man I killed was a victim?"

I inch closer, keeping my gaze on his instead of the gun. "Because no one deserves to die by your hand. You aren't God."

He smirks. "To most women, I am. Any woman who's had the pleasure of spending a night in my bed has called me God over and over."

I hesitate. I have no doubt Enzo is good in bed with a willing partner. My mouth waters at the thought of how he might be in bed. Powerful, strong, and merciless. He would ensure his partner came, while also taking everything he wanted from her. Fucking her harder than she's ever been fucked, spreading her wider, pushing her beyond her limits. There would be spanking, a rough taking, and rope to tie her up like they were in some Fifty Shades of Grey novel.

A willing partner is the key. *I wouldn't be willing? Would I?*

I snatch the gun before I answer my silent question. I take a step back at the same time as I aim the gun at Enzo.

He doesn't move. He doesn't offer his surrender or try to take the gun from me, even though I'm sure he could easily.

"Do it, pull the trigger. Put me out of my misery," he says.

His misery?

He doesn't know what misery feels like. He can't with a body like his, a mind that has been through schooling, and a company, albeit an illegal organization, he runs that makes him millions.

"Don't tempt me. I should. You are not my master."

He shakes his head. "I'm not your master. No one could control such a creature like you. You are like the sea; you can never truly be owned by any man." His words seem to sadden him, like he's just now coming to this realization.

I can't kill him.

Just as he couldn't kill me.

But I can kill myself.

I change the direction of the gun. I point it toward my heart.

One squeeze and I'll be gone. Even if I miss my heart, my body couldn't take the blood loss.

I see Enzo's body tighten. He doesn't tell me to stop, but every muscle in his body is pulling, forcing him to stay when he wants to snatch the gun from my hands.

I sigh.

I can't fucking kill myself. Not after everything I've survived.

I drop the gun.

He doesn't go to pick it up. Instead, he walks to the bathroom. When he returns, he has a wet washcloth and a glass of water.

He holds them both out to me.

I take them carefully before taking a seat back in my corner of the room. I use the washcloth to wipe the sweat from my body, and then I drink the water.

He watches me carefully until I'm lying on the floor again, and then he exhales sharply.

"Can you at least put a shirt on around me?"

"Huh?"

"Just...fuck. I know for whatever ridiculous reason, you feel more comfortable naked than wearing clothes, but I just can't—I can't."

"You can't look at how disgusting I am?" I spout my anger.

He rubs his neck. "I can't look at how attracted I am to your brokenness."

My eyes widen at his admission. I knew he was attracted to my pain, but now I've confirmed it.

"I'm twisted, Kai. I'm not your savior, and I'm not your monster. I may have been the boy who saved you only to turn into the savage who destroyed your life. But now, all I want is for you to disappear again like before."

Shit.

"I'm not going to sell you. Though sometimes we don't get what we wish for."

His eyes bury into mine, and I can feel everything. His lust at wanting me, his fight at holding back. And his desire to go hunt and kill the man who hurt me. Enzo Black may be a monster, but he may be the kind that protects me instead of hurts me—at least this new version of him. I can see the regret in his eyes at selling me, but I can't forgive him. I can never forgive him.

Never.

He seems to regret that too.

But I can't make his life easier. I won't wear a shirt, because it will make sleep harder, even if I'm tempting his self-control. Even if I'm risking him fucking me by exposing my body to him.

I lay down in the corner, naked.

He sighs.

"What am I going to do with you, Kai?" he says to himself.

I'm broken, you don't have a choice of what to do with me. Just let me go. Stop hurting me.

I expect him to leave—find a different room to sleep in.

Instead, he starts removing his clothes.

Shoes, then tie.

Then the slow unbuttoning of his shirt, until his rippled body appears. And then his pants slide down his thick legs.

I expect him to stop.

He doesn't.

He removes his boxer briefs.

My eyes burst, and my heart pumps wildly at the sight of his thick, long cock. It's only partially erect, but it's the most glorious thing I've ever seen.

"What are you doing?" my body freezes. He's told me many times he won't fuck me. Or even touch me. He's disgusted and turned on at the same time. *But then why is he naked in my room?*

"I'm going to sleep. I prefer to sleep naked too. If you get to sleep naked, then so do I."

I frown.

"This isn't your room."

He rolls his eyes. "Are you going to be able to sleep without me here?"

I flame. "What?! You are one cocky ass if you think I can only sleep with you here."

He raises an eyebrow at my explosion. "The last time I stayed with you, you slept for three days straight. How much sleep have you gotten since I was gone?"

I don't answer him.

"That's what I thought."

I watch in horror as he pulls the pillows and blankets from the bed and starts making himself a cot on the floor next to my spot.

"You really don't need to be here," I say.

"I do. I need you healed."

"So you can fuck me?"

"No," his eyes sear.

"So you can sell me?"

He groans. "I'm not going through this with you again." He fluffs his pillow and then lies down on the pile of covers and blankets. But doesn't cover himself. His perfect round ass sticks straight up in the air.

"I'll have a new door and locks installed for you in the morning."

"You're not mad I had them installed?"

"No."

"Why?"

He shrugs. "This is your room now; you can do whatever you want with it."

"Because I'm never leaving this room?"

He doesn't answer, which means his answer is yes.

I sigh and decide not to continue our circle of usual conversation any longer.

"Sleep, Kai."

I curl up on the floor watching him as he closes his eyes. He looks so peaceful lying on top of the covers like that. I don't ask why he doesn't cover up. I know how hot he runs. He doesn't need covers to be warm.

I'm the one who needs covers, but I can't tolerate them.

I need to be warmed.

Enzo could warm you. But I won't ever ask or risk the burn I felt before.

I'm alone.

Always alone.

I close my eyes and try to sleep, but I already know what I'll dream about, and in some way it will be a worse nightmare. One of the only things that kept me sane all those years was Enzo. I'd dream of him, his kiss, his body. I'd imagine his cock as I rode him. I'd imagine the look he would give me, the want. I would fantasize about him saving me, fucking me when the other men were touching me.

Enzo saved me more than once in these last few years, and now that I've seen his real cock, I've seen the glaze of his eyes as he imagines fucking me, I won't be able to stop fantasizing about him. Even though I can never have him. Even though he's the worst kind of man, he still saved me numerous times in my dreams—once for real. As much as he's a monster, he will always be my savior.

I can pretend I can never forgive him for selling me, but he did it to save my life. To give me a chance to stay alive. He was hiding me from someone more dangerous than him. And someday soon, I will get my answers.

20

ENZO

Kᴀɪ'ѕ ѕᴄʀᴇᴀᴍѕ will forever live in my head.

I always thought the next time I'd hear her scream was with me thrusting in her tight cunt. But that will only ever happen in my dreams. I won't hurt her.

Instead, the scream I heard hit me to my core. I thought someone had broken into the house and was torturing, raping Kai.

My feet have never flown so fast up the stairs, determined to kill the intruder for touching what was mine. But I was met with a door that wouldn't open. I couldn't protect her.

I chewed Westcott out big time for allowing Kai to install such locks on the door, even though I knew why he did it, and it was the right move. Then again, I couldn't stand to not be able to save and protect her from whatever devil was on the other side of the door.

Breaking down the door was easy when I had that much adrenaline and willpower running through my veins.

And then I saw Kai. Alone. No torture was happening, at least not in the present. It was a nightmare.

A nightmare I couldn't save her from.

Fuck, fuck, fuck.

How did I let this happen? How did I let her get hurt? And why have I grown so soft as to care for her when I've only ever cared about my own survival? This girl threatens my survival more than anything.

I will never forget the agony on her face, and her naked body still bearing every mark the bastard laid on her. It makes me want to return Jarod from the depths of the ocean only to kill him again for hurting her.

Then she found my gun. I wish she would have pulled the trigger and ended my life, but when she turned it on herself, I realized how much more she mattered to me than I was aware. *Why do I think her life is worth more than mine?*

It made me admit how much I want her, even though I'm fucked up. I'm the worst possible man in the entire world to want her. I thought telling her one bit of the truth would warn her to stay away and hide her body from me. Of course, Kai did no such thing.

And then I did the stupidest thing I've done in a while. I decided to sleep on the floor next to her. It's the middle of the day, but it doesn't matter. The sun no longer shines in due to the blackout curtains. And my sleep schedule is fucked up. I work more nights than days. I'm used to sleeping in the daylight.

I slept on the ground next to her; it was purgatory. Not just because the hardwood floor is the most uncomfortable place to sleep, even with my pile of blankets, but because I was so near to Kai and couldn't touch her.

The last time I slept next to her, I got to touch her. I got to feel her cool skin, and it slowed my unsteady heart, cooled my veins, and relaxed me. Being so close, but not being able to press against her was excruciating, even if it was for both our benefits. It's not something I want to repeat.

But even that wasn't the worst part. The worst part was worrying she might have another nightmare—one I couldn't save her from.

It's obvious from spending time with her she doesn't want to be touched. And I'm happy to oblige. *But what if she's in the middle of a nightmare and it's the only way to pull her out? Then what would I do?*

Thankfully, I don't have to answer that question, because Kai sleeps undisturbed—whether from my presence or sheer exhaustion.

I watch her sleep. It's been almost eight hours since I've laid down next to her. She's been asleep the whole time. While I've struggled to keep my eyes closed for more than an hour at a time. I don't need much sleep, I've adapted to survive. You don't get to sleep much when dangerous men with guns are hunting you down. And I'd rather watch her sleep than rest my own eyes.

Kai coils her body tightly into a coil; I'm sure that's the only thing keeping her remotely warm. I'm desperate to cover her with a blanket to warm her if she doesn't let me touch her. But I resist.

I try to look past the bruises and scars, but I want to feel every one. I deserve to feel the pain for what I did.

I deserved that pain, not her.

I was the coward.

I chose my life over hers.

If only I could change the outcome.

"Enzo," she whispers.

My attention draws back to her. I expect her to wake, but she doesn't. She's still asleep, dreaming about me.

"Yes, Enzo, like that."

Wait? Is she having—

"Fuck yes, Enzo. Fuck me harder."

A sex dream.

I smile. *God, please don't let this be the last time I hear her curse my name like this in anticipation of coming.* It probably will be the last time, so I revel in it. I let it fill me for all the times I will never get to experience her beauty, her passion, her rage.

I want to feel everything Kai has to give. She would have the passion in bed most women lack. Most women I've been with only go through the motions. They think it's all about how big their boobs are or how they sway their ass or the sweet coos that leave their too plump lips as I fuck them. I don't give a shit about any of that. I've always wanted a woman who could equal me—who would fight me in bed —a woman I'd have to tame in order to touch. Worship to be worthy. Love to be her king.

Kai Miller is the only woman who ever seemed like she could fit the bill.

Maybe because she was always off the table, it was just a fantasy I could never confirm or deny. Never realize if Kai is just like all the rest of the women or not.

Hearing her beg for me in her dreams is enough confirmation to know exactly what I'm giving up by not consuming her. She is the woman I've pined for all these years. All it would take is for me to turn into the monster she already thinks I am.

Kai's eyes open, and she smiles at me sweetly.

I smirk. *You wouldn't be smiling at me so sweetly if you knew what I just overheard.*

I lay on my side, and her eyes widen as she notices my rock hard cock. Her mouth waters as she stares openly, not hiding her shame at gawking at me.

"Don't be getting any ideas. My cock is off-limits."

Her smile vanishes, and she scowls at me. "I wasn't thinking about wanting your cock. Trust me; I could live the rest of my life without fantasizing about another cock."

"Hmm, somehow I don't think that's true."

I stare between her legs, even though I know I'm playing with fire.

She doesn't cover herself up.

"So if I asked you to put a finger between your thighs, you wouldn't be wet right now?"

"No."

"Prove it."

"Why? What do I get if I win?"

I shrug, overly confident. "Whatever you want."

She smiles. "And if you win?"

"The pleasure at being right."

"Deal."

She places two fingers between her legs. Her face immediately drops. She's soaked.

I smirk. "Told ya."

I continue to smile as I walk into the bathroom where the cold tile hit my feet. My cock is hard as a rock thinking of her desperate moans.

Fuck.

I pride myself on my self-control, but this is impossible. *How am I going to keep resisting her when I have to be so close to her? How can I resist her naked body?*

Avoidance.

I turn the shower to cold and step inside. Not even allowing myself to jack off to her—that would be giving in and showing weakness. I am not weak. I will not let her or anyone else control me.

The cold droplets should help. Instead, they just remind

me of her.

Jesus Christ, I curse as I squeeze my eyes shut. I can't even get relief from a shower. I need to get the fuck out of here. So that's what I do.

———

Day after day passes, and our routine only fortifies into the same.

During the day I sleep on a cot on the floor next to a naked Kai. And at night I get work done. I'm ruthless in my endeavors. I work harder than I've ever worked, turning my money into more money and ruling the underground, sparking more fear at the sound of the Black name.

I should be thrilled Kai is fueling such dedication to my work, but I'm not happy. I can't keep going on like this. I try my best to be a machine. I turn off my feelings and work, but it's impossible to keep Kai from my mind when I get a new image of her naked body every night.

She's started healing. Her body has begun to fill out now that she's eating and sleeping properly. If she wore clothes, it would be easy to think of her as normal, albeit a little skinny. But she never clothes herself unless I demand it—which I haven't. It's like she wants to taunt me with the scars I allowed to happen on her body. I have my own scars, so there is no need for an imagination for me to understand the pain she endured in getting hers. It makes my skin crawl thinking about Jarod hurting her. *Thank fuck he's dead.*

I've spent the night turned away from Kai, but I can still hear her heavy breathing. It almost sounds like panting.

I squeeze my eyes tighter, wishing I could do the same to my ears. I'm a wreck. I'm sweating; my cock is hard, my balls blue from not allowing myself to jerk off to her.

It's been weeks now.

Weeks.

I've gone this long without sinking my dick into a woman before, but it's different when I'm so desperate for such easy prey right next to me.

My alarm goes off, and I don't care that its blaring wakes her up. She's gotten enough sleep.

"Morning," Kai says. "Or should I say good evening."

I frown, ignoring her pleasantries. I need to get out of here faster than usual today. I need to find a new solution because I can't keep sleeping next to her on the floor. For one, my back can't handle it anymore.

I stomp to the bathroom, preparing myself for another cold shower. But at the last minute, I change the water to steaming hot. I've tried cold too many times. It only reminds me of Kai's icy skin. I need hot.

And then I step under the steaming water.

"Hey!" I hear Kai's voice.

I close my eyes, *ignore her.*

"Hey, asshole! You aren't even going to talk to me anymore now?"

I count to three.

One.

Two.

Three.

It usually helps me gather my rage before I speak. I am in control—just not around her.

"No, I'm not going to fucking talk to you, Kai!"

My rage overwhelms me. I know Kai has questions, and she's just lonely. Well, she wouldn't be so alone if she would ever leave this fucking room, but she hasn't since that first day.

I have questions too.

Like why the hell does she sleep on the floor instead of the bed?

Why won't she let anyone touch her?

How did she get every bruise?

And most of all, what happened to her that made her forget the truth of what happened to her?

I turn the water off and step out.

Kai stands with her arms crossed as she glares at me.

I grab a towel and start drying off, not caring to hide my body from her. We are both too comfortable with each other's bodies now. There is nothing left to hide.

"What do you want, Kai?"

"You know what I want," she breathes.

I roll my eyes. "You don't always get what you want or even what you need. You of all people should have learned that by now."

I walk to the closet and begin getting dressed in a dark gray suit.

She follows.

"Why do you sleep on the floor?"

Her eyes widen, and her head whips back. "What?"

"You heard me. Why?"

She doesn't answer me, she just blinks.

I huff. "You want your questions answered, well I have questions of my own."

Her breath rises and falls in her chest, pushing her hard nipples toward me.

I close my eyes again, trying to think of anything but her tempting body. In my angered state, I can't help but want her. And I know my self-control is growing dangerously close to losing.

When I open my eyes, she's somehow made her body even more appetizing. Her lips are parted, I can see her taunting tongue between her teeth begging to be in my mouth. Her nipples are pointing at me, and her legs are squeezed together as if hiding a secret.

I stride toward her with a look meant to scare her. She doesn't back down.

She stands taller, stronger.

I growl.

She huffs back.

This is never going to end. I'm never going to be free of her until I understand what she went through—seeing that bastard and the yacht she was tortured on isn't enough. Only once I hear her story in her own words can I heal her. Only then can I leave and never look back. My favorite house will become hers; I will sail away on my yacht and leave Miami in Langston's control. I prefer the sea anyway.

I need this to end.

I need to get away from her, stop thinking about her. Then I can go back to fucking any woman and return to my normal life of self-control.

What would end this?

I smirk as the answer finally comes to me.

"How about a game of truth or lies?" I ask.

A slow grin forms on her face. "Stakes?"

"Winner gets to ask the other three questions. *Any* three questions."

Her face lights up. I don't care if she wins. Her winning might actually let me leave faster. But even if I lose, I will still end up with more answers, because in the game, she always reveals more about herself. And I need to know everything about Kai to free us both.

21

KAI

Enzo wants to play.

It seems the only way either of us will share information is through the game. And I'm ready for redemption after the last time we played and I lost.

I'll do anything to get answers. And I've already lost everything, my freedom included, and got nothing in return.

Enzo continues to dry his dripping body off with a towel, feeling free to show me every inch of him.

I don't like being touched, but it doesn't stop my body from aching to be stroked by him. I want to sink my claws into his sculpted abs. I want to outline the mysterious wounds marring his body. Run my tongue over his thick jawline until I taste his salty lips.

"I'll meet you in the bedroom when you're finished getting dressed," I say, turning to leave. If I'm not gaping at him, I won't be as tempted. He doesn't thirst for me anyway. And I don't want him to crave me. If he did, he would have already forced himself on me. And neither my body nor soul could handle it.

"No."

I pause, snapping my head toward him. "Change your mind?" *Please tell me you didn't.* I need more information. Even if I lose, I'll learn more about this strange man. And I'm tired of being alone. Our nights together are our only interaction. And we barely speak one sentence to each other.

The only real conversations I have are with Dr. Miranda and Westcott. Although neither talk about anything other than whether I'm healing or not. I'm tired of being alone. Even if it just means playing a game where we both try to hide the truth.

"We aren't playing in the bedroom," he says.

I gape.

"You will need to leave the bedroom," he continues.

He wants me to get dressed. To wear clothes, so I don't distract him.

"I'm not wearing any clothes," I say defiantly.

He smirks and drops the towel. "Neither am I."

Shit. Why did I think this was a good idea again?

Because now as much as he's going to be tempted by my body, I'm going to be distracted by his. And I can't let it show. I can't let him see my weakness.

Enzo winks at me like he knows the dirty thoughts plaguing my head. And then he strides past with his glorious, godlike body.

I follow, chills running through my body as I walk. My body feels sore and stiff. I haven't left the bedroom in weeks, or has it been months? I've forgotten how long I've been here, unlike when I was taken before and counted every single day.

Being held captive by Enzo isn't that bad, but the loneliness is the same. I still feel like property. I'm still owned.

Enzo just doesn't act on his dark desires as my previous master did.

We step into the hallway single-file. The lights are off, and only the moonlight shines through the window overhead.

We continue in silence down the stairs that are no longer my adversary. The swelling in my ankle has reduced and other than an ache of stiffness, I'm able to keep up with Enzo's quick steps.

My eyes dart around on the first floor, looking for Westcott. I don't know what he does except bring me regular food.

"Westcott's room is separate. He lives in a small cottage on the grounds. He isn't here."

I exhale. I don't know why I care if Westcott is here. He's seen me naked almost every time he's brought me food. It's not about that. It's that this feels different. This game we are playing is ours—our secret. I don't want anyone else to know.

I don't know where we are headed. I have yet to tour the entire house. So when Enzo makes a sharp turn, I suck in my breath as I stand in the double door entrance to a grand room.

He steps inside, but I gawk. Not at his tight bare ass I want to lick, but the room. The room stretches two levels and has floor to ceiling windows that seem to float out over the ocean. Large bookcases line both walls, the kind where you need a ladder to reach the top shelves. The room is dark, and Enzo doesn't turn the light on. The only light illuminating the room is the moonlight, which is more than enough for both of us to see. I've learned that Enzo prefers the night almost as much as I do. Probably because it's easier to attack people in the dark than the light.

"You like books?" I ask, stepping inside.

"No, I hate them," he says stone-faced.

"That would be a lie. I win round one," I say smiling.

He grins as he pulls two chairs up, right next to the window overlooking the sea.

"We should sit back here. That way you're supposed hatred for the books will keep you distracted," I say barely stepping into the room.

He shakes his head. "The ocean can't hurt you."

I cringe, hating that I told him my secret about hating the ocean.

That's the problem with the game. No matter if you win or lose, you always reveal more about yourself.

He takes a seat and waits.

I edge closer, like I'm waiting for a lion to jump out and eat me. I stare at the surf knocking about in an endless calm of rolling waves. We are high above the water. There are panes of glass and several yards between me and the sea.

The water won't hurt me.

I sink into the other chair. I swallow hard, pushing the ache in my throat down.

"This isn't fair you know. You have the advantage."

He raises an eyebrow. "No, it's a fair game."

"How?"

"You are afraid of the ocean. And I'm afraid of you."

I huff. "Afraid of me?"

"Of what I would do if I lost my self-control."

"You mean you would torture me?"

He's silent—*which means yes.*

I look away from him and back to the ocean.

"How you can be more frightened of the ocean than of me, I don't understand."

236

I glare back. "Because all you've ever done is threaten. You threatened to kill me, you sold me, you held me captive, yet you've never once physically hurt me yourself. And although I don't know why, I do know for some reason, you can't hurt me."

He growls and jumps out of his chair, stopping only millimeters from burning my skin.

"Be lucky all you've ever experienced is a threat from me. Trust me; you may be the only human on the planet I've threatened without following through. You think you've experienced pain, but I'm the king of pain."

"You won't hurt me," I spit back.

His eyes trail all over my body. "Not today; I can't promise I won't tomorrow."

He sinks back in his chair.

I tremble a little from the booming voice that just fell silent.

"Let's just play," I say.

He nods.

"Ladies first."

I let my mind still as I think of my lies. I should try to appear sexy, use my body to try and distract him, although he only seems attracted to my injuries because he thinks about how much enjoyment he'd get from breaking me again.

I clear my throat and focus. I want to win. I want my answers. And he won't give me much truth in what he reveals about himself.

"I never want to be touched.

"I enjoy sleeping on the floor.

"I want to fuck you."

His throat growls when I say the last one. His body monitoring mine as if searching for some hint of truth to any of my words, relaxing after seemingly finding what he was looking for.

"My turn," he says.

I nod.

"I'm never letting you go.

"I hate that I let another man hurt you.

"You were taken for six years, not three."

I gasp.

He looks pained—like every word he spoke was fire from his mouth.

Suddenly, my truths and lies no longer matter. Because all I can focus on are Enzo's. *I was taken for six years, not three. How is that possible? It can't be true, can it? It has to be a lie, but then why would it hurt Enzo so much to say it?*

I'm never letting you go is obviously true. He's told me as much before.

And he's also implied that he hates the scars on my body. That he wasn't the one to cause them, because he's a fucking sadist as well as a cruel bastard.

Six years...

I lost three years more than I thought.

Three whole years.

Fuck.

What else was I wrong about?

I ticked off the time in my head so clearly, but I remembered wrong. *Did I block it out? What else don't I remember? What did I get wrong?*

I can't speak, but thankfully Enzo can.

"The third one is your truth, the rest are lies."

He doesn't call me out. He doesn't prolong the inevitable. He doesn't say why he believes that to be true. Or even brag that even though he's my captor, I still want to fuck him.

Just because I want to doesn't mean I will ever act on it. It's just lust after a hot man. Because two-seconds after I want him, I remember all he's done, and I go back to hating him.

"Your turn, Kai."

I could win. Actually, we would tie if we both guessed correctly. I know the truth. They are all truths. I just refuse to say it. Because if I say it, then it makes it true. And it can't be true. None of it can be.

"All of yours are lies," I say unable to meet his eyes, which leaves me looking at his bare feet.

"Kai," he commands.

One word and my head raises.

"Are you sure? That's your choice?"

I nod.

He sighs, knowing I just threw the game.

I narrow my gaze. *Did he want me to win? Well, I can't! I can never win! Because I'll never be free.*

"You win," I whisper. *I lose. I always lose, even when I win.*

22

ENZO

Kai let me win.

Because she can't face the truth. She wishes every word out of my mouth was a lie.

She hates that I care that another man hurt her.

She hates that I've claimed her forever.

And she hates, most of all, that I know something she doesn't. That six years have passed instead of three. That the reason time seemed to move so slowly over the years was because it was standing still for her.

My choice was easy, even if she hadn't thrown the game. I know her well enough to know even though she needs to sleep on the floor, she yearns to find comfort in the soft cloud of fabric covering the bed. Even though she's afraid of my touch, her body begs to feel that exquisite warmth she remembers from our first encounter all those years ago.

Six years ago.

And I saw the way her body heated when she said she wanted to fuck me, I've heard her cries for me to fuck her in her sleep. Those were the hardest words I've heard leave her mouth. It pushed my restraint to the limit. Because I'm desperate—for anything. A touch. A caress. A brush. *Anything*. I need that spark that occurs when cold and heat mix.

I need more.

I need her lips pressed against mine as I suck on her swollen lip. I need her body aligned with mine, writhing beneath me. I need to watch her gasp and moan as I flick her harden nipples between my fingers. And most of all, I want to watch the tears well in her eyes as I spread her wide with my cock. And I want to watch the tears change as her eyes roll back in her head and the pain changes to ecstasy.

Yet I don't get to touch her. She's just desperate for a chance to feel any pleasure after being denied joy for so many years.

I need a drink.

Kai shouldn't drink when she's this weak, but the only way I'll get to drink without her protests is to offer her some too.

So I walk over to the bar cart in the corner. I grab two glasses and pour some scotch into both before I bring the drinks back. I hand one to Kai.

She takes it with shaky hands. She doesn't even focus intently to ensure our hands don't brush as she snatches the glass from my hand. I should have brushed my fingers against hers since she wasn't on guard. That might have been my only opportunity to touch her.

I sigh as I sit and sip mine.

Kai's hands continue to tremble violently as she brings it to her lips. I know she tastes the liquid, but her eyes have glazed over into a blank expression.

I take the glass from her hands and set it down on the floor beside her. Her body is too focused and unsteady for the alcohol at the moment.

"Six years," she whispers.

I want to speak to explain. I want to take away the last six years for her, but I can't. *I want to take it away for myself.*

Finally, her head whips toward mine. "It's been six years since we fell into the ocean off the side of your yacht?"

"Yes."

She closes her eyes harshly, as she sucks in a breath. Her knees come up to her chest, trying to reassure herself.

I could comfort her so easily with a hug. I'm sure a hug would help. But it's not something I'm used to giving, nor have I experienced in recent years.

And then I see why her eyes are closed so tightly. Tears. Tiny droplets are escaping out the side of her eyelids.

I gasp.

Out of everything she's endured, I never imagined she cried. Kai's too proud and strong to let any man see her pain —including me. The only reason I get to see them is because this revelation took her by surprise. She spent her time in captivity trying to remain in control, I'm sure, but now she realizes she was never really in control.

She brushes the tears from her cheeks as they roll down, but no audible sob escapes her lips.

I shake my head, admiring her strength.

I wish I were as strong.

Her eyes open after several minutes pass. The redness in her eyes the only sign remaining that she cried.

"I was taken at sixteen. Just two weeks shy of my seven-teenth birthday. I thought I had only lost three years, but I lost six. So instead of twenty, I'm twenty-three years old."

There is nothing to say, so I say nothing.

"I'm twenty-three." She laughs at herself as if that is the only logical thing to do. Then she looks at me with wildness in her eyes. "Age is nothing but a number. Twenty isn't that different from twenty-three. That's not what makes it hard. It's realizing how long I was gone. How much I endured. How much control I lost."

I disagree. Twenty is very different from twenty-three, at least the three years made a huge difference in my own twenty-four years on this earth, but I won't tell Kai that. She needs to deal with the realization on her own.

She slumps back in her chair, her legs falling back to the floor. Then she turns her attention back to me. "You won. Ask your questions."

And then I realize why she let me win. This answer, finding out she lost more years, was enough for tonight. She can't endure any more truths.

What do I want to know? I get three questions. I start with what I assume will be an easy answer.

"Why do you sleep on the floor instead of the bed?" I assume it has to do with the six years she was taken, but I need confirmation.

Her eyes go blank again. "Because for three—I mean six years—I was never given a bed, pillow or blanket. The floor I slept on was hardwood. Over time I guess my body adapted. Anything else is too soft for me."

I nod. I appreciate the truth, but I need more. And the only way to get more is to push her out of her comfort zone.

"Why don't you like being touched?"

She bites her lip. "Get touched against your will for six years and then tell me how you like other people's touch."

My eyes darken. "There's more to it than that."

She shakes her head. "No, that's it."

"No, that's not it."

"How do you know? You've never been through the torture I have."

"Yes, I have!"

Her eyes widen, our bodies halt, but my voice carries, bouncing off the walls, echoing through the room. We wait for the reverberations to stop.

Her tears threaten again. This is what I need an answer to. *This.* I've finally hit a lie I need the truth of. It's the key to healing her.

"Why don't you like being touched?" I slow my voice.

She looks down, ignoring me.

"Why don't you like being touched, Kai? I've experienced torment before, but it doesn't make you stop hating other people's touch. If anything, it makes you seek it out more. It makes you desperate for pleasure, comfort, love, anything that can erase the pain."

Nothing.

"What happened, Kai?!"

I grab her forearm before I realize what I'm doing.

Kai screams, but I'm not sure if it's from surprise at being grabbed, pain, or pleasure. Her scream carries, as the electricity pulses back and forth between us. Pushing us to the edge of joy before ripping us down with the sharp ache as the heat and cold fight with each other.

I only touch her for a second, before I correct my mistake, but it's enough to know she is definitely hiding the truth from me. Because her reaction is beyond anything normal.

Instead of pushing her again, I change my tactic. "Why come back to the barbarian who sold you?"

She holds her forearm carefully in her other hand, as she stares at the spot where I touched her. A single tear rolls down her cheek.

"Because I am nothing. I can't be healed. They broke me, permanently.

"I used to think someone would save me. My father or

best friend would come and rescue me. I even fantasized you might come and take me away. But when I broke, they said I was free.

"When I came back to Miami, I knew I wasn't. I was alone, surrounded by people who didn't care enough to come for me. I didn't want to go back to them. The only thing that seemed to matter was my need for answers. I risked everything to learn the truth. I risked my life because I already knew no one would save me. I couldn't even save myself. The truth became my everything, but now that I know one truth, I realize the truth isn't worth my life."

More tears fall down her rosy cheeks.

"If you could take our previous game back, where you lost your life to me, you would?"

"Yes."

.

23

KAI

"YOU SAVED YOURSELF, that's how you got free," Enzo says encouraging me despite me never having asked a question, trying to pretend like my life isn't the mess that it is—trying to give me some sense of encouragement.

My eyes glisten with the tears. I didn't cry for six years— hardly a single tear fell. And now, I feel like I can't shut them off for the stupidest of reasons.

"No, I didn't save myself."

"Then, how did you get free?"

I've already told him, but he wasn't listening, or he needs confirmation that the words I spoke were true, and I wasn't exaggerating.

"I was deemed broken. It was a game to them. Jarod wanted to break me, and then the men had no use for me anymore. Jarod said I could be free if I broke, so I broke. And then they dumped me on a park bench."

Enzo curses under his breath. It's beautiful how he feels all of my agony. It makes me more attracted to him than solely his physical allure. It's a stupid thought to think he could be more than a beast.

"Where did they keep you?"

"In a room with no furniture."

"Where?" he asks again.

My eyes flutter down as I think of the yacht and why I hate the water so much. I glance out at the ocean in front of me.

"Okay, no more questions," Enzo sighs.

He stands, and I think I should follow him, but he motions for me to stay seated. So I do.

I hug my knees to my chest again as I try to self-soothe. I wish I could let someone embrace me. I would love to feel comforted again. I look out as the moon rises higher over the sky. I don't know what time it is. Usually, Enzo leaves by this time of night and heads to Surrender or to kill whoever dared to cross him.

I don't know what he's still doing here with me.

A few minutes later, Enzo returns. I gaze at him as a pair of sweatpants now cling to his legs a tray of food in his hands.

Neither of us has worn clothes around each other in weeks. It was a silent protest, a game we both wanted to win when one of us backed down. It seems I at least won one game.

"Come outside with me, Kai."

My eyes widen. My body stiffens at the thought. "No."

"The sun won't warm you as it's not out. And I promise not to toss you into the ocean like before," he smirks trying to lighten the mood. It doesn't exactly work.

I bite my bottom lip. I can't go outside. I'm a prisoner. And I'm afraid. *Can't you see that, Enzo?*

"Do I have to win another round of truth or lies to get you to go outside?"

"No, I hate that game."

He nods.

"Come eat some food and drink some wine on the deck with me," Enzo says.

I can't.

"You can ask me questions while we eat."

It's tempting, but I know what he's not saying. I can ask questions, just not the question I need an answer to.

"Kai," his voice warns. I don't know why he's so insistent on me going outside with him. But I know if I don't go willingly, I will be forced to go. And on some level, I want him to force me. I want to see him as the devil again. Not the man who seems concerned about what happens to me.

And also because I want to feel him touch me again. The last time he did, sparks flew. I wasn't sure if I was experiencing pleasure or complete agony. It was a mix of both. But I could see the potential in the touch. With time, I could crave his touch.

"I'm not going to hurt you, Kai."

"Why?"

He shrugs. "Because I can't. You should be dead. And when you returned, I should have tortured you for information about your master. I should have ensured you weren't a spy. I should have used you and disposed of you a long time ago, but I can't."

"Why?" I whisper again.

"Because you are the only one who could save me."

He doesn't elaborate. He just carries the tray out through the glass window that turns into a swinging door, when he pushes against the pane.

I could run back to my room and lock him out. But I'm tired of being afraid. I won't live in fear. I'm safe, even if I'm only safe because I'm in a new prison with a guard who won't touch me.

My feet touch the rough wood of the deck, and I want to recoil back inside. *Push through; you can do this.*

I take another step. Then another, then another. And then I feel the cool ocean breeze hit me.

I freeze.

The salt is rough against my skin; it tangles in my hair and makes me want to run.

I don't run, but it doesn't mean I can move.

"Sit, Kai. The ocean can't hurt you."

I know his words make sense, but I can't. I can't move.

"Kai, you can do this. Sit."

My legs collapse, and I fall onto the couch outside next to Enzo. Tears stream down my face again.

Dammit!

This isn't what I want. I want to be strong. I want to face my fears with courage, not weakness.

"I'm such a coward."

Enzo growls, forcing my head to look at him.

"You are the strongest fucking person I know. I still don't know the whole story, but I know enough. Don't let anyone, yourself included, ever tell you you are anything but strong."

"All I ever did was survive."

"That's more than anyone else in your position would have been able to do."

I shiver as the cold spritz from the water hits me again. It's windier than I would have expected from inside; the weather looked so clam. Or maybe it's because I haven't felt fresh air in so long that everything feels more intense.

"Do you want a blanket?" Enzo asks, with hope in his voice.

I don't.

"It will protect you from the wind and salt in the air."

"Okay."

He dashes inside and returns with a lightweight blanket before I change my mind. He hands it to me, and I take it. I wrap it around me instinctively and close my eyes as I feel trapped beneath its material.

"Here, I made you a sandwich."

I open my eyes and see what appears to be a grilled cheese sandwich on a paper plate that he removes from the tray on the coffee table in front of us.

I smile. "A grilled cheese sandwich? Are you a chef or something?" I tease.

He smiles back. "Nope, I just decided to fix the worst thing for us. It's all grease, processed bread, and gooey cheese. It is the worst thing for our stomachs, but hopefully, it will put some more weight on your bones."

I frown. "It bothers you how skinny I am, doesn't it?"

"Yes," he hisses.

I take a bite of the grilled cheese; the cheese immediately melts in my mouth before sliding down my throat.

"How does it taste?"

"Better than most of the stuff Westcott has been trying to get me to eat. Except the bacon. I like bacon."

Enzo smiles. "Everyone likes bacon. I'll tell Westcott to add grilled cheese to his menu for you."

I nod and continue to scarf down the sandwich. Maybe if I eat quickly, we can go back inside.

When he's satisfied that I ate my entire sandwich, he pours me a glass of red wine.

I take it and smell it first. I've never had a good glass of wine, but I expect this is more expensive than what most people drink. I've seen enough people smell it first before taking a sip to know that's what you are supposed to do.

I sip. It tastes bitter and dry, but soothing at the same time.

The sadness overcomes me immediately.

"What's wrong? Do you not like the wine? I can get another."

"No, the wine is fine. I just…"

I look up at Enzo. "This is the first time I'm drinking, legally."

He holds out his glass. "To drinking legally as an adult. May we drink smarter than our previous, reckless selves."

He waits, but I don't know what he's waiting for. "You are supposed to clink your glass with mine."

"Oh." My cheeks burn as I clink my glass with his.

Enzo Black, what are you doing to me? My eyes travel up and down his bare chest again, and I give a silent plea for him to find a way through my walls. To make it so he can touch me again. So one day, he can fuck me. And I can find the pleasure I've been missing all these years.

We both sip our glasses, while our bodies yearn to touch. Like a magnet, I feel my body reaching out and trying to join with his. But I'm not brave enough to even brush my hand against him.

"How has work been this week?"

"Huh?" Enzo asks.

"You never talk about work. I don't even really know what being the all-powerful ruler you are means."

"It means I make the rules and all the men follow. It means I make millions of dollars a day. It means I own the underground, the darkest places in Miami and the ocean surrounding. No one takes a foot in this town without me knowing about it."

I nod. "I know that, but what do you do every day? Where do you go?"

"Surrender mostly. That's where I can get information and gather my team to ensure everyone is doing their jobs, which mainly means running the clubs and yachts and protecting those that have paid us for protection. I spend my day looking as menacing as possible, so no one dares defy my rule, and if someone does, I make an example of them."

I sip more wine.

"And women, you can't forget the women who dance all over you and let them fuck you at night," I force a smile to my face as I say the words that hurt more than they should.

Enzo isn't yours. He can fuck whoever he wants. And even if he were yours, he shouldn't be. You can't forgive him for selling you.

"Yes, the women make the job more enjoyable," his jaw hardens as he speaks.

"Ever had a serious girlfriend or someone you considered making Mrs. Dangerous?"

"No."

"Why not?"

"Because there will never be a Mrs."

"It seems a King needs his Queen."

"Not this King."

I take a long swallow and finish the wine in my glass. I hold it out, and Enzo pours more into my glass.

"You should come with me," he says suddenly.

"Go with you?"

"To Surrender. It would be good for you. It would help you heal faster."

"How would watching naked women dance on the most disgusting vile men help me?"

"Because you need to face your fears to heal."

"I'm not afraid of Surrender."

"No, you're not. But you are afraid of clothes and light and going outside. I'm sure being around strange men isn't exactly your idea of a great day either. You need to push yourself to heal."

"You trust me enough to go and not run away?"

"No, I don't trust you. Try running and see what happens."

"That sounds like a threat you will never follow through on."

He smirks. "Maybe I won't, but Langston will."

"Fine. As long as I don't have to strip, I'll come with you."

He laughs. "You walk around naked all the time in front of me and anyone else who enters my house. Why would stripping be so bad?"

I laugh. "I guess it wouldn't. My strip show would end quickly though since I'm already naked."

We both laugh at the ridiculousness. And then Enzo's gaze turns serious.

"Stop looking at me like that," he says.

"Like what?"

"Like you want me to take you to bed and pound you until you come screaming."

"I'm not looking at you like that."

"Liar."

"I'm not."

He sighs. "I will never fuck you, Kai. I will do my best to never touch you. I can't have you, Kai. I will ruin you."

"I'm already ruined."

He reaches his hand out.

I freeze.

He stops short of stroking my black hair like I want.

"No, you're not ruined. You're just hurt. You're just in

pain. Someday soon you will break free of the walls you put up to protect yourself. And when you do, you'll realize just how amazing you are."

I try to cling to his words, but I can't. My eyes are growing heavy. I just slept almost eight hours. I shouldn't be so tired, but I am. So, so tired. My body starts loosening like jello, and I fall into a heavy pile on the couch.

24

ENZO

I TIGHTEN the rope around Kai's wrist. She moans as the sharp pain digs into her flesh.

My eyes glaze at the sight, knowing she'll wear a bright red scar tomorrow because of me.

I stand back and admire my work. Kai is spread eagle on my bed. Her arms and legs are tied by a crude rope to the bedposts. My tie is around her mouth so she can't speak.

She doesn't move, but her eyes beg me—don't hurt me.

I'll do my best princess. The pleasure will be worth any pain.

She swallows hard, her neck muscles flexing as her saliva slides down her throat.

My eyes can't stop soaking her in. Her hardened nipples are begging to be licked. Her stomach has flattened, preparing for my kisses. And her pussy is dripping with anticipation.

And then I see the scars...

On her neck, her breasts, her stomach, her legs. They are everywhere. Reminding me of what I gave up. I let another man touch her.

Wild hunger stirs deep inside me. I don't know why I've

waited all these weeks to touch her. I'm hungry and desperate for her, and her body is more than ready for me.

I climb up on the bed and settle between her legs, careful not to touch her. I want our bodies to connect in one swift movement as I slide inside her. I want an explosion.

I warn her with my eyes, and she braces herself on the bed but doesn't tell me to stop. She wants this.

I grab her hips and slam my cock into her body in one long stroke.

Damn, she's tight. So fucking tight.

"Jesus, Kai. I've never felt anything this tiny, this chilling to my bone, this comforting." Her pussy molds to my cock in cool perfection. Christ, even her pussy is cold compared to my skin. *But it's the perfect balance for me.*

She sucks in a rough breath through her nose; her whole body is tense. I've hurt her.

I've hurt her.

I need to stop. Give her time to adjust.

Stop, I can stop. I'm self-control. I'm not a monster.

I stop, but then her pussy tightens, a soft cry escapes her throat, and a tear trickles down her precious face. Any normal man would stop seeing her react like that, but I'm not normal. I was raised by the devil and revel in the darkness. So instead, I lose myself.

I pump hard, my full-length inside her.

Her gentle tears turn to streams. She's fighting inside, trying to get me off her, trying to make me stop.

But now that I've started, I can't stop. I won't stop. Not until I've destroyed her.

In.

Out.

Harder.

Faster.

Her tears are spilling from her eyes, but I need more. I love to see her in pain, knowing I'm the one to give her that experience. I'm the only one who gets her tears.

"Cry for me, baby. Beg for me."

"Stop."

"Yes, just like that."

"Stop, Enzo. Please."

I freeze, staring at her mouth still tied up. She can't talk. It's not possible. But I know I heard her speak.

"Please."

————

I open my eyes.

"Enzo," Kai whispers in her sleep on the floor in her usual spot in the corner of my bedroom.

It was a dream.

My body is pressed against her as I hump her leg like a sixteen-year-old horny boy.

Shit.

I scurry away, shocked that I haven't woken her up. I'm a sick, disgusting prick. My dream alone is reason why I can never touch her, or permit myself to fuck her even once. I'm not a good man.

I remember last night. How many secrets were revealed, and how many more are left to say.

She passed out so easily. At least this time I don't think it was from exhaustion. She's just a lightweight after not drinking alcohol for years and having lost so much weight.

But it gave me another excuse to carry her to bed. Well, the floor since she won't sleep in a bed.

But I can't even carry her anymore if this is the result— me humping her while dreaming of torturing her.

I'm sick.

I need to find a way to get her out of my life quickly before I do more damage than I've already done. She doesn't deserve any more pain.

I stare down at her still sleeping body. She reaches out like she's trying to grab something, but I'm no longer there for her to grab onto.

It's for the better, Kai. You don't want me. Maybe before, if we had fucked on that yacht before she was taken. *No, she was too young then.* She wasn't ready to be fucked.

If she hadn't been taken by a man as sadistic as I am, then maybe I would have a chance. She could learn to enjoy how twisted I am in bed. Many women before her have enjoyed my sick fantasies. But Kai never will. She's been through too much. She will always see me as the same monsters as them.

Kai was a virgin. She'd never been with a man. Never even been kissed before I hurt her.

It makes me nauseous knowing her first time was with a man set on breaking her. And I was the catalyst to that happening. I'm the reason she isn't still cleaning boats and stealing to make enough money to eat.

Either way her life would have sucked, but not as bad as now. I took her innocence and gave it to a man who didn't deserve her.

And now she's lost.

Destined to break beyond repair if I don't get her away from me.

"Are we going to Surrender today?" she asks with big eyes.

I don't know how long she's been awake, but I don't know what to say. I don't want her to come to the club with me. I can't be around her. But I told her to come. She needs to heal; that's my best plan for being able to leave her—by continuing to lie.

"Yes."

She fidgets with her fingers.

"We will leave in twenty minutes. You need to get dressed."

I walk into the bathroom, grab one of my suits, and then head to one of the other bathrooms to get ready. I can't be near her. I can't help her put clothes on. I doubt she will wear anything suitable to go out in public in any way. I'll just tell her she has to stay, and I'll deal with her a different day.

I glance at my watch after twenty minutes exactly have passed.

"I'm leaving. You ready?" I shout up the stairs. I continue fidgeting with the watch, remembering the one Kai stole when I hear her footsteps stomping down the stairs. Even as light as she is, she has no idea how to be quiet on her feet.

I look up when her feet still in front of me.

"Fuck," I curse.

"That bad?" she asks.

I don't know what to say. I thought at most she'd wear a loose T-shirt. Maybe she'd find an oversized dress I had Westcott pick out to fill her closet. But I didn't expect this.

Kai is dressed in tight dark jeans, a flowy black halter top that pushes her boobs up, and strappy heels. She's not wearing any makeup, but she's combed her hair into shiny tendrils framing her face in dark lines.

"I couldn't find any makeup, and my hair could use a trim, but I thought I looked alr—"

"You look beautiful, Kai. You don't need makeup or anything at all, but I'll make sure Westcott buys you some before your next outing."

She smiles with a nervous lip.

"You going to be able to walk in those shoes?"

"I didn't figure I'd be walking far."

"You never know when you'll need to run away from danger at Surrender." *Or me.*

If she would find a way to disappear, then I could let her go. I'm just not sure she's strong enough to leave alone.

She follows me to the garage and hops in my Porsche without waiting for me to tell her to. It's like something has changed in her overnight. She's tired of living scared. It's like knowing that more of her life was taken than she realized made her want to start living her life now instead of waiting.

I'm in my own head on the drive over, trying to decide why I want her at the club.

Because Surrender is where the truth will eventually come out—whether that's today or a year from now. Eventually, she will learn the truth here.

I pull up outside the back entrance to the club. No one knows of this entrance but me, and now Kai. Everyone else enters through the single entrance at the front.

"Ready for this?" I ask.

"I don't know. I'm guessing I will pass out in fear and you'll have to carry me home again."

"Please don't do that."

"Why?"

"Just don't. I won't push you. If you need a break, just tell me or Langston or Zeke, and we will find a private room for you by yourself."

"No, push me. I need to be pushed to heal."

I lead her inside. Through the dark hallways that only she and I can see in. It's nice not to have to touch her to lead her or turn on a light. I prefer the black.

We walk to one of the main public rooms, and I find Langston prowling.

Kai stalks in behind me, holding her head up and proud.

"Katherine, would you like a drink?" I ask using her true name instead of the one people might recognize here as the dead coming back to life.

"Sure," she says.

She doesn't tell me what she wants to drink, but I decide something light like champagne that she hopefully won't drink too quickly. It's more for her to have something to hold and be more comfortable. I give Langston a look to watch her before I retrieve our drinks.

I grab her champagne and me a whiskey. When I turn back around to give her her drink, I see Langston reaching his hand out to touch her.

I drop the glasses and run to her. Her body is frozen in fear at the looming touch.

I don't know how I reach them just in time. I don't know how to stop Langston except to tackle him to the ground, so that's what I do.

"What the hell?" Langston wrestles me, trying to push me off him.

All eyes in the club are on us.

"Sorry," I say, before I throw a punch at his face. I need to send a clear signal no one touches Katherine. And even though I stopped Langston, I need everyone else in the club to keep their distance. So the punch was necessary.

"No one hits on my girl. You hear me—Katherine is mine," I yell, making it clear why I hit him, even though he's my best friend, and what will happen if anyone else touches her.

I stand up and wipe the sweat from my knuckles. I give

Kai a look and walk out of the room. Turns out it wasn't Kai who would need to go cool off in another room; I needed it.

I leave her with Langston without explanation. She's free to wander. But she won't run or escape. As much as she wants freedom, I saw the look on her face when I punched Langston—thanks and relief. She's come a long way, but she's still terrified of the world. She won't leave, because she feels safe with me, the monster she knows. That's a mistake.

25

KAI

I hate Enzo.

I can say that with certainty now.

Hate.

I hate the contradictory feelings he stirs inside me.

I hate that he is the only person who I can truly talk to.

I hate how he makes me lust after his muscular body.

I hate that he tries to heal me, never allowing me to stay broken.

I hate that he protected me from a single touch by acting like a jealous lover.

But most of all, I hate that no matter what he does, it will never be enough for me to forgive.

My heart has blackened because of him. My soul tormented, and my body changed. I'm thankful that he spared my life, although the consequences he faced for that seem inconsequential. But I can never forgive him for selling me.

It doesn't seem Enzo does any of these things because he expects my forgiveness. More like it's a meticulous plan that will somehow end in me out of his life again.

Despite how I hate Enzo, my heart softens every time he does something to save or protect me. And he just saved a night or possibly weeks of pain by preventing Langston from touching me. And my stupid heart likes Enzo more than it should for protecting me from that pain.

Enzo stormed off without a word to Langston or me. All eyes in the club are on us. It's a strange feeling, after being alone for so many years. I'm not used to so many people in one room, especially when all the attention is on me. But I refuse to show weakness. Or hide the scars or marks on my body.

I want to chase after Enzo and find out why he prevented Langston from touching me. And why he stormed off afterward. He brought me here to push me, to heal me faster. He thought that would happen sooner if he made me face my fears.

"Are you okay?" I bend down to ask Langston, who is still lying on the floor in shock.

Langston nods slowly, as he stares at me with large eyes. He stands up quickly, and I give him a wide berth, so he doesn't touch me. Langston gives one look to the crowd, and the stares stop, the voices begin again, and the dancers continue as if the last few moments didn't happen.

"I'll get you some ice for your face," I say.

"No, I can't show weakness."

I study his eye; it doesn't look too bad right now. But it will swell up and blacken my morning.

"I'm sorry," I say.

"Why are you sorry? You weren't the one who hit me. I just didn't realize you and Enzo had gotten so serious so fast. Enzo isn't exactly the dating type."

I snort. "We aren't together."

Langston frowns as his eyes dart around the room at

men who are most likely listening to our conversation. "Follow me."

He walks down a hallway to a locked door, buried in the depths of the club, but not as far as Enzo's office. Langston unlocks the door and then steps inside. I follow while keeping my distance. I shut the door behind me.

The room is small compared to Enzo's office, but Langston's office appears more for regular work than Enzo's. Langston's has a desk, laptop, papers, and a small seating area. But Langston doesn't sit down. Instead, he walks over to a mini-fridge in the corner where there is a bar setup. He opens the freezer and pulls out a bag of peas, placing it over his eye.

I try to hide my smile, but I can't. "You a big fan of peas or does this happen often?"

He walks over to the rolling chair behind his desk and slumps down, as he continues to hold the frozen peas to his face.

"In my line of work, this happens often—although Enzo isn't usually the one throwing the punches at me." Langston pauses, studying me as if trying to understand who I am and what I'm doing in here.

"Should I call you Katherine or Kai?"

I shrug. "Ask Enzo."

My feet are aching from standing, and the only seats in the room are the small couches in the corner, not close enough to talk to Langston. He notices my stares and gets up from behind his desk; he collapses down on one of the couches in a lump of pain. His head is obviously throbbing. He wouldn't crumble in such exhaustion from a simple punch if it didn't have force behind it. I know the difference between a weak punch and one with the full weight of a body behind it.

I walk to the other couch, but I'm not used to my heels and my feet are already twinging. I step, and the heel moves out from under me, causing me to stumble.

Langston reaches his arm out to catch me. I see it the split second before I would crash into his hand. But I can't let him touch me. I contort my body and fall away from his hand to the floor.

We both stare openly at my reaction to his almost touch.

"What is going on? Why don't you like to be touched?"

My eyes drift down to the now visible marks on my arms and chest, my clothes not hiding them this time. This time when I entered this club, I didn't want to hide behind my clothes.

"You know why. You saw me that day naked. You saw how broken my body was and how it continues to be. It shouldn't come as a surprise that I don't like to be touched."

"No, I guess not. It still doesn't explain who you are or what you are doing in Enzo's life."

I settle myself on the floor and lean against the couch rather than sitting on it. The floor is more comfortable for me anyway.

"If you figure out what I'm doing here, let me know."

Langston continues to study me with his one good eye. "Enzo and I have been friends a long time. We've both taken bullets for each other. Committed the worst sins together. Trust me; I will learn why you are here. So you might as well tell me now and save me the trouble."

I cross my arms as anger floods my eyes. "You want to know what I'm doing here! It started six years ago. Enzo was looking for someone by the name of Kai Miller. *Me*. He was sent by his father to kill me. Except when it came down to it, he couldn't do it. He didn't kill me. Instead, he had me kidnapped and sold. A few weeks ago, I was returned to

Miami. I was pissed and went in search of Enzo. I wanted to know why. We played a game of truth or lies. I lost. Now I'm forced to live my life as his prisoner. That's why I'm here, because I lost a stupid game. And I will never understand why."

Langston freezes as I tell my tale. I hope he has the answers. He will be able to tell me why, if he knows Enzo as well as he claims. Langston should know why Enzo's father ordered him to kill me.

Langston's mouth eventually drops as he realizes the truth. He knows my answers.

"Why? Why was I ordered to be killed?"

A knock followed by a head poking through the door halts our conversation.

"Langston, there has been a security breach," a man says while entering Langston's office. I don't recognize him. I haven't met him before.

Langston stands, dropping the bag of peas on the coffee table as he starts walking to handle the issue.

"Langston? Answer me?"

He stops at the door and turns and faces me.

"Please," I beg.

His lips thin as he stares like he's seeing a ghost. "It's not my truth to tell. I'm sorry."

And then he's gone.

I slump, my shoulders rounding over my chest.

Now what?

Enzo won't tell me. Langston won't answer me. But someone in this club knows my answers. I just have to find the man willing to answer me. I'm not going to wait here for the men to return. I'm going to get my answers.

I force myself up onto wobbly legs. I really shouldn't have worn these heels, but I knew after the last time I came here that I wanted to look my best. I wanted to fit in, instead of standing out.

I make it to the hallway, but I have no idea where to wander. I know where Enzo will be. I remember the string of corridors that lead to his lair, but do I want to find him?

I start walking, being drawn this way or that way, not thinking as I walk, just feeling and letting my body wander through the hallways. The hallways are mostly dark, and occasionally I'll walk by a room that is lit up and noisy. I walk by the entrances quickly, not ready to be in the throws of large groups of people again. If I'm going to get my answers, I'm going to need to do it one on one.

Slowly, I realize I am indeed headed toward Enzo's office. I stop just outside the solid door to his office that is now closed. I consider knocking, but that doesn't feel right.

I grab the handle, just as I hear sounds behind the door.

I pause my hand on the door as I listen, hoping to catch the end of a conversation Enzo is having. Hopefully, a discussion that will give me answers.

But I don't hear words.

Moans escape through the cracks in the door. Then panting.

Sounds I would only recognize in my dreams.

I squeeze my eyes shut, trying to keep the tears in my eyes. I manage to keep them on the edge of my eyelashes.

I shouldn't be upset that Enzo is inside fucking a whore. He has every right. He's not mine, and I don't want him to be.

I just don't like that he gets to experience any amusement after what he did to me.

My hand tightens again on the door handle. I should leave and find a man who might talk. I'm sure there are plenty of drunks around here that would be willing to spill

Enzo's secrets with the right persuasion. But I can't. I'm too focused on what's happening behind the door.

I turn the handle slowly and crack the door open. My eyes focus in on the dark room and the shadows moving on the lavish couch. Enzo and his whore don't notice me.

Maybe Enzo does, but he doesn't care that I'm watching.

I don't have to step inside to see, I can see just fine through the dark slit in the door.

I see Enzo flip the woman over, spreading her legs wide, her ass in the air. He pushes his pants down and then sinks his cock inside her. He gathers her hair into a ponytail at the back of her head and pulls hard as he fucks her.

He's brutal with his thrusts, just as I would expect. He doesn't kiss her or caress her in any way. He takes what he wants without considering how it makes her feel—like a whore.

They both pant and moan as their naked, writhing bodies collide. I can hear their skin slapping together. His ass tightens as he pushes himself deeper inside.

"Sweet Jesus," she moans.

I don't know how his movements feel good to her. He's pounding into her so hard; he must be bruising her insides. But her soft cries of delight tell a different tale.

My mouth parts as his tongue licks over her ear, whispering dirty words as he fills her cunt.

I remember his tongue, how commanding and deep it went into my mouth, how he could make me drip between my legs from just his tongue on my lips.

He grabs her hips harder as her body jerks backward against his. And I remember how his hand felt against my stomach as our bodies hardened against each other, both resisting and begging to be connected together.

And then he grabs her neck—just like he did me. He

squeezes, although not to snuff out her life as he tried with me all those years ago. More to heighten her senses, to demonstrate his power, and her relinquish her control to him. Because that is what he needs above all else. Power and control.

Why would I ever dream about a man like Enzo? She may be enjoying herself, but it's not from what he's doing. He's taking what he wants without giving back. He's just like the men who took me.

I can't keep watching, but I can't tear myself away. Instead, a single tear falls at the loss of something I can never have.

"I never took you for a voyeur," Enzo's voice booms behind me.

I jump. Enzo isn't fucking the woman on the couch. He's standing behind me, and the fact that it brings me any relief at all burns me to my core.

26

ENZO

I lost control.

I never fucking lose control. And now I've done it twice in a span of twenty minutes.

I punched Langston, something I haven't done since we were kids and wrestling around testing our strength. It needed to be done. And it helps my image at the club; the men respect brute force. But I haven't had to use my muscles like that in the club in a while.

What I did after though was a complete loss of myself. I walked off in a whirlwind of rage, thinking after a stiff drink and time alone, I would be better. Composed, back to my usual controlled self.

Instead, I spiraled.

I drank four glasses of whiskey. I haven't drunk that quickly since I was a teenager. I needed to take the edge off of the restless feeling stirring in my chest. But the drinks did nothing to calm the wild storm brewing inside me.

Instead, I went to my private bedroom. I laid on my bed, took my cock out, and jacked off to the thought of Kai.

There are dozens of women, scantily clad throughout

this club. Any one of them would love the pleasure of being mine tonight. And they would do more than be mine, if I paid them well for their time with me. Most nights if I needed a woman, I'd have Zeke select one for me. She would be paid well for her time with me, although no woman ever complained about how I treated them in bed. Every woman I've been with would have let me fuck them for nothing. No money was needed, but the money bought me a sense of protection from the expectation of more. It also let me have my way with them because I was paying for the night.

But I saw the way the women I fucked looked at me. With eyes of lust when they saw my sharp muscles and rugged body. They are used to entertaining men, most of the men in the club are older, ragged with life experiences. They are wealthy, dangerous men, but the women never fear, because they know I protect them. I protect all of them. If a single woman were ever hurt in one of my clubs, the bastards that touched them would die for their mistake.

The women see me as their salvation. A way to make money they never could otherwise. I'm their defender and savior. And if they get selected to spend a night with me, they see it as winning a prize. I pay them more for a night than they earn here in a year. And I pay them well for a year's worth of work.

They think I'm a saint compared to the other men. They're wrong. I'm worse because I'm the only one with the power to save them, but I don't.

I fuck them. Give them the best night of their life. One filled with passion, pushing their limits as they take my large cock in every orifice.

And then I leave, treating them like whores. Not because I think of them that way, but because I will never date. Never marry. Never have anything more than one night.

Ever.

But I haven't had any of the women in the club in weeks. Not since Kai stumbled back into my life.

I don't understand the pull she has over me. Maybe it's because she is the only one who threatens everything I've worked to obtain. She could destroy me. And being with someone who has that kind of power over me is thrilling. It terrifies and excites me. Pushes me, and that is something I rarely experience.

So I slid my thick, rock hard cock into my hand and pretended it was Kai's lips wrapped around it instead. I came hard on my bare stomach. But it wasn't enough. I immediately fisted myself again, imagining it was her pussy I was sinking into, which wasn't hard to visualize since I've seen her naked more than I've seen her clothed. Her thin legs wrapped around my waist, and though frail, digging into me with all her might. Her fingers clawing as her legs squeezed me tight. I would drown in her body, our heavy breathing outpacing our flowing blood. I would fuck her until I simultaneously pulled a tear-filled cry and a rippling orgasm from her body. Only then would I slam my cum deep into her and adorn her with her first moment of pleasure during sex.

I came again, imaging her battered body surrendering to mine for the first time. Her eyes glittered with overcoming joy and terror at letting me be the one to show her the beauty of fucking.

When I was finished, I cleaned myself off and went in search of Langston to chew him out. He's the reason I lost control. Seeing him with her brought me to my weakest point.

Instead of finding Langston, I found her.

Kai was standing in the darkness at the door to my office. The door was cracked, and her body was stiff as she stared inside.

I heard the familiar sound of panting and heaving as two bodies fucked. It's a regular sound in a place like this—expected even.

But I could understand what it might trigger in a woman like Kai, one who only associates sex with suffering.

And I know exactly who is behind the door she's listening to. *Zeke.*

Fucking bastard.

I really need to get him a bigger office with a couch or bed. That way he'll stop bringing women into my room.

"I never took you for a voyeur," I say.

Kai exhales, as if she'd been holding the world inside as she watched. Like hearing my voice shook her to her core.

I narrow my eyes, as I study her features in the dark. Luckily, I can see so well in the night because I see the glistening on her cheek—wetness from crying. But it's like all her tears were sucked back up when she heard my voice.

My voice saved her.

I stare back at my friend and his hookup for tonight.

She's not upset because she is watching a man fuck a woman. She's not imagining that it's her or he's fucking her against her will.

She's upset because she thinks the man was me.

"I was looking for you," she says, finding her voice. It's gruff and laced with desire.

"I see that."

We are both quiet, listening to the muffled sounds of sex.

"Jealous?"

"Of what?" she asks.

"The woman," I nod in the direction. "Do you miss getting fucked daily?"

She slaps me.

And I deserve it. My words were harsh and cruel. But I need her to hate me, to be afraid of me, and keep her distance. Because I'm losing my battle at keeping her away from me, and cruelty is the only thing she will respond to. I've been too kind these last few weeks; I've begun to let her into my world. And it has to stop.

Her touch continues to sends sparks. It was a brief inter-action of our skin, but I'm dizzy with the aftershocks, the tingling her flesh offers. It was the first time she touched me willingly. And I almost want to make a snide comment again just to feel her hand against my face, no matter how sharp the sting on my face.

"Rape isn't fucking," she says.

When I gaze at her again, my eyes are heavy with tension.

"I was only pointing out you must have needs. Wants. Desires. You need to heal. And at this club, you can find whatever man you want to fulfill you. You're not ready yet, but if you want to heal, you need to find that man."

"I'm not going to find a man to fuck in your sex club."

"This isn't a sex club."

She rolls her eyes. "Yes, it is."

I resist the urge to move in on her and box her in with my body and capture her wrists. "No, one of the purposes of this club is sex, but more importantly this is a place where business and pleasure mix. Men come here for a good time, yes, but more importantly they come to meet other men who can assist them in their endeavors. They try to befriend me, so I might be in debt to them and owe them a favor."

"And the women? What do they get other than being whored out?"

"Protection. Safety. Money. Everything they desire."

"As long as they sell themselves."

I shake my head. "The women don't see it that way. They might be desperate when they come to work for me, but they live like queens. Worshiped and wanted. They are never forced to fuck or even touch a man. They don't even have to dance. They can simply serve liquor and get paid a six-figure salary to work for me."

She gasps.

I close the door to my office. I'll deal with Zeke fucking in my office later.

"You can't hide your secret lust from me. I see it as plain as I can see your tits in my mind. I've seen the look too many times not to notice."

She glares.

"There is no shame in feeling lust. Just because your innocence was taken doesn't mean you stop wanting to find the joy in a good lay. It's not sick or twisted. I'm the sick one, not you," I say.

"I agree; you're sick."

"I am, so stop looking at me like I could save you. I can't. Not with protection. Not with my body. Not at all."

"I know you can't save me from the demons that haunt me; nobody can. And even if I get better, I'm still a prisoner in your home with no hope to work off my debt."

My eyes darken. I can think of plenty of ways she could work off her debt to me.

"Langston will drive you home. The club was too much for you. From now on, you can stay a prisoner in my house," I say, my jaw clenching as I say the word *prisoner*. But that's what she is, until I release her. Or someone else figures out the truth.

"Why not you?"

"Because I have work to do. And Langston owes me."

"Thank you for stopping Langston," her words explode out of her in a whisper.

I huff. "You obviously haven't learned anything if you are thanking me. I'm not your protector, Kai. You should know by now that I could set you free; I just never will."

And then I walk away, despite my urges to stay. To drag her into a spare room and make her realize what it's like to be fucked and enjoy it.

I feel her staring as I round the corner. *I can't save you, but you can save us both.*

27

KAI

ENZO SAID I need to have sex in order to heal. I need a man to pleasure me. That's the only way to truly get over my fears.

I'm sure he's right, but I can barely tolerate clothes, I can't sleep in a bed, I hate the sunlight. I'm not ready for sex. I don't think I'll ever be.

I stand frozen in my spot after Enzo leaves me at the closed door to his office. I can't believe I thought the man in the room was Enzo. I can't believe I cared, but I do. I'm not even sure I'm jealous because I want Enzo to be the one fucking me. I'm clearly not ready for sex. I just don't want him fucking anyone.

If I'm his possession, then I want him to be mine. But it doesn't work that way. Only one of us gets to be the object, the other a person with a life.

"Katherine," Langston says cautiously from behind me.

I turn, and it's clear from his stoic expression he's been given orders from Enzo. I'm now Katherine instead of Kai. *Why am I Katherine here? What does my name mean? If I spoke my name aloud to the men in this club, what would happen?*

"Are you ready to go home?" he asks.

Home.

Enzo's place is anything but home. I don't have a home. Even if Enzo would let me go, I don't know what I'd do. I don't have a high school diploma. I have no money, no experience, and I can't even tolerate being touched. I don't know how I'd get food if I were truly free. I should be thankful Enzo keeps me, even if I don't understand the purpose.

I nod.

Langston leads me out the front, but not through the crowded rooms at the entrance. Through the door and outside into the night, he doesn't walk slowly or wait for me at all as we stride down the street. My feet ache in the shoes. I feel the flicker of early light, as the sun slowly begins to rise. *How is it already almost morning?*

I'm exhausted. The night was long, even though the time spent away from the house was relatively short.

Langston stops in front of a Maserati and opens the door. I slide into the passenger side before he hops into his side.

My heart races fast, my palms sweat, and my pupils dilate as Langston eases onto the road. Driving here was easier with Enzo at the wheel, but I don't know Langston, I don't trust him. But Enzo didn't offer to drive me home. Because I'm nothing to him. I need to remember that even when he offers me a brief moment of kindness.

I close my eyes to try to block out the car ride. My plan works, because we arrive at Enzo's house before dawn breaks.

Langston hesitates as the car idles, he's looking at me. And as much as I want to run out of this car and into the safety of the house, to my room, I don't. I can tell from Langston's hurried breath he wants to say something to me, but he's not sure how to say it. I wait, hoping it will give me some insight into Enzo, the man they all call Black.

"Be careful."

I narrow my gaze. "Careful?"

"Yes, careful. This is a dangerous world you are now a part of. Black may be a king. He may rule all, but Enzo is different than the man he portrays at Surrender. He's frailer than you realize. Don't hurt him."

"Don't hurt him! Are you serious? Shouldn't you be telling him not to hurt me?"

Langston looks me over. "It doesn't appear you have been hurt in weeks. Enzo is helping you, not hurting you."

"I wouldn't say keeping me as a prisoner is helping."

He leans across me, and I freeze trying to keep my chest from bumping against his arm. He's careful not to touch me as well. He opens my door.

"Then leave. Go. Be free. I won't stop you. Enzo won't stop you."

He smiles smugly when I don't move. "That's what I thought. You need him to survive. So stop thinking of your-self as a prisoner. You're as much a prisoner as Enzo is."

I frown, and then I realize Langston thinks of Enzo as a prisoner as well. *To what, I don't know? His father? His job? What?*

Slowly, I step out and walk inside. Langston waits until I close the door before he speeds off.

Westcott welcomes me with a smile. "Can I get you a coffee or tea? Some breakfast maybe?"

Does the man sleep? Why is he up so early? And hasn't he realized it's not morning for me? The sun is up, which means it's time for bed.

Except, I don't know when or if Enzo is coming home. He seemed pissed off the last time I saw him. He may leave again for weeks just to avoid me. And I haven't slept alone on the floor in weeks.

I scrunch up my nose at the thought of tea or coffee. "No, I'll just be in my room."

I practically run to the stairs before I kick out of my heels, leaving them on the floor as I dash up the stairs. I get to the bedroom and slam the door shut. I lock the six locks Enzo had installed again. And then I begin to strip the constricting clothes off. When I'm free of them, I sigh.

No.

I need to continue to make progress. I lost six years. I need to make up for it. Get my life back.

But I'm tired of wearing tight jeans. So I walk to the closet and let my hand stride over the fabric. Half of the closet is filled with Enzo's suits, jeans, hoodies, and sweat-pants. The other half is filled with clothes I'll never wear. Dresses, jeans, skirts. I tolerated the jeans, pushing myself. I need to settle now on wearing clothes, any clothes. Something I can sleep in.

I pull the largest T-shirt on my side of the closet I can find, and I slip it on. It hangs down to my knees.

It's a start.

I walk back to the bedroom and stare at the bed. It still looks like the most uninviting thing.

One step at a time. Today I wear clothes. I went out in public. Soon I can try the bed again.

I stare at the blackout curtains blocking the sunlight. *Maybe just one more step?*

I walk to the curtain, grip the edge, pull it open and let the light in. I lean against the window forcing myself to feel the warmth, forgetting some windows in the house turn into a door when the appropriate pressure is applied. The window falls open, and my body trips out onto the balcony.

I wince as the brightness of the sun burns my eyes. It's so fucking sunny. But it's warm and relaxing at the same time.

Just five minutes. I'm already out here. *Five minutes.* Tomorrow it will be six, then seven, then eight. *I will get my life back; I'm not a prisoner.*

There is a couch with a small table and chairs on the balcony. I want to sit on the hard chair, but I choose the soft couch. I curl my legs up, compelling myself to try and get comfortable.

Four minutes. Just four more minutes.

I am strong.

I am not broken.

I can heal myself.

I don't need Enzo.

I don't need anyone.

I close my eyes, trying to block out some of the sun's rays.

But my body shakes at the heat. I shift in my seat trying to get comfortable. I grab the hem of the shirt I want to rip from my body. It itches and scratches, driving me mad.

I try to adapt to my old ways. Shutting everything out. Squeezing my fists to the point of pain to distract myself. Counting. Blocking. Guarding. None of it works.

Enzo.

I know it's the one that will work, because it's what saved me time after time. There is nothing wrong with it. Fantasizing about him doesn't make me sick. It's just because he's the only man in my life. The only man who hasn't physically hurt me.

That's not true—Mason didn't hurt me either. But I'm not attracted to Mason like I am Enzo. He doesn't have that rugged, beckoning, mysterious look Enzo has. Enzo is the only boy I've ever kissed. He's the only one whom I can imagine.

————

Kiss me.

His lips brush against mine, stopping just shy of giving me what I fully want.

Kiss me, *I say in my head again.*

This time, he doesn't resist. His lips devour me; his tongue slips deep inside, threatening a groan to escape my throat. I hold the sound in, not ready to show him how much pleasure a simple kiss gives me.

More.

He tangles my hair in his fist as our bodies rub against each other. I shift my weight, pressing my body closer.

Want me, fuck me.

He pushes me back, and I fall against the soft fabric of the couch. His dangerous eyes leaving me dazed as he exposes me, pushing up my shirt.

"*Touch yourself,*" he says.

I nod.

I want this. *The fire between my legs is begging to be touched, stroked until I explode.* I need this.

I slide my hands down between my legs.

"*Like this?*"

"*Yes baby, just like that.*"

I begin rubbing slowly over my swollen nub. Small circles and then bigger, I move my fingers, stroking faster. And then I reach inside, pulling some of my liquid out, and drag it over my clit, intensifying the feeling.

Yes, God, yes. *This is what I've been missing—an orgasm to pull me from my shell.*

"*Faster,*" *Enzo commands.*

I do as he says. I can feel myself growing with need and tingles ripple through my body heating me and bringing me closer to the edge I seek.

I look up at Enzo with heavy eyes, I'm close, but I need his help to get me to the brink.

"*Your turn,*" *I say.*

He frowns, looking at me with disgust.

I stop. "*What's wrong?*"

"*Why would I want to fuck a whore like you? You're disgusting. You have no curves. Your skin is battered, permanently. You have no fight left. No man will ever want to touch such a revolting whore like you.*"

I pant heavily. No, I'm good enough. Touch me!

"*No.*"

—————

I jolt, my eyes waking from the fantasy I was playing in my head. I breathe recklessly in and out, knowing I can't get enough oxygen to calm my body any time in this century.

I stare down at my body wide-eyed, which doesn't help my anxiety. My hand had slipped between my legs, trying to act out the fantasy. Of all the times I've imagined Enzo in my head, I've never attempted to act it out. That's what went wrong.

I can't tolerate touch—not even by myself. That's how fucked up I am. That's what those men did to me.

I wipe my moist hand on the edge of the T-shirt I'm wearing and pull it down as I sit up, my body still spinning a million miles an hour. I need to go back inside and try to sleep. Forget this day even happened, but I'm not sure it's possible.

A loud popping sound startles me. I curl into the farthest corner of the couch, as I hesitantly look over the edge of the railing to see what is happening below.

I don't see anything.

"Fucking ladder," Enzo curses.

A metal ladder thumbs against the railing again, this time staying against it.

I bite my lip, and try to remain calm as I watch Enzo climb up the ladder to the balcony. I'm not sure he knows I'm up here. So I stay silent.

But he came back. I smile.

He reaches the top, swings a leg over the top, and then jumps out of his skin when he sees me. He starts falling backward, and I reach my hand out, trying to grab him to keep him from tumbling over.

He rights himself before I reach him.

We both stare at my hand outreached to help him. I would have never offered to touch him in order to help him before. *This is a step.*

"Progress," he says, smiling.

"What are you doing?"

"You locked the door."

I nod. "Yes, I locked the door to keep you out."

He shrugs. "That's not how this works. You lock the door to keep yourself safe. You've already decided I won't hurt you."

He stares at me wearing a white T-shirt sitting on the couch. "The better question is, what are you doing?"

I tremble. "Pushing myself."

"I see." His tense eyes travel over me. "I think you've had enough."

I nod.

He walks to the door and holds it open for me as I step

inside. I immediately run to my corner and fall to the ground, my body shaking violently.

Enzo rubs his neck, looking frustrated. I don't know if the look is for himself or me.

There is a knock on the door, and I freeze. *What the hell?* Westcott never comes up here and disturbs us if Enzo is here. Enzo always calls him if he wants him.

Enzo looks at me with a silent sorry on his lips.

I hug my legs, bite my lip, and let my hair fall to my face. I'm done with people today. I've pushed myself far enough, and now I'm about to shut down.

Enzo slowly undoes each of the locks, his eyes cutting to mine at the sound of each mechanism unlocking, making it easier for them to get to me. *The monsters.*

I close my eyes.

I'm safe.

I'm fine.

Slowly, the door opens, and Enzo slips out through the crack. I'm alone.

I consider racing to the door to slam it shut and lock out Enzo again, but as much as I want to declare my independence from him, as much as I want to run away, I can't. I'm not strong enough to survive on my own, not yet.

And I need Enzo to sleep next to me in order to rest myself. Especially tonight after getting myself so worked up. I need the edges of his muscles to focus on, his rippled chest, his gruff face covered in dark shadows. I need to hear his soft snores rocking me to sleep. I need him.

The bastard. Maybe this was his plan all along. To get me to rely on him. So I could never leave. He wouldn't need a cage or guard to keep me trapped. I would do it myself.

I need to form a plan to stop relying on him, but right now I just want to sleep.

The door creaks open, and Enzo returns. He considers for a second and then walks over to me. He kneels down in front of me like I'm a child.

He bites his lip before he speaks. "Can you do me a favor?"

"No."

He smirks. "Then do yourself a favor. Let's go to the bathroom."

I raise an eyebrow. "Got a new fetish? Like watching me pee or something?"

He laughs. "No, just trust me. I need to change before we try to sleep."

"And you need me for that?'

"Yes," he sighs.

I stare at the door. He's hiding something from me behind it. But whatever it is, I don't want to be in here alone when it arrives.

So I stand and walk awkwardly to the bathroom.

Enzo shuts the door and locks it, something he never does. I stand silently as Enzo begins removing his jacket and tie.

"How was the car ride with Langston? Did he drive as cautiously as I told him to?"

Why is he asking about Langston? We seldom talk about normal things.

"It was fine. Yes, he drove like a grandma." Even though it didn't help me trust him or feel safe.

"Good. Has his eye started turning black and blue yet from my punch?"

"No, it was just swollen and red."

"Damn, I didn't hit him hard enough then," he smirks, a hint of a dimple on his cheek showing.

I open my mouth to thank him again for preventing his

touch, but then I remember he told me to stop thanking him, so I don't.

Enzo kicks out of his shoes, leaving them a mess on the floor. It isn't like Enzo. He's organized and controlled. He usually hangs or folds his clothes when he's done with them. Even the dirty ones are folded in a pile for Westcott to collect.

"What's going on?" I ask.

He frowns. "I'm talking to you like a normal person while I get undressed."

"Except we don't do normal."

He shrugs.

The bedroom door slams. I flinch.

He sighs. "We can go back to the bedroom now." He hasn't finished getting undressed for bed. He's still wearing his shirt and slacks, but since it was just a distraction anyway, it doesn't matter.

I unlock the door and open it, terrified of what I will find. The way I'm acting, you would think there would be a wild animal on the other side ready to attack me.

I open the door but don't notice anything different about the room. The room is empty; no animal or person jumps out at me. I hesitantly enter the room, and that's when I notice the bed.

It has a different mattress on it than before. The covers have been removed and replaced with silk, thin and light. There is no comforter or blanket on the bed. And the pillows look like rocks.

"What's this?" I ask.

Enzo steps behind me, staring at the new bed.

"I'm fucking tired of sleeping on the floor. So I found the hardest, most uncomfortable bed I could find for us to try."

Us.

That word is dangerous. There is no us. *No we.*

There is Enzo, the man whose last name fits him—Black, like his heart. My new master who will soon snap and stop treating me like his damaged queen.

And then there is me—the woman filled with secrets and shame.

There is no us.

Us would mean we have a future together. Us means he thinks of me as more than his property. Us means I forgive him. And I can never do that. No matter how kind he's being, I can't forget about the cruelty inside.

28

ENZO

The bed was a mistake.

Kai's not ready to be pushed any further. She's been pushing too hard already. She's going to crack if she keeps going at this rate.

Six years she was hurt and beaten. It's going to take more than a few weeks to bring her back to life after that cruelty.

It's all my fault Kai is pushing beyond her limits.

I put her up to this when I brought her to Surrender. And now she's going to lose any progress she's made by going too far.

The bed sounded like a good idea in my head, when I was driving back. I called and ordered the firmest bed on the market to be delivered upon my arrival back home. Normally, the mattress company doesn't deliver so quickly, but when you have money as I do, the impossible easily becomes possible. I only wish my problems with Kai were as easily fixable.

Langston and Zeke are out meeting with a new gentleman in town who wants to acquire a yacht. I would usually meet with a new client, as this man is willing to pay big bucks for what he wants. I intended to meet with them after delivering the mattress for Kai to try. But seeing her now, I know I can't leave her.

Even though I should.

I feel unsettled no matter what I do, stay or leave.

Fuck.

I don't know what to do. Not when it comes to Kai. I want to help her, but it's as much about helping her as helping myself get rid of her.

I try to stare at the bed, instead of her. I can't believe she's wearing clothes now; even if it's just a T-shirt, it's more than I've seen her in since she arrived.

I should let the issue of the bed go, and continue to sleep on the cot I've made on the floor. But my back is killing me, and I'm more irritable than usual after our outing at the club. I doubt I'll be able to sleep, but if Kai sleeps, it will be worth it. She needs as much sleep as possible to continue to heal.

I walk closer to her, careful not to get too close and accidentally brush against her. I inhale her scent, knowing this is the best I will get tonight, or ever. But her scent will stay with me in my dreams.

Kai usually smells of the wildflower shampoo she uses. But tonight she smells different. She smells of lust, desire, and sex.

My eyes widen, and my heart races. *Did someone touch her? Rape her? No, I would have known.*

"Show me your hands, Kai."

She turns with concern on her face. "What? Why?"

"Just do it." I give her a warning look.

She hesitantly holds up her hands.

I lean down, lowering my head to her hands stopping

just above them. I inhale deeply. Her fingers are laced with the same scent that hung in the air before.

I straighten, studying her face. She blushes and bites her lip nervously.

I cock my head, realizing what happened. She pushed herself even further than I realized. She pleasured herself, but from the anxious look on her face, it didn't appear to go successfully.

I suck in a breath. I could fix her problem so easily. Make her come with a few strokes of my fingers. Give her undo pleasure. But that would require her to be touched. Tolerate a bed.

"Didn't go successful, did it?" I ask, raising an eyebrow at her hands.

Her blush deepens. "No."

I'm surprised by her honesty. We both know what I'm talking about.

I stare at the bed and then back to her. I don't know what's gotten into me. My own sexual frustration has heightened. And I'm afraid what I'm about to do will make it worse.

But I know how healing it could be for her, how freeing to let go of one tiny bit of her own frustration.

"Get on the bed, Kai."

She blinks and swallows slowly. "What if I can't?"

"I'm not asking you to sleep. Just lie down on the bed."

"I'm not sure—"

"You can. It's not an option; it's an order. Get on the bed."

Kai slowly walks over. She takes her time climbing up, her legs moving awkwardly. And then she lies down flat on her back. Her breathing speeds as I walk over, her body trembling slightly.

I have an uphill battle if I'm going to have any success with my plan. I don't even know if it can be done, but if anyone can do it, I can.

I smirk, *I'm a cocky son of a bitch.*

Kai must see something on my face. Something that makes her say, "I trust you."

Those words crush me. Because I haven't earned her trust. *Not ever.*

"Good, because I'm going to give you back something that never should have been taken."

29

KAI

I TRUST YOU.

I don't know why I said those words.

Trust.

I don't trust Enzo.

But it seemed those were the words he needed to hear to carry out his plan. And it seemed I would be rewarded if I let him get his way.

So despite every bone in my body begging me to run, I stay. I lay on the cool bedsheets face up. I expected to hate and curse the bed the second I laid down on it—but I don't hate it.

The bed is firm. The sheets feel brisk, my skin adapting to the temperature easily. And the pillow is supportive under my head and neck, not soft and mushy.

I'm not sure what Enzo has planned as I lay face up on the bed, but I'm tired of living in fear. Today, I will claim something back. Something bigger than wearing clothes or stepping out into the sunlight. *But what?*

"Turn off that brain of yours," Enzo says.

"I can't."

He sighs. "What was the last good memory you have?"

That's too invasive of a question. My last good memory should be the time Mason and I played hooky from school and spent the whole day at the beach getting sunburned and drinking vodka. That day should have been the day I got my first kiss.

Or maybe it should have been a memory with my father. Sharing a simple meal I cooked, and not worrying about bills and payments, before watching Jeopardy together on the TV.

Neither were my best memories.

"Kai? It doesn't matter what it is; I just need you to think of a positive memory. Something that will help you relax."

My one good memory bubbles up; it's the one I've played in my head every day for years. The memory that saved me from death. The one I could use to escape when my body couldn't.

"You kissing me."

He shakes his head. "Not your happiest memory with *me*. Your happiest memory *ever*."

I swallow, hating myself for the words I'm going to say, because I'll be giving him a lot. But I say the words anyway. "You kissing me *was* my best memory."

He gasps. His eyes latch onto mine, and I swear I see moisture in his eyes. It's sad that my only good memory is my first kiss with a man who moments later tried to kill me —who succeeded in selling me. But there it is. My life is too tragic to be true.

He nods. "Okay, that's good. It will make this easier."

This. What's this? What are you doing, Black?

"We are back on the water."

I tense—*fucking ocean.*

He notices and changes the narrative. "We are here, in

bed. In the only place you feel safe. The door is locked. No one can get in."

"The ladder?"

"It's gone. No one can use it to get to you."

I nod.

"Close your eyes."

I do.

He pulls the curtains tight, blocking out the last strips of light poking through. I feel the darkness descend around me before he walks back to the edge of the bed, standing over me, but not touching.

I open my eyes when he nears.

"Tell me what you remember of our kiss," he says, his voice thick with desire.

"I remember how unexpectedly good it was. How powerful I felt even though you were in control. I could push back against you. I remember the collision of our lips. How good it felt to enjoy the scolding hot for once. How your lips made me surrender to you, no matter how much disdain I felt for you. In that moment, I wanted you. I would have given you everything. Trusted you with my body. Let you take my innocence."

"I should have," his voice is pained. "I should have taken your innocence. Then, Jarod wouldn't have. You would have at least had that."

My lip trembles. *Would it have been better? Would I be as broken as I am now if Enzo would have taken my virginity?*

Yes, it would have been better. Even if he sold me afterward, it would have been better.

"Take off your shirt," Enzo says.

I hesitate but give in. I don't care that he can ogle my body. He's done it a million times before. But for some reason after telling him one of my most intimate of memories, it's harder to strip naked in front of him.

I pull the T-shirt over my head and hand it to him; he sniffs the shirt slowly then tosses it on the floor.

Enzo starts undressing—pants, buttoned-down shirt, and underwear.

I should be freaking the hell out. Alarm bells should be going off, warning me of what a naked man with a predatory gaze wants with me. *To fuck.*

Something I imagined a million times, but can't let happen. I can't touch myself; he would ruin me if he tried to fuck me.

He smirks, noticing my reaction. "It's a good thing I can't touch you. Otherwise, I'd have you tied up, and bent over this bed, while I sink my cock into you with no apologies at how tight the fit would be in your petite body."

I nibble on my bottom lip. "If you aren't going to touch me, what are you going to do?"

His eyes brighten, a wicked grin spreads across his scruffy face, and I know without him saying what he plans.

"Make you come, of course."

"But how? If you can't touch me? I'm not ready."

"Because the only way you won't be truly terrified of life anymore is to experience some pleasure."

"Giving me my freedom would make me happy."

"No, it wouldn't. Stop lying to yourself."

I glare. "How would coming make me happy?"

He freezes. "You don't remember, do you? I know your last few memories have destroyed you, but you don't remember before?"

I suck in a breath giving him a silent answer.

"Don't you remember when you'd lie in your bed at night with a boy you thought you could love in your head?

One who would smile at you in the hallways at school, hold your hand innocently. One whose crotch you'd stare at enough times to get the general sense of how big he was beneath his jeans. With that image in your head, you'd let your hand trace circles all over your body, priming yourself for what comes next. You'd let your breathing get heavy, and your head floats away in the clouds, imagining that one special boy was the one gently and carefully removing the clothes from your body like he was unwrapping the most precious gift.

"Then as your hand slipped between your panties, you'd pretend it was him. His fingers finding your clit and knowing how to rub to make your juices spill from between your lips. Maybe you'd imagine he'd go down on you, putting his head between your legs, his tongue taking the place of his fingers. You'd writhe beneath your fingers as you circled that beautiful pink clit of yours faster and faster. Building yourself up to images of him. You'd take your time because you wanted to drag out the feeling. You wanted the dream to be real, and yet you didn't because you were afraid reality with a boy wouldn't be as good as you could experience on your own. You'd be right; boys your age wouldn't be able to find your clit, let alone know what to do with it. And then you'd come. That tiny explosion would start at your core and then grow as it trickled outward to the tips of your fingertips and toes. Don't you remember, Kai?"

My breath is caught in my throat. "No, I don't remember." I want to, desperately. I want to own my body again. I want to be able to touch or have control over my emotions and feelings. *But I can't.*

His face drops. "Then let me help you."

Enzo rounds the bed; my eyes follow him as he climbs up on the bed next to me and lies down. I stare at his naked body with muscles so defined he looks like he competes in wrestling matches. His body isn't flawless. It's marked with scars, but no tattoos that I can see. I don't let my eyes drift down to his cock. I keep my eyes up, like if I don't stare at his cock, I'll be saved. From what I don't know.

Maybe if I had met Enzo earlier, I would have dreamed about him in high school. He would have been the dangerous boy that everyone knew they should stay far away from, but secretly pined for at the same time. He would have been every girl's crush and every boy's nightmare.

Enzo's eyes aren't as forgiving as mine. He doesn't shy away from staring at my body. And the way he slowly licks his lips lets me know he likes what he sees.

"Moisten your lips, beautiful."

Beautiful. I focus on the word. Hold onto it. I haven't heard a compliment like that in forever. But I'm not beautiful. The healing has made me more human but not attractive.

He scowls. "If this is going to work you have to trust me. You promised you would. You have to believe every word I say is true. I won't lie to you. Not now. You're beautiful, Kai."

I moisten my lips, but I'm not sure I believe him.

"Good. Part your lips, run your tongue over your bottom lip slowly. Take your time."

I hang onto his words, my body responding before I have time to process them. I let my tongue explore my own mouth, running my tongue over my bottom lip slowly, like it's the most delicious popsicle I want to taste.

"Good girl. You're so fucking sexy when you do that. I remember how you taste. I've never forgotten."

I raise an eyebrow. *Not possible.*

"I haven't. You tasted like the sea. Like salt and cool,

refreshing water. You were the most invigorating woman I've ever kissed. So eager and yet so in control of your own body."

Control, I want that back.

"Now, take a deep breath and exhale slowly with me." He sucks in a breath, and I do the same. We hold our breath for what seems like forever before he steadily lets us exhale. In and out we repeat, until I'm breathing slowly on my own.

"You are so beautiful, so fucking strong and in control."

Beautiful and in control, I repeat his words in my head.

"Now let your hand fall against your body wherever it wants. Don't force it anywhere."

My hand rests against my chest, feeling my speeding heart beneath it.

"Perfect, Kai. Let your fingers dance across your flesh. Let it feel the tingles as you trace the scars, but more importantly, the untouched skin that will heat your body."

My fingers barely move at first, focusing too much on a scar over my chest on the left side. A knife wound. I thought it would kill me, that I'd bleed out.

"Move your fingers, Kai."

I do, letting them move to skin that feels good instead of evil. My fingers trip over the point of my nipple.

Enzo sucks in a sharp breath, and his eyes deepen with his own lust. "See that hard nipple? It's hard because it knows what it wants. It wants to be flicked, stroked, touched. It's peaked in anticipation of what you will do to your own body."

I pause over my pointed nipple. *How did it get hard?*

"Squeeze it between your fingers."

My thumb and fingers squeeze.

"Ah," I cry at the unfamiliar sensation.

Enzo grins seductively. "Good girl, see how your body

reacts. Your other nipple has hardened. Ready for its turn. Lick your finger this time before you touch it."

I slowly lick my finger, letting my saliva soak it before dripping it over my nipple. It feels better than the first, as I move my finger in slow circles.

My body arches into my hand as my nipple tenses beneath my touch.

"You're so beautiful taking control of your body like this, Kai. You're making me use all of my self-control to not touch you. Because goddammit, I've never wanted a woman more than you."

His words are like my own special chorus singing to me. I want him to want me, even if I never want him to touch me.

"Now what do you want, Kai? What are your fingers eager to touch next? Let them go."

Down. My fingers slip down.

"Part your legs."

I let my legs fall to the side, as my fingers slide down my marred stomach.

"Wider."

I spread my legs as open as I can and realize I'm opening not for my fingers, but for Enzo's dirty gaze. His tongue licks his lips, and I feel the sensation in my core.

"Fuck," I jerk at the unexpected sensation even though he didn't touch me.

He bites his lip in an evil grin.

"Touch yourself, Kai. Show me how you like it."

"What if I don't remember?"

He shakes his head. "Trust your body. You do. And if you don't, I know what you like. How you like to be touched."

My fingers are between my legs, and I let them move as one, caressing my cunt, taking all of my lower lips in.

"You're wet," he says, and I confirm with my touch.

"Yes."

"Move your hands in big slow circles."

I do, as I exhale the intensity of the touch and his devouring stare is too much.

I can't.

I stop and start moving my hand away to give myself a break.

"Don't you dare. Keep your hands on your pussy. You don't get to stop until you've come all over your delicious fingers."

I clench my teeth together at the overwhelming sensations I can barely handle.

"You're ready."

"For what?"

"To sink your fingers inside. To feel the walls of your pussy."

I nod. *That sounds incredible.*

"Start with one finger at your entrance."

Yes, one finger.

"Now slide it in through your slickness."

In my finger slides as he growls deeply, and my skin burns. His growl urging me on as if knowing this step was going to be hard for both of us.

My finger stills. It's just one finger. I can barely even feel it inside me, but its enough to send me into a frenzy of anxiety.

"You got this, beautiful; hold onto my voice."

But I can't. A tear burns my eyes. *Why is this so difficult? Why can't I touch myself?*

I start panicking. Sweat drenches my body, and I start pulling my finger out.

"Look at me, gorgeous."

I blink back my tears as I turn my head to Enzo. *I failed. I can't.*

"Look at my cock."

I do, and I gasp.

His hand has his cock firmly in his grasp, and I've never seen him so hard. "This is what you do to me. You make my cock hard and thick. You make it ache to thrust inside of you. You make me into a fucking desperate son of a bitch who only bursts for you."

He strokes himself. *God, he's so big.* Bigger than any man I've seen. His cock is long, thick, and veiny. It grows the more he strokes it, as he devours me with his wolfish eyes.

"I haven't had another woman since you arrived. I used to get laid weekly, daily if I wanted it. But not one single woman since you."

"Why?" I breathe.

"Because of you. All I think about is you. Your naked body. Your fight. You drive. Your tears. I want it all, Kai. Every buried emotion, I want it. To claim and own myself.

"Don't let me take it. Your emotions and experiences are yours—not mine. No matter how much I want you, only you can give yourself to me. And I don't deserve you. Take back your body. Take back yourself."

He continues to stroke himself, and I realize my finger starts sliding in and out of myself the same as his rhythm stroking his cock.

"Add another finger. Stretch that pretty cunt."

Another finger slides in and out, but I don't stop at two. I add three.

His heavy growl at my addition drenches my fingers.

My other hand drops lower and begins to circle my clit finding the swollen nub easily now that I'm so turned on.

"Yes, Kai. Touch yourself. Feel how incredible your body feels beneath your fingers."

"God," I moan as another surge makes my toes curl. The sensations start coming back, and I remember how it feels. I remember what to do.

My back arches into my hand as my fingers work. My lips part and my legs spread wider as my fingers sink deeper.

"Beautiful, are you close? I'm so fucking close because of you." He's stroking himself so hard I don't know if he's pleasuring or punishing his cock for wanting me.

"Take it back, Kai. Take back what is yours."

I feel my body clenching around my fingers, my body tensing, arching for more. So close, but even though I'm the edge, can I really fall over the cliff? Can I let myself feel the intense joy and feel the peace afterward?

"Let go with me, Kai. Let go. Come on those dirty, filthy fingers. Come because you control your body. No one else, just you."

I hear his words. And they help. But I also feel myself stirring inside—a voice of my own stepping out of the dark shadows of my heart.

I'm here.

I'm strong.

I'm in control.

I scream as I finally push myself into an orgasm. My muscles squeeze my fingers rhythmically as I come. My body clenches and then releases my orgasm as it bubbles then bursts in tiny explosions throughout my body, releasing all of the darkness of my past and giving me back my body—giving *me* back.

I gasp as I try to regain my normal breathing, and then I watch Enzo jerk his own beautiful orgasm from his body.

His eyes roll back, no longer focused on me, as his cock hardens before the thick, white liquid spills onto the tight muscles of his stomach.

God, what would it feel like for his cock to spill his seed inside me?

I'm not sure I've seen anything so breathtakingly attractive as a man coming on himself when he wanted to fuck me instead. He could have. He could have taken me and destroyed me. Fucked me into oblivion. But he didn't.

He didn't touch me.

And it's never made me want a man more. I just came, just experienced that sensation again for the first time in years, but I think I'm already crazier with need than before. I'm horny and lusting after the handsome man lying next to me.

I can never forgive him, but this...giving me back a piece of myself is as close as I will ever get to absolving him.

But right now, I can't think. The heavy pull of sleep is too much. And I let it consume me.

I wake up to an empty bed.

Enzo is gone.

But I slept in a bed; albeit a hard, cool one.

And I made myself come.

I'm healing, faster than I thought I would heal in a lifetime, and it makes me want to think about a future. *What does my future look like?*

Will I ever be free? Finish school? Hold a job?

Or will I end up a whore? A slave again?

I climb out of bed, before I realize my legs are woozy from last night.

I smile. I have a new favorite memory. The only way it could have been better would have been to combine the two memories. Kissing while coming would have made it better.

I don't know what time it is. I fell asleep in the early morning. I pick up my discarded shirt from last night and put it on before I walk over to the curtains and pull them open. The sun is low in the sky. It's almost sunset. I slept all day, no wonder Enzo left the bed. He's probably at work.

I don't hesitate, I push the glass open and step outside. I take a deep breath of salty air, feeling like a new woman as I walk over to the edge of the balcony and lean against the railing. Today is a new start. I don't need answers to heal anymore. All I need is me.

I can decide my own future. And Enzo will just have to deal with it. He won't stop me. I'm his kryptonite. I can have anything I want, and he'd give it to me. I just need to figure out what I want.

Him.

Shit, I think.

"You're entering a brave new world," Enzo says from behind me in his suit.

I smile. "Thanks to you."

He frowns. "No, I had nothing to do with it."

That's not true. He gave me back myself after being the one who took it in the first place. I feel settled for the first time in years.

"Here," he says holding out a tall drink with a straw to me.

"What's this?"

"Try it."

I take it from him and sip. It's crisp and sweet and delicious.

He grins, his dimple showing as my eyes light up. "It's

iced coffee with cream and sugar. I know Westcott has been trying to get you to drink coffee or tea when you wake up. But I knew you would enjoy something cold more than hot at the moment."

"Thank you."

He sighs. "Stop thanking me."

"I can't. You helped me. Why do you keep being so nice to me?"

"Trust me; I'm not nice. If you knew what was going on in my head, you wouldn't be thinking that way. I have my own devious reasons for helping you. And in the end, you will hate me again. So don't let yourself like me for a second. Because I will just use it to destroy you."

I don't believe him. I misjudged him. He's my savior.

I step toward him.

Closer.

Closer.

Closer.

My hand outstretched as I hesitantly lay my hand against his chest.

Spark.

Fire.

Fuck.

The sensation of only our touch is more than the explosion I felt last night when I came. His heart squeezes at my touch—his dark, dangerous heart. The one that can be cruel or kind.

"I'm glad you didn't take my innocence that night. The kiss was enough to survive on."

He looks pained as I continue to touch his heart.

"Sex with a worthy man was something to look forward to. A goal to get back to."

He grabs my wrist forcefully. The most forceful touch I've felt since I was released.

"Stop looking at me like you see me bringing you chocolates and flowers. I'm not your knight in shining armor. I'm not your savior. I made a mistake all those years ago. One I plan to rectify very soon. I just need you healed before I carry out my plan. Because I'm not so ruthless to destroy a broken girl."

He releases me and steps back. "You aren't broken anymore. Now I can ruin you."

He walks away.

I want to be fucked by a worthy man. Enzo Black isn't that man. He never will be.

30

ENZO

KAI IS NO LONGER AFRAID.

She can walk in the light.

She dons clothes instead of going bare.

She slept in my bed.

And her body is hers again.

She's healed. There are still fragile parts, pieces that will take longer to fit back into her body. Pieces that still appear broken and can't be fixed in a single night. But she doesn't need me anymore. She's healing on her own.

There is no denying she isn't broken. The shattered pieces of her icy cage are being put back up, but this time, she let me in first.

It was the one thing she shouldn't have done—trust me.

Healing her broke me in ways I wasn't expecting. She's no longer shattered, but I am. Because as much as I want to pretend it's better that she's healed, it's not. I know what darkness comes next, even if I don't want to face it.

The door to my lair at Surrender opens, and Langston walks in, followed by Zeke, Westcott, and Archard, my lawyer.

I motion for all the men to take a seat at the long conference like table I have brought in for meetings like this.

"You all know why I gathered you here for this meeting," I start.

"The girl," Langston answers.

I nod.

"She's the one? Kai? The one you killed six years ago?" Langston continues.

"Yes, one and the same."

"But how is she alive, if you killed her?" Zeke asks.

All of the men stare at me with bated breath as they wait for my answer.

"Because I didn't kill her."

"Why not?" Zeke asks.

"Because Black's in love with her," Langston slumps back in his chair. "I told you that pussy would be what destroyed us. Everything we've spent our entire lives working for. All the shit your father put us through will be lost because you want to fucking get laid."

I slam my fist down on the table. "No, I don't love the girl." *Truth.* "And I sure as hell don't want to fuck her." *Lies.*

"Then what, Mr. Black? Why didn't you kill her?" Westcott asks this time.

"Because it's not who I am. It's not who any of us are. I didn't want to start my reign by killing someone who didn't even know what could be hers. It didn't seem fair."

The men nod.

"I was a boy. I was stupid. I won't make the same mistake again."

"So you're going to kill her now?" Zeke asks.

"No, I'm going to follow the rules and earn my kingdom the way the contract was written. I'm tired of feeling like a fraud."

"Kai's not ready for that. She's weak. It would be kinder just to kill her," Langston says. He's the only one who truly got any insight into who Kai really is. Westcott may have spent time with her, but he doesn't know her. She never opened up to him.

"She is now," I say.

"What changed?" Langston asks.

"Everything," I answer.

I turn my attention to Archard, my lawyer. The real reason I brought all of my most trusted men together. To understand what my next steps are now that I know the last few years have all been a lie.

"So tell me what happens now," I say to Archard.

He thumbs the papers. "Well, the contract you signed three years ago is void now that we know the conditions haven't been met."

I nod, I knew they would be. But everyone else in the room gasps, realizing what it means.

"What are my choices now? What are the conditions for me to regain everything I just lost?" I ask.

Archard looks concerned as he pulls the paper and slides it over to me. The paper I haven't seen in over twenty years. One I only faintly recognize. I skim quickly, already realizing what I have to do.

It's the same choice as before. *Save her or save myself. Never both.*

I'm used to surviving. I don't know how not to survive. I don't know how to lose.

Kai is stronger now; it could be a fair fight.

Liar. It would never be a fair fight. I should have just killed her all those years ago. I should have snuffed out her life like you put a wounded dog to sleep, because it's kinder than letting them suffer.

I could choose her this time. I could save her, and find a way to lose.

But it's no longer just about me. I look at the four pairs of eyes focused on me. Their lives rely on me too, as well as the hundreds of other men who work for me. The entire city's survival depends on having a strong Black at the helm —protecting them from the evil. And as much as I'd like to think you need good to drive out the bad, it isn't true. Only the cruelest, darkest of men can do what is needed to drive out the darkness.

I'm the worst kind of man. Because I brought Kai Miller back to life, only to destroy her. She thought she was broken before, but when I'm done with her, she will never recover. This time she will remain broken.

31

KAI

"Meet me in the library," Enzo says, poking his head out on the balcony where I drink another iced coffee as dawn ascends. I don't know why I've resisted sitting out here for so long. *Why have I resisted everything?*

"Okay. Why?" I ask, not tearing my eyes from the still haunting ocean.

"For once, can you just do what I fucking say without asking any questions?" Enzo snarls before leaving.

I frown. *What the hell is up with him?* The last time we were in the library we played truth or lies. *Is that what he wants again?* We still haven't talked about what happened the last time we slept when he made me come. He vanished afterward.

I hate following orders, but right now it seems necessary to get my answers.

I run my hand through my long black hair that now reaches almost to my butt. I could really use a haircut. *But why does it matter what I look like?* I'm a prisoner. He wants me locked away, even if I won't stay hidden much longer.

I'm wearing jean shorts and a spaghetti strapped shirt.

The same type of outfit I was wearing the first time I saw him. I thought my life was devastatingly horrible then, but I didn't realize how tragic my life was destined to be.

I carry my iced coffee to the library doors, which are closed surprisingly enough. I raise my hand to knock but stop myself. This is my home—at least for now. And Enzo invited me to the library. He's expecting me.

I push the heavy door open and step into the dream-like room. I've never been a big book lover. I've never had time to read books; it was hard to find the time when I was focused on finding enough food to fill my belly. And I never had money to spend on lavish things like books. But being in this room makes me want to get lost in the spines. I want to go on an adventure and never return. Books might be the only way for me to do that.

Enzo is the only silhouette I see in the moonlit room, but with every second that passes, light continues to pour in as the sun rises in the sky. We will only be veiled in darkness for a few more minutes.

I walk and notice the chairs we sat in before are gone. Instead, there is a small table with two chairs at either end. This is business. Whatever he brought me here for, it's not casual.

Neither is he. He's dressed in a suit. Usually, when he arrives home, he loosens the tie or kicks off his shoes. He doesn't today. His tie is still done up to his neck. His jacket still buttoned. The only hint that he's already put in a day of work is the scruff of shadow on his chiseled jaw.

Enzo notices me. His eyes take every drop of me in from head to toe. He notices the clothes and the way they still hang loose on my body. He notices that I tried to brush my hair and that my skin has slightly more color after spending a few hours sitting out in the sun. But he doesn't speak. Words are reserved for the meeting.

Instead, he sits in one of the chairs. I mirror his movements and sit in the other. I expect now that I'm seated he will start explaining why I'm here. He doesn't.

The door opens, and Westcott enters. I cock my head. He never enters when it's just the two of us.

He carries in a large tray with what looks like orange juice in tall skinny glasses, a tray of fruit, and cheese and crackers. He hands each of us a glass and puts the food on the table before leaving. I watch intently as he goes.

Enzo holds out his glass, and I clink mine to his before sipping. It's bubbly as it goes down. There isn't just orange juice in the glass; there is also champagne. It tastes nice going down.

"Since it's morning, I figured mimosas would be more appropriate than wine or liquor. Even though we will both be going to sleep in a couple of hours."

Mimosas, that's right. That's what these things are called.

"Stop stalling. What am I doing here?"

His lips thin as he cautiously sets his drink on the table. "Isn't that the question you've been dying to know the answer to?"

I bite my lip. *Is he finally ready to talk? Will he tell me why I'm here? Why he was sent to kill me in the first place?*

"Want to play a game?" he asks.

My lips part in anticipation. *Do I? More than anything.*

I clear my throat. "Stakes?"

"The usual, winner asks all the questions. *All of them*, until they are satisfied."

I nod. I feel like this is a setup. Like he's going to lose on purpose in order to tell me his truth. *But do I want him to win?* Because after he made me come, I realized I want to tell my own secret.

I want to spill all of my secrets. I want to tell Enzo what truly happened, every painful memory. I want to tell him why I don't like being touched. Why as much as I've healed, I will always be broken too. My secret could change everything. How Enzo feels about me. How he treats me. How he looks at me. And I'm not sure I'm ready for that. But I'm not sure I'm ready to hear his truth either.

Because I care about Enzo, I've learned to hate him less, and knowing the truth will probably cement his place in my send to hell list.

So I'll play the game as always. I'll do my best to deceive and figure out his truth. This time, I just don't know if I want to win or lose.

"I've never been sold.

"I've never been raped.

"I've never been tortured," I say.

He gasps as each word is spoken. Obviously not understanding any of my words or how a single one could be true. But we've bent the rules before. Last time we played, all of his were truths. So he knows that all of mine could be lies. Or all truths. And he doesn't get to protest the results.

That's how we play the game now. The truth is always well hidden, even from the game itself.

"Your turn," I say, raising an eyebrow.

"I will never fuck you.

"I don't regret letting you go.

"My real name is Rinaldi."

I don't react. I knew whatever he chose to tell me was going to be shocking. But after our last game, learning I've been gone six years instead of three, nothing he says will surprise me now. *Nothing.*

But his words still hurt. And all of them hold an air of truth.

He's said plenty of times that he won't fuck me. I'm damaged to him. *Why would he want a woman another man's touched and abused?* He has plenty of playthings back at his club.

And of course, he doesn't regret letting me go. Nothing touches him. Even the complication of me returning.

The last one makes the least sense. His real name is Rinaldi. *Is Enzo his middle name or nickname or something?* It seems completely out of left field if it isn't true.

They could all be truths. They could all be lies. But I've made my decision.

From Enzo's hungry stare, it's apparent he has as well.

"They are all lies," he says.

I take a deep breath in and out. Deciding how to answer so he will believe me. Because one of them is the truth, the rest are lies. I shake my head slowly, waiting for the confusion and acceptance to clear his face.

One second passes, then another as we both stare. He tries to read my face. Tries to understand which of the three is the truth—which pain I never suffered. Or how I could make one of them fit my truth in my messed up head, even though it truly happened.

Finally, he slumps in his chair and says, "You were never tortured. At least you don't feel you were because it would make you weak. It is the narrative you can control. They beat you, but torture requires the other person to submit to it. If you blocked them out, they never got in."

I don't confirm or deny his statement. I just choose my answer, preparing for the answers I've been waiting years for.

"Your name is Rinaldi."

"Good answer. Yes, my name is Rinaldi."

I narrow my eyes, not understanding. And it's clear he feels he needs to give me more confirmation. But I believe him. My true name is Katherine after all, even though I've always been Kai.

He clears his throat loudly, and the doors open again. Langston, Zeke, and Westcott all walk in.

I cock my head. *Have they all been outside listening this entire time?*

"What is my name?" Enzo looks to the men.

"Your name is Enzo Rinaldi," Langston says.

Zeke and Westcott, both nod, confirming the statement.

"Thank you; that will be all for now."

The men file out of the room.

"What was that about? If you say your name is Rinaldi, then I believe you. No need to drag out men that would lie for you to prove your point."

"My name has everything to do with it."

"Okay?" I say slowly. "Then explain. Why do you go by Black if your name is Rinaldi? Did your father change your last name or something because he thought it sounded more menacing?"

He shakes his head.

"Black wasn't my father's true name either. We were both born Rinaldi. There is only one way you get to become a Black. You earn it. Black is a legend, a myth. The name alone sparks fear in anybody who understands the true origin of the name in this city. Black has been around for hundreds of years—passed on from leader to leader. It's the name assumed when a new leader is born to Surrender. To the sea. To Miami. *The world.* It has to be earned."

Black. Living in Miami, of course, I'd heard the name. I knew Black was the most dangerous man in the city; myth said the world. He offered no mercy. No prisoners. No survivors. But I never thought the myths were true. Always over exaggerated to get people to do his bidding. I thought he was Enzo's father and that Enzo now became Black because his father either died or got too old to do the job properly. If Black doesn't truly exist, it's only a name assumed by a family of men when they take power; it makes more sense why all the rumors exist around the name.

But one sentence he spoke concerns me more than the rest. *The position has to be earned.* My eyes flutter up, my jaw clenches, and my hands fist.

"What did you do to earn the title?"

"I took out my opposition."

I exhale. That doesn't seem so bad. And it doesn't seem to have anything to do with me or my predicament.

"Who was your opposition?"

His jaw tightens. "Only one of two people can take over the title—from two families with an arrangement. The most powerful offspring of each fight, in each new generation, for control."

I nod, understanding more about him. How he felt trapped in this world from birth. He was. Destined to fight for a crown he may not have even wanted. But only the strong survive. So he had to be ruthless to gain his freedom. But he's free now as their leader. Free to make any decision he wants.

"Ask," he says.

"Who are the families?"

Maybe I know the other family, and that's why this pains him. He killed someone he thinks I cared about.

I silently laugh.

He doesn't realize there is no one I care about anymore —no friend worth saving. He could have killed Mason, and it wouldn't have hurt me much after Mason failed in rescuing me. It may be heartless, but I lost my heart six years ago.

"The Rinaldis," he says indicating his own family.

I nod, of course.

"And the Millers."

I gasp.

"What? Miller as in…"

He nods. "Your family."

"No," I shake my head viciously as I laugh out loud this time. "You're joking. My family isn't strong. My family has nothing and is nothing. We have no money, no power, no control. We wouldn't know the first thing about running an evil empire. This is ridiculous."

"Your family was strong the generation before your father. They had money, power. Your grandfather was Black. He ruled the empire, but then your father lost to my father, and that started the Miller's downward spiral."

What?

"Usually, the loser helps the next generation out, getting ready to fight for the next battle by preparing them. Ensuring whoever becomes Black is the strongest of all the men."

"But my father never told me. He never spoke of this to me. I had no idea that…" I can't even say the words.

"That you are heir to a criminal empire."

I nod.

"You are."

"No, I can't be. And you said *man*. I'm not male."

"Usually, it's a boy chosen as the one to fight. But since you are an only child and have no cousins…"

"I'm the only choice." I drink down the mimosa with

shaky hands not understanding any of this but needing something to soothe my nerves.

He sighs and then clears his throat again.

The door once again opens. A different man enters carrying a stack of papers. He brings them to me.

"I'm Archard, Enzo's lawyer. These are papers going back generations explaining how control of the Black name and empire works. Here's your father's signature. And—"

"Mine," I say looking at the ridiculous signature. It might as well be in crayon as big and half written as it is. But there it is—*Kai M.* I couldn't write Miller yet, it doesn't look like I'm much older than five from the way my name is written.

"We've met before?"

"Only once when we were kids. Our fathers were the ones to set out the rules for the next generation. That's how it is done."

I nod, my new world sinking in as Archard leaves.

Why didn't you tell me the truth, dad? Why didn't you prepare me for this? For the evil in the world? Why didn't you protect me at least?

"This doesn't matter anymore," I lift the papers. "You won. You're Black. You defeated me when you sold me. And even if you didn't, the Millers aren't strong enough to run an empire. We would have lost."

"The Miller family has been weak for a long time, but it's strong again." His eyes stare at me. He means *me*; I'm the strong Miller he's talking about. "But you don't belong in this world."

"I'm in it whether I want to be or not. But I don't know why you are telling me this. You're Black. You won."

"No, I claimed the name wrongly. If I had killed you, I would have won. I would have a rightful claim to the name.

The contract would have been finished, safe for another generation."

"But there wouldn't have been another generation of Millers."

He nods. "The Rinaldi's would have claimed the name forever. The old ways would have been over."

"Why didn't you kill me?" I whisper.

"I don't remember signing those papers any more than you do. But I've known since I was a kid what my destiny was. My father trained me hard, assuming that when the battle came, I would win no matter my opponent. The families are usually tight-lipped on the number of children each has. Keeping secret who will fight in each generation. But in this generation, only a single child was born to each."

I nod. He's a machine, I don't even know what the battle would entail, but I assume it's dark and dangerous. It would involve using a weapon, having other men attack. It would involve killing and blood—not things I could ever do.

"Of course you would win. But why didn't you kill me? That would have ensured you the name and title—your freedom."

"When I was given the assignment to kill you, I didn't know who you were. I didn't know you were the one to be my opponent. But when I met you, I sensed something. Something wasn't right. I wanted the truth, but it was clear you didn't know your own truth."

He sighs.

"All I had to do was kill you, and the empire was mine. I couldn't. It didn't seem fair. You obviously didn't understand what you had a claim to."

Enzo could have killed me. He could have won without making it messy. Defeated me and taken the name. But he didn't. He showed me mercy, something I'm sure his father punished him for. But when he sold me, he was given the title. I used to think death would have been better than what I went through. But I'm not sure anymore.

"Thank you for sparing my life. I can't forgive you for what occurred afterward, but I understand now the position you were in. And I thank you for doing the only thing you could to keep me alive while winning your own life back. But now that you have won the right to call yourself Black, to be the leader of savages, you can let me go. You don't have to worry about me sticking around. I have nothing to stick around for. I'll leave Miami forever."

"I figured you would say that, but there is one important part you don't understand."

I stare at the papers in the middle of the table I have yet to read thoroughly. *What's the catch? Do I actually have to be dead for him to retain the Black name? Is he really going to kill me this time?*

"I'm no longer Black. The second you were confirmed to be alive, I lost my title, my empire. I'm just Enzo Rinaldi again. I have no more power than you do."

"I don't understand."

"You're alive. The rules of the contract have not been met."

"Then I surrender. You win; just let me go."

He frowns. "It doesn't work that way. I can't. Too many people know you are alive."

"Then what do I have to do?"

"You choose. You have three choices."

I don't like where this is going.

He pulls out his gun and lays it on the table.

"One, I kill you now, and claim what I've spent my entire life earning."

Not going to happen. If he couldn't kill me before, he can't now.

"Two, we fake your death, and you stay locked away in my room forever. The men will think you are dead, and I will keep my power. But you will wish you were dead. I've been kind and merciful for the past few weeks. That time has passed. You've healed, and I will claim that tight little pussy as mine as many times as I want. And as you said before, you will surrender to me. I will take it, and you will beg for more."

His lips twitch, and I know that's the most appealing option to him. The fucking part is appealing to me too, even though he's the devil. A night or two in his bed doesn't sound so bad. But I would be trapped. I would be taken. I would be a prisoner.

"Or three, you play the new game and lose. In the end, your surrender will be taken. I will rightfully and legally claim my empire. And you will go free."

I sigh, three is obviously the only choice I have if I want to be free. This isn't about me choosing. It is about Enzo getting his way—as always.

"But know, this new game isn't like our truth or lies game. This game is dangerous. Your life will be on the line every single day. If you play, and aren't strong enough, you'll die. And there is nothing I can do to prevent that. More truths and lies will be revealed. And they will hurt worse than anything I've told you so far."

I smirk, I've experienced pain. I can handle any truth.

"If I chose three, where will I live? Will you let me free?"

He growls as his eyes bare down on me, and I know his answer.

"No, you're *mine*. You already lost one game. You don't get to back out now. And I'm done playing a nice host.

Any choice other than death will leave you tied up in my bed."

"I only get to go free when the game is over?"

He nods, but it pains him. He doesn't want me to go free *ever*. But I assume it's one of the fine prints of the contract I should be reading before I agree to anything. But I don't. Because as I thought before, this isn't a choice. I've never had a choice. Never been able to dream or fantasize about my life. My life has been predestined from the start.

"And what if I win the game?" I ask. I don't know what this new game entails. But if it involves truth or lies, we both know I'm just as capable of deceit as he is. If it involves pain, then I can survive agony and torture. I've lived it longer than him. Enzo only wins when it comes to weapons and killing.

When he brought me here, I wouldn't have had a chance. If he brought out this contract then and forced me to play, I would have lost before the game started. But that's not what Enzo wanted. He wanted a fair fight. That's why he was so determined to heal me.

He's not a kind man; he just wants to sit on his throne, knowing he earned it like every generation before him.

He smirks. "You won't," his cocky ass mouth says. But there is a hint of a smile and glimmer in his eyes. He's more than ready for a fight—a battle—both in and out of his bed. His dark desires read all over his face.

But he won't win both battles. I'm strong enough to win one—whether it's saving my body or claiming an empire I don't even want. I just don't know which fight I will win. Because as much as he can only win one battle, I can only surrender to one. Will it be my body or my life I surrender to him? And which will I claim?

"Let the games begin," I say with a smug smile. I'm going to enjoy kicking his ass.

The End

Thank you so much for reading! Enzo and Kai's story continues in Betrayed by Truths #2!

TRUTH OR LIES SERIES:

Taken by Lies #1
Betrayed by Truths #2
Trapped by Lies #3
Stolen by Truths #4
Possessed by Lies #5
Consumed by Truths #6

Want to order signed paperbacks? Visit: store. ellamiles.com

BETRAYED BY TRUTHS

I'm a lost bet.

His to own. His to claim.

Nothing but property.

But I'm only beginning to understand the truth.

I can choose my own fate.

And claim a future I never thought was possible.

I just can't let Enzo lie to me.

I have to find the truth, even if it kills me.

FREE BOOKS

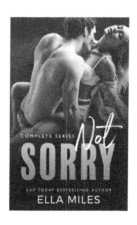

Read **Not Sorry** for **FREE**! And sign up to get my latest releases, updates, and more goodies here→EllaMiles.com/freebooks

Follow me on BookBub to get notified of my new releases and recommendations here→Follow on BookBub Here

Join Ella's Bellas FB group for giveaways and FUN & a **FREE** copy of **Pretend I'm Yours**→Join Ella's Bellas Here

ALSO BY ELLA MILES

TRUTH OR LIES (Coming 2019):

Taken by Lies #1

Betrayed by Truths #2

Trapped by Lies #3

Stolen by Truths #4

Possessed by Lies #5

Consumed by Truths #6

DIRTY SERIES:

Dirty Beginning

Dirty Obsession

Dirty Addiction

Dirty Revenge

Dirty: The Complete Series

ALIGNED SERIES:

Aligned: Volume 1 (Free Series Starter)

Aligned: Volume 2

Aligned: Volume 3

Aligned: Volume 4

Aligned: The Complete Series Boxset

UNFORGIVABLE SERIES:

Heart of a Thief

Heart of a Liar

Heart of a Prick

Unforgivable: The Complete Series Boxset

MAYBE, DEFINITELY SERIES:

Maybe Yes

Maybe Never

Maybe Always

Definitely Yes

Definitely No

Definitely Forever

STANDALONES:

Pretend I'm Yours

Finding Perfect

Savage Love

Too Much

Not Sorry

ABOUT THE AUTHOR

Ella Miles writes steamy romance, including everything from dark suspense romance that will leave you on the edge of your seat to contemporary romance that will leave you laughing out loud or crying. Most importantly, she wants you to feel everything her characters feel as you read.

Ella is currently living her own happily ever after near the Rocky Mountains with her high school sweetheart husband. Her heart is also taken by her goofy five year old black lab who is scared of everything, including her own shadow.

Ella is a USA Today Bestselling Author & Top 50 Bestselling Author.

Stalk Ella at:
www.ellamiles.com
ella@ellamiles.com

Made in United States
North Haven, CT
24 January 2022

15191881R00211